40-LOVE

OLIVIA DADE

PRAISE FOR OLIVIA DADE

With richly drawn characters you'll love to root for, Olivia Dade's books are a gem of the genre—full of humor, heart, and heat.

KATE CLAYBORN

ABOUT 40-LOVE

This match is no game.

When a rogue wave strips Tess Dunn of her bikini top, desperate, half-naked times call for desperate, please-cover-me-kids-are-coming-closer measures. Enter Lucas Karlsson, AKA that flirty Swede in the water nearby. When he prevents her bare buoys from being exposed to fellow vacationers, even an ocean can't drown the sparks that fly.

Lucas, a former top-level tennis pro now giving lessons at the resort, fled there after the abrupt, painful end to his injury-plagued career. But he's finally ready to move on with his life —and after a few late-night, hands-on sessions with Tess, he's eager to prove he's the ace she wants.

But this match comes with challenges: She's forty, and at twenty-six, he's barely old enough to rent a car. Worse, they only have two weeks together before Tess returns to her assistant-principal life in Virginia. During that brief time, they'll have to play hard, take a few risks, and find out whether their chemistry is a one-shot wonder...or whether they're meant to be doubles partners for life.

For Emma Barry, my ever-patient, ever-supportive, ever-wise, ever-talented friend, who guides me safely through the thickets, holds grudges on my behalf, and has the most joyful, infectious laugh in the world. This story is dedicated to you, with so much love. Thank you. ♥

ONE

JESUS, THIS STUPID BIKINI WAS KILLING HER.

Tess tugged on the bow digging into the back of her neck. "Dammit."

She could only conclude that women with ginormous boobs, a long history of neck issues, and a decided intolerance for wardrobe-related discomfort should *not* wear halter tops. No matter what her friend Isabelle might argue about how the style flattered her body and the color suited her skin, blah blah blah.

Belle still harbored starry-eyed dreams of meeting her soulmate under swaying palms, a handsome hero of a man, one who would take one look at her cleavage and fall to his knees in worship to such mammarian bounty.

As of tomorrow, Tess was forty. She should know better.

Maybe a little adjustment might help. Could she tighten the back hooks to take more of her breasts' weight and then loosen the neck ties? All without flashing some nip and traumatizing innocent spectators?

Dawn had broken mere minutes ago, and pink still streaked the eastern sky. Other than one oblivious guy a good distance away, she was all alone in the water, far from the other early-birds just now choosing their beach chairs and adjusting their umbrellas. Very few people on vacation, it seemed, rose before the sun. She wished she hadn't either, but there was no escaping her body's internal clock.

You could take the assistant principal out of the high school schedule, but you couldn't take the high school schedule out of the assistant principal.

One last scan of her surroundings established that no one was looking her way, and her boobs were about to break her neck. She needed relief, stat. Belle also deserved to sleep longer on the first full day of their vacation, rather than have her foolish roommate reenter the room and wake her a second time.

Screw it. She was doing this here and now.

Tess waded farther into the turquoise depths surrounding the island, taking a moment to appreciate the natural beauty around her. This private, luxurious retreat off the Gulf Coast of Florida was famous for its clear, warm water, as well as its spotless beaches and countless amenities. And given how much of her savings this trip had consumed, she'd been relieved to confirm the truth behind all the hype.

Everything was perfect. Everything except the Bikini of Torment.

But she would fix that within seconds.

The island's white sand slid between her toes, silky and soft, as the water moved over her waist, then her chest. Once the gentle waves lapped at her neck, she unhooked the back of the top, praying no one came closer. She'd keep an eye on the shore, just in case.

Under the circumstances, she couldn't follow her usual bra-donning procedure: hooking in front, then rotating the entire garment one hundred and eighty degrees. Too great a risk of revealing her tatas to the world. Instead, she fumbled blindly beneath the water, attempting to locate the innermost eye with her top hook.

None of her increasingly frantic passes caught on anything, and her shoulders were starting to hurt. She lowered her arms for a moment, squeezing them tight against her sides to hold the top firmly in place. In a minute, she'd try again.

This bikini would *not* defeat her.

Probably.

When she'd shopped online—local brick-and-mortar stores didn't stock cute plus-size swimsuits—for her upcoming birthday trip to the island, Tess had allowed herself to be persuaded by Belle. Yes, perhaps she *could* wear a bikini top without the usual buttresses and pulleys and cranes required to hoist her girls north of her navel. Yes, perhaps the thin strap fastened around her torso *would* take all the weight of her H-cup boobs. Yes, perhaps she *should* buy and pack a halter-top, in lieu of a standard bikini with thick straps and underwire that could serve as a garrote under different circumstances. Or, even better, a utilitarian tank with soft cups that would let her breasts hang virtually unhindered.

"Next time, I'm letting my sweet chariots swing low," she muttered. "Or just going to the nude b—"

A wave suddenly rushed over her head, and her lungs filled with salt water. Choking and coughing, she flailed for the surface.

She caught a quick gasp of air before another abnormally high wave sent her under a second time. She scraped and tumbled against the sand, trying to figure out which way was up, before finally finding her feet. But then, as if nothing had happened, the ocean grew calm again, and she was standing once more in neck-deep water with only gentle undulations caressing her nape.

But something *had* happened. Four things, to be precise.

First of all, she was fighting to catch her breath through her coughing, but that was temporary. No real problem there.

Second of all, the tall dude in the distance was looking in her direction, but he couldn't see her clearly from so far away, and he turned his back to her again as soon as he ascertained she wasn't drowning.

Thank Christ for that.

Because third of all, her goddamn bikini top was...gone. Totally, irretrievably gone. Nowhere in sight. Either the knot at her neck had unraveled or the top had simply slipped over her head while she was underwater.

And that *was* a real problem, because fourth of all, a group of freakin' kids—why the hell were they up so early?—was suddenly splashing into the water, shrieking happily as they tried to dunk one another. A couple of them were carrying floats and boards, and they appeared bound for deeper water.

Where she was. Topless. A high school assistant principal on a family beach.

She could see the mugshot and the local news headlines now: *Buoys of Terror: Assistant Principal Dunn Corrupts Innocent Children with Her Enormous, Naked Gozangas.*

No school would make her principal then. Certainly not Marysburg High.

Crossing her arms, she tried to cover as much surface area as she could, but there was no hiding that amount of boobage. Anyone who came close would know she wasn't wearing a top, even if they couldn't spy her nipples.

The room keycard tucked into a secret pocket in her bikini bottoms wouldn't help her now, and neither would the towel she'd carefully spread onto her chosen beach lounger. Belle was still asleep in their room.

Sure, Tess could move further out into the water until the kids left, but they might follow her. Besides, she wasn't a strong swimmer, and Shark Week had left certain indelible impressions on her brain. From what she'd seen through her fingers, braving deeper waters meant becoming human sushi.

And at some point she was going to have to return to shore, children or no children.

There was only one thing that could help her. One person.

Shit. This was going to suck worse than the school's last audit.

Careful to keep both nipples covered with her right arm— a harder task than she'd anticipated, given how her boobs' natural buoyancy and the waves made them shift in the water —she waved her left and raised her voice loud enough for Oblivious Guy to hear.

"Hey! Excuse me, sir!"

He didn't move.

She tried again, abandoning diplomacy in favor of specificity. "You there! The really tall dude with the brown hair and that cowlick in the back!"

At that, he turned and squinted in her direction.

The children were getting closer, their shouts becoming ever more piercing.

"Yes, you! With the, um"—no other good descriptor came to mind, since water covered most of him, including his swimwear—"shoulders! And the face! Can you please come here?"

A lazy smile dawned on that face, a face she now realized —to her vast regret—was both handsome and smugly amused. Dammit, the last thing she wanted was help from a twenty-something bro. But it wasn't as if she had much of a choice, did she?

"Thank you for noticing my best features." He raised a cocky brow, moving a few steps toward her. "The ones you can currently see, anyway."

He emphasized his vowels in a way she didn't entirely recognize. The accent sounded kind of British, but not exactly. And was he...was he *winking* at her?

It didn't matter. She could survive a bro, European or not;

she couldn't survive losing the principal job because of public indecency charges.

"Please come here!" she repeated, desperation in every syllable. A few dozen feet more, and those kids were going to see everything. *Everything*. "I need your help! Now!"

That self-satisfied grin still playing on his lips, he flicked her a salute. "On my way."

Finally, he began a slow crawl in her direction, and God, she didn't have enough time for this man-shaped tortoise to get up to speed. So she dove toward him and began—appropriately enough—a quick breaststroke, hoping the splashing of her arms and legs would disguise her topless state from any onlookers.

He arrived in front of her sooner than she'd expected, those long limbs propelling him through the water with enviable ease.

Then he stood, and water poured from his broad shoulders and glinted from his dark lashes as he scanned her up and down. Oh, Lord, he was tanned and muscular and way too pleased with himself.

Whatever. She only needed him for one simple task: grabbing a towel.

Arms crossed protectively over her chest once more, she attempted a polite smile. "Thank you so much for coming."

His gentle snort of amusement rippled the water near his chest.

"No problem. I see you've experienced a—" He scratched his stubbly chin. "What do they call it? A wardrobe malfunction?"

His voice was low and husky, his words unhurried. The urgency of the situation did not seem to have punctured his equanimity in any appreciable way.

"Yes." She dug deep for her poise and didn't let her smile falter. "I lost a key component of my swimsuit in those rogue waves just now, and there are kids getting way too close. Is there any way you could—"

"Well, let me think about it." He raised his broad hands from the water, eyeing them consideringly. After another glance at her partially covered breasts, he shook his head. "I may not be man enough for this job, but I'm more than willing to take it on."

What?

Her smile collapsed. "I don't know what you mean. I just need you to—"

"Oh, love," he said, dimples creasing his cheeks. "This isn't my first lost-bikini-top incident. If you want my hands on you, you don't have to come up with an excuse. Just ask."

Ah. *Now* she understood. Arrogant asshole.

While she searched in vain for a suitably crushing response, he kept talking. "No need to be embarrassed. They're very good hands." He flexed them a bit, as if in demonstration. "Besides, I admire a woman who pursues what she wants."

She summoned her most fearsome stern-administrator tone and her most arctic former-schoolteacher glare. "I don't want you to cover my, um"—her voice faltered—"*assets* with your hands, sir. I just want a towel." She narrowed her gaze even further. "That's it."

He looked down at her, his heavy-lidded olive-green eyes skeptical. Behind her, the sound of splashing water was getting louder by the moment.

She enunciated very clearly. "Please. Get. Me. A. Towel. *Now*."

"All right, then. One towel, coming up." Flicking her another lazy salute, he turned for the shore.

Thank God. Finally.

He'd only taken a single, indolent stroke toward the beach, though, before she glanced over her shoulder and realized the terrible, terrible truth. She didn't have time for him to slow-poke his way to a towel and come back to her. The kids were almost upon her, and her naked boobs were almost upon *them*.

They weren't paying her any attention right now, but that could change at any time.

No more hesitation. A worthy principal-to-be should snap into problem-solving mode in an instant, and she was choosing to treat this circumstance like a particularly enthusiastic cafeteria food fight. An emergency, all hands on deck.

Lunging forward, she snatched the man's ankle just before he swam out of reach. He jerked to a halt and sank a little beneath the water. But soon he was back on his feet, dimples popping and mouth open, no doubt in preparation to say something loathsome.

She didn't give him the chance.

Before he could get out a single brotastic word, she'd grabbed his waist and maneuvered him until he was facing the kids. Then she leapt onto his broad back, her arms wrapped tight around his neck, her legs around his waist, and her breasts smushed against his shoulder blades.

A silent moment passed. Two. Then he started laughing uproariously, his shaking body rubbing against hers in unexpected and intimate and embarrassingly pleasurable ways.

Oh, Jesus. She'd done it. She'd plastered herself, half-naked, to a random bro.

With his unwitting help, she'd managed not to flash innocent children.

But who was going to save her from her savior?

TWO

THE BRO COULDN'T HAVE PEELED TESS OFF IF HE'D tried. Which he didn't.

"Keep me behind you at all costs," she hissed into his ear. "I don't want those kids to see me."

His back had gone tense at the first contact of their bodies, every muscle delineated on those powerful shoulders. But when he finally stopped laughing and relaxed, her body melded to his with surprising ease.

"No flashing the children with your, uh, remarkable charms," he murmured, his cadence as lackadaisical as ever, despite the situation. "Got it."

Then he didn't say more for a few moments. Enough time for her to regret her sharp tone.

Yes, he'd made some conceited assumptions about what she needed from him, but he was young and handsome. Women—even women her age or older—undoubtedly threw themselves at him on a regular basis. And if he was inclined to catch them, who was she to judge?

She'd snapped at him. She'd tackled him, half-naked. She was using him as a human shield. And he hadn't uttered a word of complaint, even though she was disrupting his vacation.

Much as she hated to admit it, clutching him wasn't exactly a hardship either. He was strong and warm and a formidable barrier between her and possible jail time.

His smooth, firm back felt good against her breasts. Too good. It was all very irritating.

Still, she knew her duty.

"Listen…" Her sigh pushed her breasts even tighter against him, and he went very still. "I'm sorry I was waspish. I panicked a little when my top fell off." Before he could reiterate his preferred theory, she emphasized, "By *accident*. I'm an assistant principal. I can't afford to be brought up on charges of indecent exposure and corrupting a minor and exceeding the maximum allowed volume of bare tatas in public."

The rumble of his laugh vibrated through both their bodies, and to her dismay, her nipples responded.

"I'm not familiar with every American law, but I don't think that third one exists. If it does, though, consider me a conscientious objector." He gave her shin, currently resting somewhere along his flat belly, a pat. "And don't worry. You're not the first woman I've infuriated, and I'm certain you won't be the last."

She couldn't resist. "I'm certain of that as well."

He laughed again, and she found her lips twitching too.

"So what brings you to the island?" To her relief, he didn't wiggle or take advantage of his position in any way. Instead, he seemed to be keeping close watch on the kids only a few feet away. "Are you celebrating something, or just taking a topless vacation?"

Nipping at his neck in retaliation for his smartass remark was *not* a good idea, she reminded herself. "I'm here with a friend to celebrate my birthday. I turn forty tomorrow."

The number didn't bother her, because it didn't alter one

iota of her demanding but comfortable life. It only marked the passage of time—time better spent achieving her professional goals than bemoaning the inevitable creep of age.

Besides, she liked those sparse threads of silver that had begun to appear in her hair. She was choosing to consider them free highlights.

"Happy early birthday, Ms. ..." Pausing so she could fill in the rest, he turned his head until she could see his profile. His smile.

"Dunn. But under the circumstances, I think you can call me Tess." She lowered her right hand to grab one of his and gave it an awkward shake. "Nice to meet you."

"I'm Lucas Karlsson." He let go of her hand and hesitated. "But maybe you already knew that?"

Cocky son of a gun. "Sadly, word of your good looks and charm hasn't spread throughout the entire resort yet. Give it a few more days."

"Fair enough."

He didn't sound offended. If anything, his shoulders seemed to drop a fraction.

"So why are *you* here, Lucas? And where are you visiting from?"

Good. She was getting this conversation back on impersonal footing, despite the way his satiny back caressed her breasts and how easily her legs cradled his narrow hips.

"I'm originally from Sweden, although I've lived in the U.S. for a few years. Miami, most recently. I became a permanent resident last year." His hand swirled beneath the surface of a gentle wave. "I'm here for this beautiful water, I suppose. Sun. Sand. Relaxation."

That explained the vaguely-British-but-not accent, although she wouldn't have guessed Sweden. Then again, she probably shouldn't take her linguistic cues from a Muppet spouting gibberish and hitting pretend meatballs with a tennis racket.

11

"Are you celebrating something?" she asked.

Jeez, she hadn't even considered whether he might be here with someone else. The fact that he'd eagerly volunteered to hold her naked breasts didn't preclude a significant other, and she didn't want that someone to catch her plastered to Lucas's back.

This little farce was enough drama for the entire vacation. She didn't need more.

"Nope." His voice sounded tight, for some reason. "Not a thing."

That tanned, strong hand in the water...it was scarred. A neat T marked the wrist. And if she squinted, she could see something on the opposite wrist too. Another mark of... something. Surgery?

Not her business. "Well, I hope the rest of your trip goes well."

"I don't think my time here will get much better than this, to be honest." She could hear the grin in his voice. "Consider yourself a highlight of my sojourn on the island."

"How long are you staying?"

Would she see him around the resort again? Did she want to?

She shouldn't. Scratch that, she *didn't*. He was a cocky twenty-something bro from Sweden, and she was a comfortably settled American thirty-nine-year-old contemplating the purchase of reading glasses. They had nothing in common, not in temperament or life experiences.

He shrugged, his skin sliding under her hands. "For another while yet. I'm not sure how long."

Another sign of the vast gulf between them. If he was staying indefinitely at the resort, he clearly didn't have a full-time job, and he clearly had plenty of money.

Neither of those things detracted from the kindness he'd shown her, however. "Good for you. I have to get back to school in two weeks. Students and teachers may get the summers off, but we don't."

When he turned his head again, she caught a glimpse of his stubbled cheek. Seen up close, it was craggier than she'd expected, and he had slight bags under his eyes.

Maybe she'd been wrong. Maybe he was older than she'd—

He interrupted her thoughts. "Do you enjoy your work?"

"I do, actually. Quite a bit. I love the staff and the kids at my school. I want to become the principal soon, if I can." How to explain her feelings to someone like him? "How old are you?"

"Twenty-six."

Ah. Just as she'd initially thought. Although his features seemed a little more worn than she'd have expected for such a young man. For a moment, she'd wondered whether—

Well, it didn't matter.

"Establishing myself in a profession I love has been a joy and a privilege, Lucas. The greatest of my life. Once you've worked for a few years—" She paused and rephrased, uncomfortable with the implication he hadn't been working. Maybe he was one of those young tech entrepreneurs and could simply afford an extended vacation. He didn't really seem like the type, but what did she know? "Or for a few more years, I hope you have that experience too."

He didn't respond, and the silence grew uncomfortable.

Dammit. Of course he didn't want to talk about the satisfaction and meaning she found in her career. He'd asked a polite question, and she should have simply given him a polite, surface-only answer, not a too-personal motivational speech.

Time to lighten the mood. "I'll bet I sounded like your mom just now."

There. She'd given him the perfect opening to tease her about her advanced age.

His back lifted and lowered beneath her as he took a deep breath. Then he gave her foot a little squeeze, and she squeaked.

"Believe me, you don't remind me of my mom." His voice was warm, and she let it surround and comfort her like her favorite quilted blanket. "For one thing, you're—"

For a single foolish instant, she was sure he was going to say something like *hot*. Or *stacked*. Or *sexy*. No offense to his mom, who was probably all of those things too, at least in the eyes of people who weren't her offspring.

"—ticklish," he finished.

Then he was flicking his fingers over the soles of her feet as she laughed helplessly. And even when he stopped after a moment, his own laughter shaking his shoulders, his right hand continued to cup her foot. He held it in a light but secure clasp against his belly.

She smacked him on the arm. "Shame on you, abusing your elders like that."

"My apologies, Assistant Principal Dunn. I couldn't resist such cute toes."

Her brows drew together. "They aren't cute."

She peered at them. They were short and stubby and didn't even have polish on them. Not horrific by any means, but cute? Nah.

"I beg to differ." After one last squeeze, he let her foot go. "I think the kids are gone."

Startled, she peered over his shoulder. When had the gaggle of children left the area? And why hadn't she noticed their departure?

"Do you still want a towel?"

"Uh..." She looked down at herself and laughed. "That would be a yes."

He turned his head enough to meet her eyes. "Because if so, I'd better grab it now. I need to get going soon."

Why? Wasn't he on an open-ended vacation?

Maybe he had a date. Or maybe he was just looking for an excuse to end this encounter. God knew, he'd already spent an inordinate amount of time helping a cranky middle-aged stranger who couldn't keep track of her bikini top.

"Okay." She gave a halfhearted nod. "Thanks."

Oddly deflated, she unwound her legs from his waist as he returned his gaze politely to the front. And then she was standing on her own two feet, arms wrapped around herself once more.

"Do you want me to get your towel, or will any towel do?" Although he swiveled to face her again, he kept his eyes on her face. "Since we don't know when a new batch of kids will decide to drift in your direction, I suggest the latter."

"You can grab one of the resort towels. They're plenty big enough to cover all the important bits."

His lips curved. "Barely. And before you wonder, that's a compliment."

"Whatever." She rolled her eyes. "Just bring me a towel, Don Juan. Or whatever his Swedish equivalent would be."

He nodded solemnly. "Ah, the story of Lars Larsson and his many lovers, all named Pippi. It's a sweeping tale of seduction. Also, interestingly, rotten herring."

"That's total bullshit," she told him.

The dimples reappeared. "But how will you ever know for sure?"

To the right of his tall frame, she caught some sort of movement under one of the beach's many palm trees. When she squinted, she could make out a curvaceous woman in a sparkly pink swimsuit with pale skin, a curtain of blond hair, and a waving hand, alongside some guy in gray swim trunks with his arm around her waist.

Whatever. Forget the guy. The woman in the swimsuit was Belle. Her friend was trying to get her attention.

Now that she thought about it, Belle and Lucas would probably get along well. Belle had her own brand of swagger, one that would prove more than a match for him. She had plenty of free time right now, since teachers in her Boston-area school system didn't have to report back for several weeks. And she was only thirty-four, closer to Lucas's age than Tess.

"Do you see the pretty blonde in the pink suit?" She pointed toward shore. "That's my friend, Belle. Why don't you go over there and tell her I need a towel, so you can get where you're going more quickly?"

He glanced in Belle's direction and nodded. "I'll do that." But he didn't move. "What are you doing the rest of the day?"

Mostly brainstorming and list-making as she figured out her principalship-claiming strategy. But she and Belle had also reserved spots on a guided nature walk around the island that afternoon and planned to visit the resort's seafood restaurant for dinner. He could join them. Easily.

She almost told him so.

Despite herself, she found him charming and affable, if a bit too...

Well, she supposed the best word was *unformed*. He didn't appear to have found a purpose in life yet, which wasn't a surprise given his age. He had years ahead to gain nuance and stories and depth and ambitions.

Those years had come and gone for her already. And she *did* have professional ambitions, ones which required time and concentration and thought.

So that was her answer. She wouldn't seek out his company, no matter how sexy she found him. She wouldn't encourage him to seek hers out either.

"Nothing in particular. Hanging out with Belle, just the two of us, like we'd planned." She smiled at him, and it wasn't an effort. He seemed like a goodhearted young man, even if he was a bit too flirtatious and handsome for his own good. "Thank you again for all your help."

That cocky smile gleamed through his scruff.

"Decided to play it cool and mysterious?" Yup, he was definitely winking at her. She could tell for sure this time. "That's fine, Tess. I have a feeling you'll manage to find me anyway. Even if it takes another...accident."

Oh, Lord. They were back to this again?

"It *was* an acci—" she started to tell him.

But he'd already begun to swim, his long arms slicing through the water in a slow rhythm that nevertheless brought him to shore with surprising speed. Underneath the palm, the guy in the gray swim trunks had disappeared, and Belle was standing by herself.

Lucas got to his feet in the shallow surf and strode to her side with that smile still fixed firmly on his smug, attractive face. The two of them talked for a minute before he flashed her one last grin, loped to a nearby chair, grabbed a towel, and jogged off between two of the nearby buildings. To do what, God only knew.

Right now, wondering about his rush didn't occupy the forefront of Tess's thoughts. No, she couldn't shake the image of him standing next to Belle. As Tess had speculated earlier, the two of them looked good together. Like they fit. Belle was a few years older than him, but not nearly as many as Tess.

They were both young. Both charismatic. Both at ease in their strong, capable bodies.

They belonged together in a way Lucas and Tess never could.

By the time Tess returned her attention to the water, Belle was already close, one of the resort's signature canary-yellow towels clutched in her right hand as she splashed through the warm waves.

"Hey, babe. Here you go." She handed over the towel, and Tess wrapped it around her torso with as much speed as humanly possible. "I have no clue how you managed to lose your top, but good thing you had Mr. Tall, Tanned, and Swedish nearby to help with your, uh"—she made air quotes —"*wardrobe malfunction*. If that's what it was."

Oh, Jesus. Not another one. "It was *an accident*, Belle. Lucas was helping me deal with the aftermath of my *accident*. And now you are too, so thank you."

"You're welcome. So..." One of Belle's sleek brows quirked. "You and your rescuer are on a first-name basis?"

Tess snorted. "I had my naked boobs plastered to his equally naked back. I could hardly insist that he refer to me as Assistant Principal Dunn, even though he's almost young enough to be one of my students." After securing the towel in a knot above her breasts, she began to make her way to shore. "I need a shower, woman. Let's get going."

Belle kept pace, but she wasn't ready to drop the subject. "From what I could see, he seemed interested."

"He was." Although who knew how sincere his overtures had been? "I guess."

"Are you interested back?"

Tess shook her head. "He's only twenty-six, Belle."

Her friend's strides didn't falter. "So? That's comfortably within the bounds of adulthood."

"You know most women mature faster than men. Mid-twenties or not, he's still a kid."

Belle didn't argue that point. "So his age is the main thing holding you back from a little vacation fling? He wasn't obnoxious or boring or unacceptable in some other way?"

"He's a flirt. A brazen, cocky, way-too-young-for-me flirt. And the last thing I need in my life is a player, even if he's honest about it." All true. Still, Tess couldn't suppress a small smile. For God's sake, he'd called her toes *cute*. The man clearly had no shame. "I mean, yes, he was helpful when I needed him. But he's a bit too aimless for my tastes. I don't think he even has a real job."

Belle made a noncommittal hum. "No real job, huh?"

"Nope. And even if he weren't too young, too flirty, and too immature, I don't need distractions right now. I know you keep telling me vacation time is sacred, but I have planning to do."

With a resigned sigh, Belle parroted what Tess had told her dozens of times. "So you can use this school year to prove you should get your principal's job when she retires in June. Especially since Superintendent Jones's latest pet is throwing his pompous hat in the ring."

"I wish Cressida had let us know she was leaving before last week." Tess hadn't intended to use this trip to strategize, especially given its price tag. She didn't have much of a choice, though, given the timing, and she could only hope the sacrifice would pay off next June. "But she didn't, so I need to decide now how I'm going to make my case for her job. Because once the school year starts, there's no time to think about much of anything, which you know as well as I do. And there's no way I can let Gary Goddamn Enders get the job. That man cares about kissing ass and saving money, not kids."

Belle didn't seem any more impressed by the argument than she had the last few times she'd heard it. "You're telling me one or two late-night booty calls would completely derail your planning? Really?"

Somehow, Tess didn't think Lucas was the type of man a woman easily dismissed from her thoughts, whether or not he was physically near. For example, why was she still thinking and talking about him now?

Gah. The man was a menace clad in way-too-flattering board shorts.

"Yup. So wipe him from your fevered imagination." Somehow, one of the gentle waves unbalanced her, and she stopped for a moment. "Unless, uh, you're interested for yourself."

Another vague hum from Belle.

Tess should want her friend to find a hot hookup on vacation. She *did* want that. Just...maybe not with Lucas. Really, when she considered the matter, he was too young for both of them. Belle deserved someone more mature, even for a fling.

Yes. That was why the thought of Belle and Lucas together made her cringe. Definitely.

Time to change the subject. "Who was the guy in the gray swim trunks? You two seemed friendly."

Belle's teasing smile widened. "Brian *is* friendly. Very much so."

"Brian?" Tess took a sidelong glance at her friend, her own brows raised. "I see you've also found a first-name friend."

"Yup." Belle picked her way through the shallow water, avoiding the sharp shells scattered underfoot. "He was here for some weekend corporate retreat and decided to stay a few extra days by himself. I plan to make sure he doesn't regret that decision."

Tess slowed at the edge of the waves. "You met him this morning?"

"He was on my flight here, and I've run into him two or three times since we arrived." Belle scooped up her own towel as they trudged through the sand. "He's an interesting man. Funny. Smart. And most importantly, hot as hell."

Tess stopped right before the path leading back to their room.

She wasn't Belle's older sister or mother or even her assistant principal anymore. Still, she worried. "Please tell me you're meeting him in public until you're sure he's safe."

"Of course." Belle paused. "Although privacy may be required at some point, unless I want to incur significant legal fees."

"Gotcha." Tess started walking again, and her friend kept

pace. "Have fun, but be careful. And let me know if you need me, okay?"

"I'm a big girl, Tessie." Belle grinned. "I know what I'm doing."

Tess laughed. "That's what all the boys tell me."

With a toss of her head, Belle made a show of preening prettily. "As they should."

As the two of them entered the open doorway to the hotel and turned down the hall to their room, Belle hooked their arms together. "Listen, I was thinking about what we should do the next few days when you're not working and I'm not corrupting innocent businessmen. Do you play tennis?"

"I used to." When was the last time she'd stepped foot on a court? At least a couple decades ago, from what she could recall. "Why? Did you want to play?"

"Nah." Producing her keycard, Belle waved it in front of their door's sensor until the little light turned green. "Here we go."

Tess opened the door but paused in the doorway. "So why did you ask about tennis?"

"No reason," Belle said. "No reason at all."

THREE

"THAT WAS A GREAT LESSON." THE FINAL GUEST
from his intermediate class, a twenty-something woman with
a long blond ponytail and a shy smile, slipped Lucas a twenty
during their end-of-lesson handshake. "I think I'm getting a
handle—" She cut herself off, blushing. "Sorry. Unintended
pun. Anyway, I think my backhand slice is improving. Thank
you so much for your patience. I still can't believe *Lucas
Karlsson* is giving me lessons!"

She was sweet and a generous tipper, and she was beginning to get some power behind her ground strokes. A good
client, even if he was eager for the arrival of the next one.

He smiled at her. "You're welcome, Madison. I'll see you
tomorrow afternoon?"

"Yeah." She bent to gather her borrowed gear into a neat
pile, not looking at him. "Unless you...um, have some free
time tonight?"

Another woman was occupying his thoughts at the
moment. But as a rule, he didn't like to refuse clients' invita-
tions in direct terms. Not only to avoid hurt feelings and
decreased tips, but also because he might change his mind
later.

So he used his standard response for such situations. "I'm not certain. I may have plans, so don't put your evening on hold for me. But if those plans change, may I leave a message on your room's voicemail?"

Her cheeks, already pink from exertion, darkened to red.

"Sure. That would be..." Hitching her purse on her shoulder, she shuffled her feet. "I'd like that."

Then she scurried away, and he made a mental note never to call her room, no matter how the next lesson went. No matter if he went to bed alone and aching for company.

Madison Warwick was too innocent, and she'd be too easily hurt.

If he shared his bed with a guest, he made sure both of them understood the situation, both of them enjoyed the encounter, and both of them moved on without any unfortunate consequences afterward. Including emotional ones.

In fact, he preferred not to involve emotions, period. Bodies and pleasure were enough.

Wiping the sweat from his brow with a towel, he squinted against the setting sun and checked whether his final client of the day had arrived at the tennis clubhouse yet.

Nope. A handful of people were still milling around the grounds and browsing inside the small clubhouse, but none of them boasted shoulder-length brown hair, pale skin, a round, sweet face, and a truly astounding set of curves.

Tess Dunn would most likely choose not to arrive at the courts topless, although he'd be foolish not to hope for a repeat performance of their early-morning encounter. Either way, he was eager to see her, whether she was fully clothed or half-clothed or entirely naked. He didn't even care whether she turned waspish again, or pompous. He'd take it all.

She was smart and funny and fucking sexy, whatever version of herself she chose to reveal. And interesting. Blessedly interesting, when so few things interested him these days.

The clock on the clubhouse wall was running slow. Or maybe he was just running hot. Who could blame him?

Wait. There she was, wending her way through the scattered guests. Fully dressed, sadly, in an oversized green tee, dark leggings, and sneakers. With that now-familiar frown carved between her brows, as if she were confused or disturbed or loath to see him again.

Which made no sense, since she'd orchestrated both their encounters so far.

Honestly, her decision to reserve several late-night lessons over the next two weeks had surprised him. He'd believed her protestations of disinterest earlier, despite his teasing. Sure, he'd hoped their time spent glued together, wet skin against wet skin, might change her mind about him, but she'd seemed unswayed by his charms.

By the time he'd showered at his little studio apartment, conveniently attached to the clubhouse, and accessed the day's schedule on his cell, he'd managed to banish her from his thoughts. Mostly. The sense memory of those glorious breasts against his back was hard to shake.

Then he'd seen her name listed on his daily online spreadsheet. *Tess Dunn. Room 1249. 7 p.m. Private evening lesson.*

Her sparkly friend, who'd managed a brief but thorough interrogation during their conversation at the shoreline, must have told Tess where he worked. And then Tess must have called for the appointment immediately after leaving the beach.

Damn, nothing made him feel better than being wanted by a challenging, beautiful woman. Especially when all his other avenues for satisfaction had disappeared months ago.

That warm glow of masculine pride lasted about ten more seconds.

Because then she saw him, and her confused scan of the grounds turned into an eyeroll. Her chest heaved in a sigh.

Arms swinging at her sides, she strode in his direction, those clear hazel eyes bright with evident frustration.

Which, again, made no sense. What the fuck had he done, except save her from exposing her magnificent rack to various preteens and report to his job at the time and place she'd specified?

Most women he considered completely explicable. Tess, not so much.

"Belle is a dead woman." Tess was breathing a bit hard, and he tried his best not to check how that would look below her neckline. "I was more than clear with her. You may be charming and handsome, and I may have rubbed my naked boobs all over your unsuspecting back, but I don't have time for extra socializing on this trip. Especially when that socializing involves lessons in a sport I don't actually play."

Apparently, he'd been right the first time when it came to her. Appointment or not, she didn't want anything more to do with him. Although she evidently found him charming and handsome, so maybe he should consider that a win?

He held up both hands. "Don't blame me. All I did was tell your friend my name and my job when she asked. Next thing I knew, *your* name showed up on my schedule. I assumed you'd made the appointment."

The flare of her nostrils had diminished as he spoke, but the irritation in her voice lingered. "Well, I didn't. Half an hour ago, Belle suddenly told me to stop working and come here, since she was giving me a tennis lesson as my early birthday present. For some incomprehensible reason." Her shoulders dropped. "At least, it seemed incomprehensible then. I had no idea you were a tennis instructor."

"*The* tennis instructor." A stupid distinction, he knew. But his ego had taken enough beatings over the past few years and the past couple of minutes. He needed a sop for it. "Guests can reserve the other courts for matches or practice, but this one is dedicated to my clients."

She'd gathered her shiny dark hair into two pigtails, fastened low on either side of her head, near her earlobes.

They were cute. She was cute.

Not into him—not like he was into her—but cute. And he couldn't resist teasing her, just to see those pale cheeks flush at the challenge to her equanimity.

He let a smirk curve his lips. "And please don't worry about my back. It may have been unsuspecting, but it was more than willing."

She rose to the bait beautifully, just as she had that morning. "I misspoke. My guess is that your back has been suspected many, many times over the years."

"More my front, really."

She huffed out a laugh, and he felt it like a caress of his chest.

"Do you want anything other than water to drink?" He ticked off her options on his fingers. "For one-on-one clients, I can supply juice, sports drinks, sodas, beer, or even champagne. Your choice."

"I think drinking champagne in your company would be a bad, bad idea," she said. "After a glass or two, I might forget why I shouldn't respond to—"

When she cut herself off, he tilted his head in inquiry. "Respond to what?"

After a second, she let out a long breath. "That sexy accent and automatic flirtation."

Sexy accent? Much as he adored his homeland, no one in Europe really considered Swedish the language of love. Although at least it wasn't German, a dialect that could make even declarations of undying adoration sound vaguely threatening and phlegm-y.

That said: If Tess found his accent seductive, he certainly wasn't going to argue with her.

Still, he frowned. "My flirtation is not automatic."

She raised a slim, dark brow, and for just a second, he

could totally see her in front of a classroom, confronting a student who'd blamed his missing homework on his pet chinchilla.

Not that Lucas had ever used that particular excuse. No, he'd been more partial to his imaginary moose friend, whose appetite had been remarkably vast when it came to school assignments. Or so he'd told his long-suffering teachers.

He looked at Tess again and shook his head. Dammit, that was one effective eyebrow.

"Okay, so my flirting is kind of automatic." Giving up, he grinned at her. "Doesn't mean it's not sincere."

Another eyeroll. "I'm sure."

Automatic instinct or not, he wouldn't flirt with a woman who didn't want that sort of attention from him. "Would you like me to keep things completely professional? Would that make our time together easier for you?"

An impersonal distance between them wasn't what he wanted, but neither was her discomfort.

"You mean you'd stop flirting?" She blinked up at him, hazel eyes doubtful. "Won't that cause you severe bodily injury? Possibly death?"

He considered the matter. "Maybe. But I'm willing to risk it for your sake."

"Well..." After hesitating a long moment, she waved a dismissive hand. "Nah. I'd hate for the resort to lose its star tennis dude because he experienced some sort of catastrophic flirtation backup. I can handle it."

Did she actually enjoy his flirting? Or was she merely being polite?

Either way, she deserved to know how many times she'd be weathering his charm offensive in the future. "Then we're agreed. But before we begin our appointment, I'm afraid I have some bad news for you."

Her shoulders slumped. She closed her eyes, and her dark lashes rested on her cheeks like lace. "What now?"

"Your friend didn't just buy you one tennis lesson with me."

She squeezed her eyes shut more tightly and groaned. "Don't tell me."

With her face scrunched up like that, her hair in those pigtails, she looked like a kid. He stood there and let himself enjoy the view, content to get his pathetic kicks where he could.

After he'd remained silent a few moments, she peeked through one eyelid. "What's the matter? Is it too horrifying for words?"

"You said not to tell you." He grinned at her. "I'm just following orders."

"Don't be deliberately obtuse, Karlsson." She propped both fists on her hips. "What did Belle do?"

"From what I saw of my upcoming schedule, she bought you several more lessons. Very expensive, private, nighttime lessons. The only ones still available for the next two weeks, probably because they *are* so expensive." Another groan was Tess's only response. "Unfortunately, I have to inform you that the money for those lessons is nonrefundable, due to company policy. Which the concierge would have explained to her before she booked the appointments."

This groan was more like a wail.

There was nothing he could do about it, unfortunately. Because he was a draw for the resort, the company didn't look kindly upon cancellations made less than a week in advance, whether or not they could easily fill the vacated slots in his schedule. They felt the availability of too many last-minute appointments would devalue his perceived worth.

Maybe they were right, maybe they weren't.

Either way, poor Tess had a simple choice before her: She could waste a shitload of her friend's money, find someone else to take the lessons…or suffer through several nights of his company.

They both knew how this was going to play out, at least for tonight. He just wondered how long it would take her to accept the inevitable.

To her credit, not long. Within moments, her eyes opened, her shoulders straightened, and she gave a firm little nod. "Okay, then. Multiple tennis lessons it is."

He should resist. But he wouldn't. "With me. One-on-one. At night."

"Yeah, smartass. I got that part." She gestured to the court. "How does all this usually work? I didn't pack a racket or any sort of tennis supplies."

"You can borrow what you need from the clubhouse. Part of what you pay for with those nightly resort fees." He waved her toward the building. "After you."

Clubhouse was an overly generous term for the space, which housed tennis equipment and clothing for guests to borrow and buy. Even considering the modest one-bedroom apartment—reserved for the island's famous tennis instructor—on the second floor, it resembled a small cottage more than anything else. But the resort liked its euphemistic names for amenities, and Lucas went along with it.

He went along with pretty much everything these days.

No stress. No mess. No fuss.

Opening the door for her, he held it until she walked through and then followed behind her. "What sort of tennis experience do you have?"

At this time of night, guests drifted away from the courts and toward bars, restaurants, torch-lit beaches, and bedrooms. While he and Tess had been talking, the last few clubhouse visitors had made their purchases and left. The closed sign had been placed on the inside of the door.

The two of them were alone.

Well, almost. Pat, the woman who staffed the register,

was counting her money, putting the correct amount back in the register drawer, and placing the rest in a bank deposit pouch. Soon, though, she too would leave, locking the door behind her and dropping the key off at the security hut.

Then he'd be the only person with access to both the clubhouse and his apartment, apart from security. It was as much privacy as the resort could offer. Which he knew, since he'd demanded it before taking the job.

Too bad Tess didn't want him as a lover. They'd have had all the time in the world tonight.

"I played a bit as a kid. Nothing official. Just a few lessons and hitting the ball back and forth with friends." Baby-fine strands of her dark hair fluttered around her face in the breeze of the overhead fan. "How do you choose the right racket for someone like me?"

He could have given her the answer in his sleep. "We'll pick something on the lighter end. Even though heavy rackets help with power, they can give you tennis elbow and are more difficult to maneuver."

He steered her toward the borrowed equipment wall and let her consider her options.

Her teeth sank into her plush lower lip, and her finger stroked slowly down the side of a graphite frame. At the inadvertent taunt, heat bloomed in his belly, swift and unwelcome.

"Some of the rackets are different sizes," she said.

He swallowed hard. Regained control of himself. "How much do you care about improving your technique?"

"Not at all." She laughed and turned to him. "Is that terrible of me to say?"

"Everyone has different goals." More standard instructor language. "None of them are more right or wrong than others. In your case, I'd choose a big racket head, since it will provide you with a larger sweet spot. Smaller heads are better for working on technique." He winked at her. "Although I wouldn't know that from personal experience."

"Oh, you have a big head, all right. The one above your neck." Despite her deadpan stare, her lips were twitching. "I'll never know about the other."

He leaned his shoulder against the wall and grinned at her. "Rest assured, that one is equally impressive."

While they'd been evaluating rackets, the cashier had finished her work, gathered her purse from the staff room—more like staff closet—and signed out. Now she headed for the door, shaking her head. "I'm locking up, Lucas. Behave yourself. Or at least try."

Poor Pat. She'd expected him to be classier, given his professional pedigree. "What fun would that be?"

When she shook her head again, her helmet of curls didn't move. "And fill out your paperwork when you're done. I don't want you to get in trouble a second time this week."

"Thanks, Pat." He swept her into a hug, which she returned. "Don't know what I'd do without you."

She didn't hesitate. "Get fired. Probably within hours."

After a final pat of his arm, she departed the clubhouse, and the lock clicked into place with a jingle of her keys.

"I think your amorous exploits have traumatized your coworkers." Tess sent him a chiding look. "No wonder her hair is completely grey. Mine probably will be too before I leave the island." She tugged the bottom of a pigtail, eyeing it carefully. "I think I have more greys already. I blame our encounter earlier today."

He'd noticed a few sparkly threads glinting in her hair that morning. Noticed and marveled at how unexpectedly pretty they were.

"That wouldn't be such a terrible thing. I like the little bits of silver you have. They look like…" What was the best way to describe it? "Against your dark hair, they're like stars in the night sky."

He nodded, pleased with himself.

She didn't appear impressed. "Bullshit."

"Believe me or don't. I'm fine either way." He shrugged away an unexpected twinge in his chest. "But for what it's worth, I'm telling the truth."

"Maybe." She'd bitten her lower lip again. It was red, and he could see the mark of her teeth. "But you can only romanticize my grey hairs because you're in no danger of getting some anytime soon."

Whatever. This was way too much effort expended on something that wasn't going anywhere. Not even to bed.

Turning back to the rackets, he scanned the offerings. "Let me take a look at your hands. We need to figure out the best grip size."

He'd expected her to hold them up in the air, so he could evaluate their length. Instead, she placed her right hand on top of his, where it was braced against the wall.

Was this an unspoken apology for her momentary snappishness? Or...something else?

Her mind, her motivations, were too complicated for the likes of him. He was lost.

In contrast, the feel of her was simple. Her palms were yielding and cushiony, her fingers uncallused against the backs of his. Warm. So warm.

"See? They're big. Not as big as yours"—she cast him a dampening look—"and no, I don't want to hear what you're about to say in response to that. But my hands are large for a woman, probably because I'm so tall."

She was tall compared to the average woman. Using American units of measurement, maybe a couple inches short of six feet. But compared to female tennis pros like Venus Williams or Petra Kvitová, her height wasn't particularly notable. And he'd grown up in the land of Valkyries and Vikings, so tall women were hardly a novelty for him.

He turned over his hand beneath hers so they could compare lengths palm-to-palm.

It felt electric, like every brush of skin they'd had to this point.

"I'm six-six. At least eight inches taller than you." When she was looking straight ahead, he could stare down at the part in her hair. To make eye contact, she had to tip that pugnacious chin high, like she was doing now. "As far as I'm concerned, you're a munchkin."

Then he slid his hand from beneath hers and walked a few steps away.

Even if she'd initiated contact once again, even if she hadn't pulled away from his touch, he needed to heed her spoken wishes. She didn't want him. He, in turn, didn't want their undeniable physical chemistry to confuse him or encourage him to intrude where he wasn't welcome.

And the skin at his nape was beginning to prickle, like it did when a game, a set, a match was starting to slip through his fingers.

He didn't understand it, but he didn't need to.

It was uncomfortable, and he didn't do uncomfortable anymore.

"Come on," he told her. "Let's choose a racket, grab a few balls, and get going."

FOUR

By the time they'd locked the clubhouse door behind them and reached the nearby courts, Lucas had regained his customary equanimity.

He'd flirt. Maybe she'd flirt back and touch him again. Maybe she wouldn't.

Then they'd part ways at the end of the lesson, no harm done, and he'd need to make his usual decision: Did he intend to spend the night alone? Or with company?

He could retreat to his apartment and search for something vaguely interesting on Netflix. He could call his friend Nick, who should be on a rare break between tournaments right now. He could find some of the other resort employees and ask whether they wanted to catch the ferry to the mainland for a late dinner or a drink. Or he could rifle through the room and cell numbers he'd been offered that week and opt for some undemanding female companionship.

Either way, he could relax and enjoy himself. Just like he did every day.

Just as he intended to do for the rest of this lesson.

Tess walked beside him, clutching her borrowed racket

and a can of balls. "When I asked you why you came to the island, why didn't you tell me you worked here?"

Tess, he'd found, didn't do *undemanding*. Yet another reason to keep her at a distance, no matter how unexpectedly interesting and charming he found her.

"I didn't think it was important." If he'd also wanted to hedge his bets, to ensure knowledge of his job didn't nudge her memory banks and make her recognize him, that wasn't important either. "Besides, I told you the main reasons I came here. Sun. Water. Sand. Relaxation. Everything I need."

"You forgot women." Her voice was as dry as the sand he'd just mentioned.

He grinned at her. "I never forget women. Female companionship falls under the category of relaxation. And occasionally sun, sand, or water, depending on her level of adventurousness."

She raised that single, devastating brow. "It's a miracle you haven't been arrested."

"As long as the parties involved are willing, located on the adults-only side of the beach, and not visible to other guests, security tends to turn a blind eye to al fresco shenanigans." Keeping his racket under his arm, he dumped his bag of water bottles and towels by the end of the court. "So there's no real danger of arrest. It's all pretty routine."

Her brow rose higher. "Routine? How thrilling your assignations must be."

"I don't need police intervention to make things exciting." He shook his head at her. "Trust me on that. And speaking of exciting—"

"Oh, Lord." She flicked her gaze heavenward. "Here we go."

"What?" He held up his hands, widening his eyes to approximate innocent confusion. "I was just going to offer to help you with your serve."

"And that's exciting...how, exactly?"

"Because a good serve can win you a lot of free points or set you up for success later in a rally." He gestured toward her empty hand. "Shouldn't you be taking notes or something?"

The corners of her mouth had tucked inward as she fought a smile. "So that's why you consider teaching me to serve exciting. Because of the possibility of winning free points. Not because doing so might involve physical contact?"

Well, he couldn't say he hadn't been looking forward to that aspect of the job.

Still, he tsked. "That would never have occurred to me. Assistant Principal Dunn, shame on you. You have a filthy mind."

"Yeah, right," she said. "It doesn't really matter, though. I don't want you to work with my serve."

He frowned. "Why not?"

She waved her racket dismissively. "I just don't see the point of perfecting my serve when, given my track record, I probably won't play again for a few years. Possibly ever. So spending time to improve my form doesn't make any sense. Instead, why don't we just hit the ball around a bit? I can get some exercise, and you can..." Her laugh rang through the court, plumping her cheeks and striking sparks from her eyes. "You can do whatever the hell you want. Which is, I suspect, both your preference and your custom."

That was unfair. He didn't always do what he wanted. Like right now, for instance, when he really wanted to taste the echo of that laugh on her lips.

"If a little leisurely hitting is what you want, that's what you'll get." He gestured toward the far end of the court. "Why don't you take that side, since there's less glare from the overhead lights there?"

"Sure." She handed him the can of balls and rambled over to the other side, her hips swaying in a very distracting way.

36

If he didn't get out his final question now, that hypnotic sway would make him forget it entirely. "How much do you want to run?"

"Not much. My knee can't handle it." She stretched her arms—and racket—to the sky, twisting from side to side. "Such are the travails of middle age, as you'll eventually discover."

He frowned at her. "There are professional tennis players only a couple years younger than you ranked within the top ten. Hell, the top five. Thirty-nine isn't exactly one step from the grave, and it's not that far distant from twenty-six."

"Oh, come on." She positioned her feet shoulder-width apart and bent down, stretching her hamstrings. "We share zero cultural touchstones. When I was growing up, New Kids on the Block were the boy band du jour. I had their poster on my wall. What was your era's equivalent? Backstreet Boys? *NSYNC? Or did they not make it to Sweden?"

He grabbed a couple balls, slipped one in his pocket, and bounced the other against the acrylic-covered concrete. "A Swede wrote and produced songs for both groups, so yeah. They were big there. But that happened when I was...I don't know. Six? Eight?"

"Years too young for even a glimpse of puberty." She snorted. "You're a kid."

"Hey, at least I was too old for One Direction. That should give you some comfort."

This time, when he bounced the ball, he hit it toward her. Even that faint impact zinged through his overworked wrist, but as always, the *ping* of the ball against the sweet spot of his racket soothed the sting.

The ball landed precisely where he'd intended, just within reach of her racket. She promptly hit it into the net. But when she sighed and strode toward it, he waved her off.

"This time, don't move forward quite so far. You want to stay behind the bounce, so when you hit the ball, it's in front of you. And don't try to hit it so hard. Let the racket do some of the work for you." He retrieved the ball from his pocket and bounced it a few times. "I know you don't care about technique, but even a friendly rally isn't fun if you can't get the ball over the net."

She nodded, her brows drawn together. "Got it."

Another easy shot that landed a couple steps away from her. "I'm not certain whether the reigning boy bands of different eras should be considered cultural touchstones or any meaningful gauge of compatibility."

This time, she shanked her forehand, and the ball flew off to the side.

"Shit," she muttered. "Sorry."

"You haven't played in a long time. A little rustiness is to be expected." He emptied the final ball from the can. "Be sure to swing from your shoulders, not your elbows or wrists. I don't want you injuring yourself. And picture yourself swinging through the ball, not at it."

She clutched her racket tighter, deep lines carving across her forehead.

Damn. She was supposed to be enjoying herself.

"Listen…" He climbed over the net and dropped the ball in her left hand. "Why don't you take the first shot?"

Her fingers closed around the ball, and her face brightened. "That might work better. I like having a little more control."

He huffed out a laugh. "No shit."

"I make no apologies. There's a reason I intend to become principal soon." After a couple of experimental bounces of the ball against the ground, those lines on her forehead eased, and a faint smile curved her generous mouth. "So if boy bands aren't a good cultural touchstone, what would be? Famous movies? Internet and social media trends?"

She caught the ball in her left hand, holding her racket away from her body with her right. "Because I hate to tell you this, but my family didn't get a computer until I was about eight, and I didn't send my first e-mail until I was in high school. I'm still not entirely certain what TikTok is, although I assume it involves mechanical timepieces."

He wagged his finger at her. "Don't pretend to be a technological dunce, Tess. Given your job, I'm sure you use all sorts of online educational programs and digital tools, including some I've never seen. Am I right?"

A weird sound emitted from her throat. Something between a growl and a disgruntled *hmph*. Either way, he knew what it meant: He was right.

"Maybe," she finally allowed.

With a healthy swing—from her shoulder, he was glad to note, although her follow-through was minimal—she sent the ball flying over the net. *Way* over the net, past the baseline. He scrambled backward to return it, but managed to hit a controlled shot that should land right…

There. Right in front of her and to her side. This time, she caught the ball in her sweet spot, and it sailed back over the net.

A real rally. Hallelujah.

She was still talking, still trying to prove that they had nothing in common. "When I was growing up, if I wanted to listen to a specific song, I couldn't just go online and find a YouTube video or a good streaming service. I had to listen to the radio for hours on end, recognize the opening bars of the song, hold my little tape recorder next to my radio, and pray my parents wouldn't make too much noise during the song. Or I'd have to buy the entire album, tape, or CD, depending on how old I was. When I found out about iTunes, I almost cried with joy."

He ran to reach a ball that barely cleared the net. "Too law-abiding for Napster's pirating heyday, huh?"

"I'm surprised you even remember back that far." She missed his return, which bounced past her and hit the back of the court with a rattle of boards. When he produced another can of balls from his bag, she held up a hand. "Let's take a quick break."

Obligingly, he dropped a ball in his pocket and leaned on his racket. "As far as Napster, all I can legally tell you is that my older brother had an extensive music collection around the turn of the millennium. And to tackle your broader contention, I would argue that love of music transcends the means by which we acquire it. Also its national origin."

"I take it you don't agree with my choice of relevant cultural touchstones." A few shiny strands of her hair had fallen free from her pigtails, and she tucked them behind her ears. "In that case, I repeat: What would be good ones, then?"

He thought for a minute.

"Much as I hate to say it...international tragedies, maybe? I think we both share some of the same memories, despite our differing ages and nationalities and understandings of the events at the time." Uncapping a water bottle, he took a sip. Even at night and with an ocean breeze, a Florida summer could suffocate you with humidity. "Or political upheaval. And we've both been adults and U.S. residents for the most recent example of that."

When he tossed another water bottle over the net, she caught it. "So you're going with the depressing stuff? I'm surprised at you, Lucas. I thought you were all good times and willing women."

All the *depressing stuff* had exited his life months ago. And good riddance.

"Oh, I am," he assured her with a lazy wink. "And I'm not certain any cultural touchstone can really determine how much two people have in common, or whether they'll be able to understand one another. I would think shared personality traits, interests, and life experiences would be more relevant."

"So it's not the years, it's the model and the mileage?" Her head tilted as she stared at him, and she took a long time to answer. "I hadn't thought about it that way, but I guess I would probably agree with you."

"What? You agree with me?" He gripped the net with both hands and leaned over it, squinting at her. "Who are you? And what have you done with Tess Dunn?"

She didn't answer.

Something in her eyes had shifted over the past few minutes, while he'd coached her and they'd argued about boy bands and generational landmarks. He wasn't sure what. But she was evaluating him in a different way, paying closer attention to him and his words than he remembered her doing before.

He wanted to bask in that attention almost as much as he wanted to run from it.

"Tess. Hey, Tess." He waved a hand in her sightline. "Has prolonged exposure to my handsome visage and superb body finally incapacitated you?"

She didn't bother to respond to his nonsense, and her eyes remained steady on his face. Studying him. Reading his expressions.

Then she finally spoke, her voice soft. Vulnerable. "Tell me more about why you're here, Lucas. For real, this time."

God help him, he almost told her. Almost stripped himself bare for her inspection and revisited the corners of his soul he'd shut away for good last year.

But he wasn't the same man he'd once been, so his past was no longer relevant. Particularly to a woman who was not only determined to use their age differential as a wedge between them, but also leaving in two weeks.

She was trouble. Too demanding, too defensive, and too tempting. Any entanglement with her might end quickly, but it could still damage him. He knew it already, and he should heed that warning siren of unease, the visceral instinct that had guided him through countless matches and tournaments.

Besides, she'd claimed she wasn't interested in him, so she had no right to demand answers.

Unless she'd changed her mind?

If so, maybe…

His chest hitched with his next breath. *Maybe I could change mine too.*

He rested his elbows on the net and leaned forward, his legs oddly shaky beneath him.

"First, tell *me* something, Tess. Are you interested in having lunch together? Tomorrow?" When her mouth opened, he rushed to clarify. "Not in my apartment. At a restaurant or outside. Wherever you want."

She took four slow steps toward the net, halting just out of arm's reach.

Those hazel eyes were hard to read, especially in the limited light, but they weren't narrowed with suspicion or outrage. She wasn't shaking her head, either. Wasn't telling him he didn't mean the invitation, or that it was automatic.

Which it wasn't. Nothing concerning Tess was automatic or easy, and despite himself, he liked it. Liked her. That insistent prickling at the nape of his neck be damned.

"I…" Her hard swallow shifted the shadows delineating her throat. "I'm busy tomorrow. Belle and I planned out the entire day weeks ago."

Her birthday. Dammit, he'd forgotten.

"The day after tomorrow, then." He kept pushing, determined to make definite plans before she had too much time to think. Hell, before *he* had too much time to think. "We'll do a picnic. Meet me outside the clubhouse, and I'll take care of everything."

She was wavering. Tense and uncertain. He could see it in the way her soft mouth pursed and released, hear it in the crackle of the water bottle compressing in her grip.

"Please, Tess."

Why was he pleading with her? If he wanted female company, he had plenty of options. Options who didn't respond to flirtation with an eyeroll and a truculent chin-raise. Options who'd accept an invitation to lunch without—

"Okay." Two soft syllables, spoken with a firm little nod.

As relief wobbled in his knees, he leaned more heavily on the net. "Can you do a late lunch? Half-past one?"

A tentative smile tilted her lips. "That should w—"

"Hey, tennis boy! Did you get our texts?"

The shout from outside the court made Tess jerk, her shoulders stiffening. Seemingly on instinct, she backed several steps away from the net. Away from him.

Fuck. The moment was gone, and if he gave her half a chance to consider all the reasons he wasn't a good bet for a woman like her, she'd retreat from their lunch date too.

He swung to face the interloper, his brows drawn together in warning. "Brendan, no one's supposed to interrupt my lessons. That includes fellow employees."

Brendan raised his hands, palms out. "Sorry, dude. You never work this late, so I thought this was, uh..." He scratched the back of his head as he considered his wording, jostling the brim of his backward-turned baseball cap. "An off-the-clock situation."

Lucas's glance at his watch confirmed his colleague's claim. His lesson with Tess had run way past its official end time. And fuck, she was eyeing the exit nearest the club-house, her expression guarded once more.

If he climbed over the net to her side of the court, would that reassure her? Or make her run? "Look, Brendan, can we—"

The other man was still talking. "—won't do it again. But as long as I'm here, I might as well tell you. A bunch of us are heading to Emma's place on the mainland to watch the game. I heard she made meatballs in the slow-cooker, so it'll basically be like home for you, only with less furniture assembled via Allen wrenches."

A faint snort from the other side of the net heartened Lucas.

He caught Brendan's eye and nodded toward the clubhouse, his message clear: *Get out.* "Despite that heartwarming homage to my homeland, I can't—"

This time, Tess interrupted him. "You should go. I need to get back to work, anyway." She walked to his bag and laid her racket on top. "Besides, if you ask nicely, I bet they'd even play 'Dancing Queen' for you."

He sighed. "Haha. ABBA jokes. Very creative."

"Thank you. I accept that compliment with the same sincerity with which it was offered." She shot him a half-hearted grin and walked toward the exit. "Have a good night, boys."

Boys. Yeah. That was not a promising sign.

"Tess…" He trailed off, unsure whether having her confirm their date would instead give her an opening to cancel it. "You don't have to go."

"I really do," she called over her shoulder.

It was a risk, but he needed to know. Needed that confirmation.

Just before she left the court, he spoke loudly enough to carry across the distance. "Half-past one, pigtails. The day after tomorrow. Don't forget."

Her brisk stride faltered, and he braced himself.

Then she began walking again, and her words floated through the shadows of the court. "Maybe I should. But I won't."

FIVE

Tess chose a discreet spot outside the chain-link fence surrounding the tennis courts, one partially shielded from the unforgiving island sun by swaying palm fronds. Close enough to watch and hear the tail end of Lucas's pre-picnic lesson. Distant enough to evade his notice, especially given his preoccupation with his clients, a young couple in stylish tennis whites.

If she'd picked her spot wisely, she wouldn't end up a victim of heat stroke before their date even began, and he'd never know she'd arrived thirty minutes early to spy on him.

Well, not *spy* on him. *Observe* him. Like she would one of her teachers.

Yes, that was what she was doing. Certainly there was no spying or—God forbid—ogling involved. Despite the sway of his very round, very firm ass when he bent over and prepared to return his clients' serves, or the delicious bunching of his shoulder muscles beneath his thin, sweat-soaked t-shirt as he hit a two-handed backhand.

Nope. No ogling whatsoever.

Although, if ogling *had* occurred, it would have been well worth the effort.

In between periods of not-ogling, she watched him with the couple and discovered that his patient, well-informed guidance during her own lesson hadn't been an aberration. The class had a logical, obvious structure, the clients knew what to expect, he paid close attention to both of them, and his advice was clear, practical, and stated with both knowledge and authority.

He was a good teacher, and she knew good teaching when she saw it.

He'd also left a dozen yellow tulips and a scrawled note wishing her a happy birthday at the front desk yesterday. Belle, delighted by the seeming success of her machinations, had literally squealed at the sight of the bouquet.

Tess had underestimated him.

Then again, he'd encouraged her to do so at their first meeting, and she still didn't understand why. Why he hadn't told her he worked at the resort and what he did there. Why he'd played the aimless flirt, when he was clearly more than that. Why, when he seemed interested in her, he'd chosen to hide so much of himself.

That lack of clarity—even apart from her other doubts, which were legion—had almost led her to call the clubhouse yesterday and leave him a message, canceling their lunch together. Even with those gorgeous, thoughtful tulips on her nightstand.

She'd picked up the phone in her room and dialed the relevant extension three or four times, but in the end, she'd always replaced the handset back on the cradle. And when Belle had left for a noontime rendezvous with Brian earlier that day, Tess hadn't used her limited quiet, private time alone in their room to work. Instead, after waving goodbye to her friend, she'd spent way too long contemplating her limited wardrobe options and considering Lucas's possible reactions to each before finally throwing on a simple, comfortable cotton maxi dress.

If that maxi dress showed an exuberant expanse of cleavage and its turquoise print suited her complexion, she'd told herself that was mere happenstance. But that had been a lie, and she'd known it even then.

Just as she knew an objective observer would deem her current behavior ogling.

When the lesson ended, the couple gathered their belongings. Lucas said his goodbyes and sprinted for the clubhouse, his large bag anchored to his side with one hand. With the other, he wrenched open the glass door to the little building, and then he disappeared inside.

They'd agreed to meet for lunch in ten minutes. He was hurrying. For her and to her.

That knowledge settled a few of her doubts, but not all of them, and not for long.

Taking her time, she followed his path to the clubhouse and stationed herself outside, trying not to think about the coworker who'd interrupted the end of her tennis lesson two days ago. More specifically, about how that coworker had appeared to be the same approximate age as her students. Twenty, max. Most likely around the same age as their friend Emma.

Lucas hung out with those people. Partied with them.

She was twice their age. Which was disconcerting, since forty suddenly didn't feel much different from thirty-nine. Or twenty-nine, for that matter.

Not that she'd anticipated a sudden surfeit of middle-aged wisdom as the clock struck midnight on her birthday, or foreseen her body withering and crumpling into dust with the turning of a page in her planner. But maybe, despite all her protests about the unimportance of the transition, she'd expected more *certainty* with the advent of her fifth decade on this earth. Tranquility. Calm acceptance of her life as it was, both its joys and boundaries.

That hadn't happened.

Instead, there she stood outside the tennis clubhouse, sweating in the midday heat, forty years and one day old, awash with sensations she hadn't experienced in well over a decade. After all this time, who knew she could still feel so... fluttery? So electric with possibility and doubt and risk?

She'd dated after the end of her engagement. Had sex. Even called a man or two her boyfriend.

But she'd never once reacted this way to them. God help her, but Lucas somehow unbalanced her, dizzied her until her tongue came untethered and said things—angry things, honest things, foolishly flirty things—a diplomatic, practical principal-to-be would never, ever say.

Worse, her body rioted in his presence. Bloomed. Betrayed itself and undermined her slipping grasp on equanimity. And her too-hopeful heart...

Well, the less said about that, the better.

For a woman who was, above all else, pragmatic, it was all very disorienting.

As was his sudden arrival at her side, that familiar bag once again hanging from his shoulder, the clubhouse door swinging shut behind him. The sun glinted off the wet strands of his thick, dark hair, limning its edges with copper. He smelled like some sort of outdoorsy-scented soap, and he was wearing a different outfit. Still shorts and a tee, but both were dry and unwrinkled. Heat radiated from his large body, more intense than the sun searing her scalp and bare arms.

"Hey, Tess. Sorry I'm a couple minutes late." He was smiling at her, his dimples deep, his olive-green eyes bright. "That's a pretty dress."

His forefinger skimmed her arm in a fleeting moment of contact, and her breath caught at the sudden bolt of sensation. She stared at him, aghast at her reaction to that simple touch.

Aghast and...well, terrified, actually.

He'd positioned himself close to her, his shoulder

propped against the side of the building. Only a couple feet away, people walked past them, and he didn't glance in their direction, not even when she heard his name spoken. His focus remained entirely on her. And the way his gaze caressed her features...

Lucas was still speaking, although she'd entirely lost track of his words. "—the perfect spot, I think. Will that be a problem for your knee? If so, I have another place we can go."

Wait, why were they talking about her knee?

She blinked at him. "Excuse me?"

With a graceful shrug, he lowered his bag to the ground and peered into her face, his own now craggy with concern. "Are you okay? You look kind of...I don't know. Out of it, I guess." Gently, he rested the back of his hand against her forehead, then her temple. "Fuck, I'm sorry, Tess. I should have told you to wait inside the clubhouse. Heat exhaustion can happen more quickly than you'd think out here. Are you feeling okay? You don't seem feverish."

His touch, his nearness, confused her. The echo of his words—the few she'd listened to—confused her. The explosion of damnable hope spreading sunshine through her every vein, every cell, confused her.

She caught at his broad, warm hand. Held it, needing its stability as she floundered. "I'm fine."

"I'm so sorry I ran late." Despite her answer, he was still ushering her into the shade of a nearby overhang, his fingers intertwined with hers, his other hand light on her back. "I didn't think reheating the dips or packing everything in my bag would take so long, but that's no excuse. Do you want some water?"

She closed her eyes for a moment. Took a deep breath, the warmth of his palms a tease of sensation along her spine and against her own hand.

"I apologize, Lucas. I was thinking about—" When she

licked her balm-covered lips, his gaze dropped there, and she had to shake herself free from yet another near-fugue state. "I was remembering something I needed to do for work. But I'm fine, and more than happy to go wherever you'd like for the picnic."

His brow was still furrowed as he studied her. "Are you sure you're not ill or overheated?"

She was definitely overheated. But not for the reasons he imagined.

"I'm fine," she repeated. "But thank you for being concerned, and please don't worry about being a minute late. You're fitting me into a busy schedule, and I know that."

His lips tipped up again, and his brow smoothed. "It's my pleasure. If you start feeling sick at any point, just let me know."

She waved that off. "Lead on, Macduff."

Obediently, he moved away from the wall, his hand lifting from her back. But their fingers were still intertwined, and he gently tugged her toward the sidewalk.

"You know that's supposed to be 'Lay on, Macduff,' right?" He steered them around a family stalled in the middle of the path and bickering over who'd misplaced their room keycards. "Since I'm Swedish, maybe it should be Macduff-sson instead. With an umlaut somewhere."

So he knew his Shakespeare too. Impressive. "Language evolves. Over time, what began as an error can become its own correct idiom through common usage. Different from, but equally as valid as, the original phrasing."

"Fair enough." He cast her a sidelong glance, full of what appeared to be...approval? Enjoyment? She didn't know, but it definitely wasn't aversion to her undeniable nerdy streak.

To their left, various outbuildings gave way to gardens, then the start of a nature path that wended through a nearly-untouched expanse of the grounds. To their right, the sandy beach turned rocky, the waves churning into foam and sea spray as they smacked into the boulders. Still beautiful, but wilder. Less tourist-friendly than the rest of the island, which in turn meant fewer crowds and more privacy for their lunch.

He'd slowed his stride in deference to her shorter legs, which came as a relief. She was built for comfort, not speed.

"That reminds me," he said. "I meant to ask you the other night, but I forgot. Before you became an assistant principal, what did you teach? English?"

All relief fled as they rounded a bend in the sidewalk and their probable destination came into view. It was still a five-minute walk away, but easily visible. Which it would be, as the only real high spot on the entire island.

She'd seen the steep, rocky hill and the panoramic overlook built atop it on the map, but hadn't bothered visiting once she'd read the fine print on the resort guide. *Accessible only by stairs*, the brochure had stated, and she was avoiding those as much as possible, given the precarious state of her right knee.

Dammit, she should have been paying attention earlier, not drooling at his mere proximity. Especially since this wasn't just a single flight of stairs. No, the wooden steps went up...and up...and up some more. Maybe three or four flights in total.

No wonder he'd asked about her knee. Very thoughtful of him.

Too bad she hadn't been listening.

Getting up there shouldn't be a huge issue. Given how much she walked around the school on a daily basis, her general fitness level was fine, and her knee usually didn't bother her going upstairs. Getting back down, however...

Well, that was an entirely different matter. And the tennis lesson the other night had done her joint no favors.

"I taught psychology," she told him absently. "I was part of the social studies department."

His little, interested hum vibrated through her. "What sort of things did you talk about in class?"

Shit. The stairs looked even steeper up close.

At the base of the hill, she slowed as she considered her choices. All bad. All painful in one way or another.

She could climb the damn stairs and hope her knee wouldn't protest going back down, although that seemed like a forlorn hope. But it would allow her to retain her pride. Unlike, say, her other main option.

Because she hadn't been listening as she should, she'd already said she could go wherever he wanted for lunch. Still, she could speak up now. Tell him she'd changed her mind. Explain that her knee probably couldn't handle that many steps and ask him to find a different location for their lunch.

Lucas would say yes, of course.

Lucas, a twenty-six-year-old athlete who hung out with twenty-year-olds, would definitely change his plans in deference to the creaky, temperamental joints of his forty-year-old date.

But nothing could epitomize the contrast between them more neatly than such a request, such an accommodation. All her pride would taste bitter on her tongue. It would choke her as she tried to swallow it.

Maybe her knee could handle the stairs. She'd take it slow on the way back down. Stop to faux-admire the view—which really did seem as if it would be spectacular—along the way. Let the handful of other tourists on the stairs pass her by as she took photos with her cell.

Or maybe somehow, magically, she and Lucas would never have to descend at all. They could stay up there forever, inviolate, illusions intact.

She, of all people, knew better. A reckoning would inevitably come.

But even a born pragmatist could pretend otherwise, if only for a moment.

"Tess?" Lucas was looking at her quizzically.

"Sorry." She turned to him. Offered a smile that stretched her cheeks uncomfortably. "I haven't been on this side of the island before. It's really beautiful."

He glanced up at the stairs, then back down at her. "We can go somewhere else, if you'd like. The view's great up there, but it's great everywhere else too. And the overlook's not entirely private, although there's a quieter area off to the side with a picnic table."

Last chance to be honest.

"This spot is perfect. Thank you for bringing me here." She took the first step, then another. No pain. Not yet, anyway. "Let's get going. I'm starving, and I can't wait to see what you've packed for lunch."

Screw honesty. She wanted to pretend, to believe, just a little longer.

SIX

"So what did you and your friend do for your birthday yesterday?" Lucas speared another piece of pork souvlaki from the plastic container on the picnic table. "You said you had the whole day planned out."

For the past minute, Tess had been mixing the tzatziki sauce with the eggplant dip as a sort of culinary experiment, one he'd watched with amused interest. Now, even though she had her wedge of pita piled high with the mixture and halfway to her mouth, she paused.

Then she set down her concoction, wincing. "Lucas, I'm so sorry. I should have thanked you right away for the gorgeous tulips. They're some of my favorite flowers."

He knew. When he'd finally managed to locate Belle— sans Tess—yesterday morning, she'd told him. Then he'd visited the resort's behind-the-scenes floral arrangement guy. A few minutes of wheedling and a discreet handover of cash later, he'd had the blooms in hand and on their way to the front desk.

Maybe the gesture had been too much. He and Tess hadn't even kissed. Might never kiss. They'd barely touched, for that matter.

But he hadn't wanted the day to pass without his noting it. One more year of prickly, vibrant Tess Dunn on this earth was something to celebrate, no matter what did or didn't happen between the two of them.

"My pleasure." He gestured toward her pita. "Try your special creation. I can wait on all the birthday details."

She bit down and chewed, her eyes closed, her expression thoughtful.

Thank goodness for the resort restaurant that had supplied their meal, since his own kitchen contained a toaster, coffeemaker, microwave, and scratched nonstick skillet as its primary amenities. Sure, he had a refrigerator, but it was nearly empty. The apartment's small oven probably worked too, but he owned nothing oven-safe to put inside it. Given his dearth of both food and equipment, cooking for Tess himself hadn't been an option today.

His parents had taught him how, and he enjoyed it. He still helped with their signature pork roast, applesauce, and Janssons frestelse—a creamy potato and anchovy gratin, his favorite side dish of all time—whenever he went home. But somehow, outfitting his own apartment with cooking supplies had never occurred to him.

Buying those items would imply permanency and require an eye to his future, he supposed. And he hadn't considered that future—hadn't allowed himself to consider it—for a long time now.

Tess's throat bobbed as she swallowed, and he tried not to make that image sexual. Unsuccessfully.

"Delicious," she eventually pronounced, her lashes fluttering open again. "You should tell the chef to combine both dips for a new dish of some sort."

He snorted at that. "I'm the tennis dude. If I tried to tell Georgios what he should cook, he'd use his cleaver to separate me from some of my favorite appendages."

Her gaze dropped to his lap before she cleared her throat

and looked away, cheeks now flushed from more than the sun.

"I meant my hands, Tess." He shook his head mournfully. "I'm shocked they let people with such filthy imaginations become administrators at your school."

Even as she flipped him a discreet middle finger, her lips curved in a reluctant grin.

He heaved a dramatic sigh of disapproval. "Not to mention such filthy gestures. And that's not even considering your topless escapades and unprovoked attacks on unsuspecting men's backs."

"*Shhhhh*." She was laughing now, low and sweet, her hand flapping in the direction of the stairs. "There's a family coming, and they don't need to hear about my—"

"Bouncy bits?"

One of the dip containers nearly overturned as she lurched across the table. Her fierce whisper in his ear was a taunting tease, one he fully deserved. "Zip it, Karlsson. They're almost at the top of the stairs now. And besides..."

She'd left her hair down and tumbling to her soft shoulders today. The strands, silky and fragrant with some sort of fruity shampoo, brushed against his cheek, and he couldn't resist. Where she couldn't see, he caught a stray lock of it and rubbed it between his fingers. Fought the instinct to close his eyes against the overwhelming pleasure of her proximity.

"Besides," she continued, her voice husky, "they don't bounce in the water, really. They're too buoyant for that. They float."

He'd tried not to notice. He really had. But a single glance before he'd fully understood the situation at hand—so to speak—had burned the image on his brain. Her forearm had barely covered her nipples, leaving the abundant curves of her breasts pale and wet and bare and, yes, floating deliciously close to the surface.

When she sat back, he took a hasty sip of his sparkling blood orange soda and nearly choked on the bubbles. Through his coughing, he managed to choke out, "I stand corrected. Or, uh, sit corrected."

"Are you okay?" She half-stood again, obviously ready to thump him on the back as needed.

He waved away her concern. "Fine. Just swallowed wrong."

"Thank you for all this wonderful food." After finishing her dip mixture, she sighed in contentment and surveyed the expanse of nearly-empty plastic containers covering the table. "I hadn't eaten at Georgios's yet. I've been focusing on seafood up to this point, mainly."

He lifted a shoulder. "I think his place serves the best food at the resort, other than maybe The Sands."

"The Sands is incredible!" Her arms folded on the table, she leaned forward, beaming. "We went there our first night, and I wanted to order everything on the menu. *Everything.*"

Last year, the resort's CEO had wooed Lucas over dinner there, touting the island's various amenities as the waitstaff presented gorgeous plates of perfectly cooked red snapper, spiny lobster, and pink shrimp, among countless other seafood courses.

Lucas hadn't visited since. Maybe because of his no-longer-limitless budget for such luxuries. Or maybe because food in general hadn't tasted that good or seemed that important or interesting to him in a while. Not like it did today, as he sat in the sunshine across the table from Tess, the breeze high above the water whipping that bright dress around her strong, shapely calves.

He thought back a few months. "They have a tasting menu, if I remember correctly."

"Oh, we had that. Believe me. During the school year, we live on grocery-store rotisserie chickens, frozen dinners, and occasional fast food. So when Belle and I get to visit a fancy

57

restaurant, which doesn't happen often, tasting menus are kind of our thing." Her nose crinkled in self-deprecation. "But that didn't stop me from peeking at what all the other tables were ordering and getting jealous when their food arrived."

For some reason, that thought—Tess wanting, Tess not getting what she wanted—chafed like a blister forming on his heel. "You really wanted to try everything?"

She laughed again. "Of course I did. I think I had a weird sex dream about the tuna carpaccio and lemon chess meringue pie last night. And whenever Belle sees the menu in the lobby, she kind of makes this forlorn moaning sound and mutters about scallop ceviche for a few minutes. But teachers and assistant principals don't exactly make neuro-surgeon money, so one tasting-menu dinner there will have to suffice."

If the two women didn't have enough money for sampling everything at The Sands, he could address that issue. His salary might have dropped exponentially in the past several years, but he'd been smart enough to save while he could. Moreover, he and his colleagues around the resort tended to exchange unofficial favors, and he could both collect what he was owed and hand out a few markers of his own.

Tess's pride, though, wouldn't allow her to accept that kind of gesture, especially from a man she'd just met. He knew that already.

For that reason, he simply said, "I'm sorry you won't get to taste the entire menu."

A flick of her wrist dismissed his concern. "Life is full of compromises, even on vacation."

There was no self-pity in her tone. Only practicality and resignation.

Yup. That still rubbed him wrong.

She might have accepted that she couldn't get what she

wanted, but he hadn't. And if he couldn't make her food dreams come true, maybe he could help with something else.

"Huh." He propped his elbows on the table. "You just said *compromises*. Plural, not singular. So what else aren't you doing on this vacation?"

After a glance around the outlook, now empty once more —that family had apparently left without him noticing—she grinned at him. "I really wanted to try the nude beach."

The image burst to life in his febrile brain in full color and exquisite detail, so vivid and overwhelming he was surprised his skull could contain it. In response, his pulse shot to a gallop, and the summer heat suddenly blistered every inch of him.

By all indications, if he ever saw Tess entirely naked, bathed in sunlight, he might not survive it. Hell, he might not survive this conversation.

He was willing to take that risk.

"Tell me more," he said.

SEVEN

Tess's brow crinkled. "What more is there to say? It's a nude beach. Palm trees. Sand. Water. Naked floppy bits. Sunburns in awkward and painful places."

If he thought about her naked floppy bits, his tongue would cease making intelligible sounds. "I get that part. What I don't get is why you aren't going there, if that's something you want to experience."

Tess didn't strike him as uncomfortable with her body. So why wasn't she baring it on the island's private stretch of adults-only sand?

And why didn't she invite him along for the experience? A person could dream, after all.

Silence stretched between them for a few moments before she finally spoke again.

"Can you imagine the amount of sunscreen I'd have to buy?" She huffed out a small laugh. "Besides, I'm getting enough sand in unfortunate areas. I don't need to invite a full-body scouring."

Those answers sounded like dodges to him. Red herrings. And if anyone could recognize herrings—of whatever color—a Swede could.

"Those don't seem like insurmountable obstacles to me," he said.

Her chest rose and fell on a pained-sounding breath before her lips quirked again. "You're right. I guess I was trying not to bring up how different we are."

"I don't understand." And he was no longer certain he wanted to, given what she'd just said.

Her mouth pursed. "You're a twenty-something Swede working at a resort where everyone turns a blind eye to…" She paused. "What did you call it? *Al fresco shenanigans?*"

From her lips, the phrase sounded overly glib. Blithe and careless.

"I'm a forty-year-old high school administrator in Virginia, Lucas. I can't get naked in public." She slanted him a wryly amused look, one that had grown familiar. "God bless Europeans. Do you have a national holiday celebrating full-frontal nudity in Sweden? One that involves a ceremonial dropping of trench coats in public squares before you all retire for pastries and naps?"

That particular tone, redolent with sarcasm, was also familiar. "Only on leap years. The rest of the time, we make do with just the naked parade."

"Disappointing." She shook her head. "I'd expected more, somehow."

The whole European angle was only part of what she'd said, and not the most important part either. "The nude beach is on the adults-only end of the island, so you wouldn't be flashing America's youth yet again."

He put special emphasis on the last bit, just to elicit the dirty look he promptly received.

"Can the resort guarantee that no one I know and no one I'll ever need to interact with as a school administrator will be on that beach with me?" She tipped her head as she stared at him, her gaze challenging. "More importantly, do they confiscate all guests' cell phones and cameras before allowing them onto that part of the island? Because anything any of us do in public can end up on the internet at any time, Lucas, and I can't afford to take chances. Not at this stage of my career, when I'm gunning to become principal in a year. Everything I want is so close, and I won't risk it for an after-noon in the sun."

The principal job was everything she wanted? Or was it everything she was letting herself want? Everything she'd convinced herself was practical and possible?

"I'm just lucky you were there to help me when I lost my bikini top." Unexpectedly, she reached out to cover his hand with her own. Squeezed it in silent gratitude. "I work with kids, and I have to deal with American standards of so-called *decency* and *good judgment*. That incident could have been disastrous, as could a trip to the nude beach. So no, I won't be getting naked on the sand. Even if I want to."

"That makes sense," he conceded. "I get it, Tess. You obviously want that principal position a lot."

"More than anything." Her eyes searched his in a seeming plea for understanding. "Not because I want power for its own sake, but because I think I can help the kids at my school. I can make Marysburg High a safer, happier, more useful place for them in every way." She sighed. "The other main candidate from within our school system cares more about the bottom line than education. He would be a terrible principal, and I won't let him have the job. Not if I can possibly help it."

To his regret, he had to concede her other point too: They were very different. In their lives, their work, their ambitions, the expectations placed upon them, the people dependent on their decisions.

He still wanted her. His hunger to understand the twists and intricacies of her mind hadn't eased at all over the course of the lunch. If anything, he felt more starved than ever.

If he had another half-hour to spare, he'd ask about her

plans for her students. Soon, though, his free time between lessons would come to an end, and he didn't want to start a subject they didn't have time to finish. Besides, he had one last surprise for her. One he suspected she'd enjoy.

Turning over his hand, he laced his fingers through hers and slid his thumb over her knuckles in a slow, repeated sweep. With his other hand, he reached into a bag beneath the table and produced the final container.

She peered at the clear plastic top, and after a moment, a small, tentative smile tipped her lips.

"It's not lemon chess meringue pie," he told her. "But all but one of them are for you, and I managed to get a candle for the birthday girl. Well, birthday-plus-one-day girl."

The strawberry lemonade cupcakes had reminded him of Tess. Tart and sweet. Joyously, unmistakably large. Pretty.

"They look delicious." Her fingers squeezed his as she contemplated the half-dozen cupcakes within the container. "Out of curiosity, did you remember to bring something to light the candle?"

His head dropped to his chest. "Shit."

"If you'd remembered, I was going to let you give me forty birthday spanks."

He jerked his head up so fast, he got dizzy. Maybe the new batch of tourists who'd just left the outlook had a lighter? They were halfway down the steps already, but he could catch them if he ran.

Pushing to his feet, he spared her a quick, hopeful glance. "Really?"

"No." She laughed again, her solemnity gone. "I'm fucking with you."

The wooden bench creaked beneath him as he sat back down. "Ah. That's a shame."

"No birthday spanks on offer, but lots of birthday thanks." She nodded toward the cupcakes. "Those look amazing. Thank you, Lucas, for everything you've done to make my birthday special."

Her wide smile plumped her cheeks and sparkled in those big hazel eyes, and the entire wooden outlook structure disappeared from beneath him as he sank into the sight. Into her.

He fumbled for his drink. Took another gulp and almost choked again. "No problem."

The sun was burning the tips of his ears, but that didn't explain the warmth exploding through the rest of him. Especially as she opened the container, selected a cupcake—the one with the most abundant lemon buttercream frosting, a wise choice—and took a huge bite. Her little hum of pleasure as she chewed and swallowed vibrated along his spine, arrowing to his cock.

With evident joy, she methodically worked her way through the cupcake, leaving the most frosting-intensive parts for last. He, in contrast, picked at his, too distracted by the sheer bliss etched across her expressive face to give a fuck about eating.

She wasn't shy in her enthusiasm. Within a minute or two, the confection was gone, and she was sucking icing off her fingers, then licking her thumb to pick up stray crumbs from her paper wrapper. He had to stifle a whimper.

Her gaze locked on the container once more, and he lifted the lid for her.

She hesitated, her eyes guarded. "No lectures about proper nutrition?"

"I've known you for less than three days."

Her head tilted as she watched him. "True."

"That said, even if I'd been your man for eighty years, I wouldn't lecture you. You're in charge of your body, not me." He paused. Winked at her. "Although, if you wanted me in charge of certain *aspects* of your body, I certainly wouldn't mi—"

"You're a skank, Karlsson." But she flicked him a grin as she selected the cupcake with the second-greatest frosting volume. "One with excellent taste in baked goods, however, so I'll allow it."

His heart nearly exploded before she completed her cupcake-eating process for the second time and used a wet wipe on her hands.

Then she leaned forward, and the cleavage on display made it hard to swallow. "I probably shouldn't tell you this. Your head is big enough as it is."

He opened his mouth.

"Yes, yes, I know." She flicked her hand in dismissal. "Let's just assume you already made a joke about the monstrous size of your penis yet again."

He smirked at her. "Oh, it's no joke, Tess."

"For God's sake, Karlsson, I'm trying to give you a compliment."

His mouth opened again.

"*Not* about your penis." She raised that single, expressive brow. "Do you want to hear what I was going to say or not?"

He leaned back and spread his arms. "Have at it, Dunn."

With a little, self-deprecating shake of her head, she said, "I arrived early to our date so I could observe the last few minutes of your lesson with that young couple."

She had? He hadn't spotted her. Then again, he'd have guessed she was more likely not to show up at all than to show up early. Also, both members of that *young* couple were the same age as him, but he wasn't going to mention that. Not for any amount of money.

Then she proceeded to knock a few more foundations out from beneath him. "I was beyond impressed. You're an excellent teacher. Organized, knowledgeable, articulate, and able to break complicated processes down into simple, understandable components. Respectful but friendly. Authoritative without being an ass about it. And from our few encounters,

I know you're clearly very intelligent. The resort is lucky to have you, Lucas, despite your automatic flirtiness and"—she crooked her fingers—"*al fresco shenanigans.*"

His mouth was open again, but not to say something. In shock.

An unfamiliar pressure was clogging his throat, provoking an odd prickle in his sinuses, the physical manifestations of a burgeoning emotion he didn't quite recognize. Maybe because he hadn't felt it for a couple of years now, not in reference to something outside his athletic or sexual prowess. Never in reference to...him. All of him.

"I hope you enjoy your work. But if you don't, you could do pretty much anything, given the right training." She waited, but he didn't respond. Couldn't respond. "Do you? Enjoy your work, I mean?"

A quick glance down at his tennis shoes, then at his watch, allowed him to gather himself.

"Uh..." He cleared his throat, uncomfortably aware of her scrutiny. "I have another lesson soon, unfortunately. Let me clean up while I answer that."

She rose to her feet. "I'll help."

They worked together to gather the detritus of their meal with surprising ease. And as they stacked containers, deposited trash in the appropriate bin, and consolidated leftovers, he tried to give her an honest response to her question.

"I love tennis. Always have, from the first time I held a racket at four years old." The glass bottles of sparkling soda went into the recycling container, and he took care not to break them. "Teaching is usually fun too, although—"

Damn. He probably shouldn't admit that.

She was watching him from beside the trash bin. "Go ahead. Say whatever it is you were going to say."

"All right." Hopefully she wouldn't be offended. "I usually prefer lessons with intermediate or advanced students."

She inclined her head in understanding, no evidence of offense in sight. "I'm not surprised. As I know from personal experience, you're great even with rank amateurs. I'm sure advanced students are more of a challenge, though. And with them, you're not wasting all the tennis expertise stored in that sharp brain of yours."

Her words struck him silent. Again.

Talented teacher. Expertise. Sharp brain.

Something was cracking inside him.

It kind of felt like his heart. Or at least something that had surrounded his heart for way, way too long.

After tucking the last few containers of leftovers inside his bag, she zipped it up and joined him near the sturdy wooden rail. "Are you here indefinitely as the resort's tennis guru? Or is it more of a contract-to-contract sort of situation?"

Below them, the startlingly blue ocean rushed toward the rocks in rhythmic pulses, the impact spraying water high into the air, while seagulls circled and called to one another. In the distance lay white sands and a plethora of sunscreen-covered tourists, as well as the courts where he spent virtually all his waking hours. Beyond that, the clubhouse beckoned, with the shop below and his barren apartment upstairs—the latter full of furniture and notes with various phone numbers inscribed on them, but empty of *him* in every important way.

It was gorgeous here on the island, of course. Easy.

But what was he doing here, really? How long did he actually intend to stay?

His voice emerged thick, for reasons he couldn't have explained. "My current contract lasts until the end of the year. At that point, I could sign on for another year or do something else."

What would that something else be, though?

What did he really have to offer?

You could do pretty much anything, given the right training.

In the breeze, her hair blew against his cheek, and he resisted the urge to gather handfuls of the silky strands and bury his face. Hide himself until he sorted out what he was thinking and how he was feeling, other than lost and disoriented.

She tapped her knuckles against the rail. "Do you think you'll commit to another year?"

The question sounded odd. Tentative, when Tess usually spoke firmly, with ease and authority. She was staring down at the water, her brow pinched as wave after wave piled on shore and wore away those rocks bit by bit.

"I don't know." His voice wavered, which was humiliating. So he straightened and offered her a lazy grin, complete with another wink. "You know how it is, right? I need to live in the moment. Get my fill of the sun, sand, and relaxation and not worry about what's coming next."

Even though he was willing her to look, to see how unbothered he was, how confident, she just blinked down at the water some more.

"Ah." She was silent for a long time. "I see."

He fumbled for a different topic. "You never did tell me what you and Belle did for your birthday. Did y—"

"Excuse me." A low, feminine voice came from the top of the stairs, and under the harsh island sun, a familiar white-clad figure glowed like a ghost. "Sorry to interrupt, but I need to head to my spa appointment, and I wanted to catch you before your next lesson, Lucas. One of your coworkers said you were up here."

For just a moment, he wanted to slam his head against the rail.

Fuck. Fuck it all.

He should have fucking remembered. It was the first Thursday in August, and Karolina had arrived. One of his favorite clients. Amusing. Smart. She visited the island like clockwork, reserving a long weekend every month to spend time with her equally-wealthy girlfriends, intent on being pampered, having fun, taking tennis lessons with the island's star instructor, and…

Well, she knew what she wanted, and he hadn't minded giving it to her.

"I wanted to find out when you'd be free for dinner, but you weren't answering your cell." She directed a gleaming smile toward Tess, who'd eased a step back from the rail. From him. "I didn't mean to intrude, ma'am. I'll be gone in a moment. And you picked the exact right person to ask for help. Lucas knows everything about the island."

All evidence of the picnic had been packed away. She thought Tess was a random tourist who'd cornered him for information.

To her credit, Karo's smile, her reassurance, was genuine. She wasn't mean, or he'd never have allowed even their limited sort of relationship. But Tess didn't know that, and she could surely hear the proprietary tone of the other woman, could surely see the way Karolina looked at him, as if he were her favorite toy on this island of countless amenities.

Which he supposed he was. In the past, that hadn't bothered him.

But now, wariness was blooming once more on Tess's lovely, round face.

"Karolina, I'm not—" Unsure what to say, he pressed his lips shut.

He couldn't simply send her away and tell her he no longer wanted dinner with her, that he was aching to spend more time with the silent, still woman beside him instead. Karo deserved better than a public termination of their very private—if very casual—arrangement, and she deserved an actual conversation before he put an end to what they'd had.

But if he chose Karo over Tess now, Tess would never, ever look at him that way again. The way she had mere minutes ago. With soft eyes and curiosity and openness and approval.

This was his one and only shot with her. He knew it.

Maybe he shouldn't want that shot, but he did. More than he was comfortable admitting.

He respected both women. He wanted his actions to show it. Maybe he could ask Tess to wait at the bottom of the steps for a few minutes while he had a private conversation with K—

"No worries. I've gotten answers to all my questions." Tess smiled back at Karolina. "Thank you for everything, Lucas. You kids have fun."

Kids. He closed his eyes, exhaling through his nose. Shit. He hadn't even considered the fact that Karo was in her mid-twenties. Thanks to the magic of makeup or dermatology or good genes or something, she looked even younger than that. And now that he thought about it, had she called Tess *ma'am?*

When he opened his eyes, Karo was lounging at the top of the steps in one of her usual impeccable white outfits, her blond hair sleeked back into some kind of twist.

Twenty-four. Undemanding. Pleasant. Willing.

Brushing past her with another polite smile, there was Tess, her silver-streaked hair tangled and whipping in the wind as she made her exit.

Forty. A little rumpled and sweaty from their time in the sun. Prickly and encouraging and determined and sly and funny and so fucking hot he was surprised the cupcakes hadn't melted in her hand.

She wanted more from him than Karolina did.

Correction: She *had* wanted more. For several fleeting, vulnerable minutes.

Karolina moved closer, rising on tiptoes to brush a kiss across his cheek. "So when are you free tonight?" She gave him a familiar-looking wink. "You know I always look forward to our dinners the night I arrive."

Those dinners usually occurred in bed. But not tonight, since he refused to use one woman as a substitute for another. Both women deserved better than that. Hell, so did he.

Maybe he'd feel differently tomorrow or next month.

Tonight, though, he was going to bed alone.

"Karolina..." He leaned down and kissed her on her forehead, and then moved a step back. Two. "We need to talk."

EIGHT

When Belle glanced across the room for the umpteenth time, brow furrowed, Tess ducked her head and jotted gibberish in her spiral-bound notebook, feigning intense concentration.

If she made eye contact, her friend would apologize. Again. And Belle hadn't owed her one apology, much less six of them and counting. Even if that weren't true, Tess would gladly forego penitence in favor of forgetting Lucas Karlsson existed and never mentioning his name ever again.

She'd been a fool. Idiotic enough to believe, if only fleetingly, that a barely-legal flirt might consider a woman like her anything more than a convenient distraction until something better came along. Ridiculous enough to have felt betrayed by concrete evidence of his other casual entanglements. Irrational enough to have been stung by the stark contrast between her and his...Karolina.

Apparently, she was still a fool, because her stomach churned once more at the memory of that stunning, elegant, *young* woman kissing Lucas's cheek, claiming him for her own.

But that foolishness was no one's fault but her own, no matter what Belle believed.

"Put your notebook down, babe. You need to get ready for your lesson." Belle spoke from her double bed, where she was thumbing through a paperback. "Unless you want to cancel, which I'd understand." Her wide brow furrowed as she hesitated. "It's your birthday vacation. You should do whatever you want. Again, I'm so sorry I pushed you into all this."

There it was. Heartfelt apology number seven.

It was sweet of her best friend to worry, but the contrition needed to end. Immediately.

Tess laid her notebook and pen down on the coffee table. "We worked this out already, Belle. Don't worry, and please don't apologize. I know your intentions were good."

Honestly, despite the dueling distractions of work and Lucas, Tess should have realized her friend was up to something even before that first lesson. The two of them had taught in the same department for several years and worked in the same school for even longer, besties the entire while, until Belle moved to Boston for her boyfriend-turned-ex-boyfriend. And during all that time, Belle had been a pink-clad, sequin-loving catalyst for action. Not fearless, but unwilling to be guided by those fears. She couldn't tolerate dithering, and she refused to stand by idly when she saw a problem she thought she could fix.

Tess might not have considered her current sexual and romantic drought one of those problems, but Belle obviously hadn't agreed. Which was unfortunate and, frankly, irritating.

But on the occasional teaching days when mingled exhaustion and frustration had left Tess in tears after the last bell, Belle had listened and located tissue boxes and helped however she could. No one had supported Tess more in her quest for an administrative position. And Tess had never met anyone, absolutely anyone, more loyal to her friends.

She had written Belle a glowing reference letter, celebrated when her friend landed a new teaching position in Massachusetts, and helped with the packing. But not seeing that huge smile, that bright crown of blond hair, in the halls of Marysburg High every school day had hurt. Badly.

So Tess could forgive Belle a little meddling. Hell, she'd forgive much, much worse.

Belle had just wanted Tess to have a little adventure on their vacation. A few hours of relaxation. Memories of a hot night or two she could use as a man-shaped reminder of her birthday trip. Worst-case scenario, in Belle's estimation, the appointments would roust Tess from her notebook and let her stretch her legs in the fresh air, even if she decided not to pursue her handsome tennis instructor.

No harm, no foul. Just fun and exercise and eye candy.

But Belle had underestimated Tess's foolishness. They both had.

And neither of them could have known how a simple picnic would echo the single worst, most painful moment of Tess's adult life. The moment that had ended her long engagement and demonstrated the wisdom of a wholehearted commitment to work and friends and nothing more. Especially not romance.

Even sex, she could take or leave. Unless said sex involved only her and her trusty vibrator. Or maybe two trusty vibrators, if she was feeling frisky.

"Let me say this one more time, and then I'll let it drop." Belle pressed her lips together, brown eyes soft with regret. "I should have listened to you. Your feelings and your knee both got hurt, and I'm sorry."

Since the prospect of seeing Lucas again had her tasting bile at the back of her throat, Tess couldn't dispute those hurt feelings, much as she wanted to and as unjustified as they were. But she could get over her humiliation like a grown adult and move on.

She figured the pain in her knee, courtesy of bounding down countless steps earlier that afternoon, would last much longer.

"*I'm* sorry I'm spending so much time on work, instead of hanging out with you." Tess pushed to her feet, her knee protesting the sudden motion, and adjusted her ponytail. "You deserved to take a vacation with better company."

Belle flicked a dismissive hand. "You're still hanging out with me. We're taking plenty of tours and snorkeling trips and wolfing down plenty of really expensive tasting menus. And when you need to work, I'm more than capable of entertaining myself. Speaking of which..." She pointed to the phone. "From what I can tell, you still have lots of planning to do tonight. Why don't you call the concierge and cancel the lesson?"

Tess shook her head. "I hate to waste money, and you spent a crapload of cash on those appointments, so *someone* is having a damn lesson tonight. Are you sure you don't want to go instead of me?"

"I would." Belle sounded sincere. "I know you need the time, and your lunch date today ended kind of..."

When her friend paused to find the right word, Tess filled it in for her. "Unfortunately."

Or maybe that was the wrong word, since the arrival of Lucas's playmate had stopped Tess from making a critical mistake: taking him more seriously than she should.

She should be thanking the young woman. Possibly by offering her informational brochures about her upcoming SATs and college choices.

Okay, that wasn't fair. Tess knew how to judge kids' ages, and that girl was definitely legal. Maybe even out of college. But also definitely young. So damn young.

Just like the sweet, clueless grad student she'd discovered her ex-fiancé, an ancient history professor, fucking.

She'd come home to grab her forgotten lunch and found

the two of them in the master bedroom. On the king-sized bed, which she and Jeremy had bought together. On her favorite blue sheets, the ones with the high thread count.

She'd let Jeremy keep those sheets, but she hadn't let him keep her, despite all his pleas.

"*Unfortunately* about covers it. So I would do the lesson for you, but when we thought you were busy tonight, I accepted a dinner invitation from Brian. I have plans involving room service and a complete lack of resort wear." Belle tilted her head toward her cell. "Unless you want me to cancel on him? I can, no problem."

No way Tess was vagblocking her BFF, much as she might want to.

"Nope. I'll be fine." Tess lifted her sundress over her head and began to change into an entirely inadequate sports bra. "Does Brian know what's in store for him tonight?"

Belle's smile was wicked. "Not yet. I'm going to help him see the light."

The bronze sequins of Belle's bodycon dress sparkled, set off her pale skin, and clung to her every voluptuous curve. If Tess hadn't been lamentably straight, she was pretty sure she'd have seen the light too, and it would have blinded her.

"He doesn't stand a chance." Her last pair of clean leggings lay folded neatly in the dresser drawer. She hadn't anticipated needing quite so much workout gear during this trip. "Just be sure to text me to let me know where you are and when you plan to be back in the room."

Belle executed a sharp salute. "Yes, ma'am."

After hiking the leggings up to her waist, Tess dropped another big tee over her head, this one plum-colored. "You're more than capable of keeping yourself safe, and I understand that. But if I don't hear from you, you know I'll worry."

"I know. I'll text. I promise." Setting aside the book, Belle shifted to the edge of her bed. "That color is gorgeous on you."

Tess realized. She'd chosen that particular tee for a reason. Hopefully looking decent would salve the bruises her ego had received earlier that day.

"Are *you* going to be okay?" Her friend looked worried. "I don't want you getting hurt again."

Tess lifted a shoulder. "I shouldn't have been hurt in the first place. I knew he was a player. Some other woman"— some other *younger* woman—"showing up shouldn't have surprised me, and I shouldn't have let myself get hurt. Of course I'm nothing special to him. He barely knows me. As far as he's concerned, I'm just another tourist to charm for tips. Or maybe take to dinner and fuck, as long as he doesn't have something better lined up."

Hearing her own words, the resentment in them, she paused and bit her lip.

She'd just met the man two days before. What the hell was wrong with her?

Belle's brows had drawn together again, and she positioned herself in front of Tess. "Look at me, babe. Why don't you just cancel the rest of the lessons?"

Much as Tess adored Belle, she didn't want to have this conversation. Not again. Not when Lucas hadn't owed her anything but an hour of tennis instruction and the picnic he'd promised, both of which she'd duly received. At their first lesson, he'd even offered to stop flirting, and she'd told him he could continue. That she could handle it.

Any pain she'd experienced—emotional or physical—was her own fault, and she knew it. She didn't plan to take it out on Belle or Lucas or anyone, except maybe herself.

"I'll be fine. I just got confused during that first lesson." She gave Belle a moment of eye contact and a smile before moving away to grab her sneakers. "We were talking as we played, and he was intelligent. Thoughtful and well-spoken. And he's good at his job, and you know how I feel about competent men."

"They're your kryptonite." Belle heaved a wistful sigh. "Mine too, of course."

"So, yeah, I flirted with him a bit. And yeah, I had lunch with him today, because I kept thinking…"

He'd seemed different in those last few minutes of their lesson. During most of their picnic, too, until she'd asked about his future at the resort. He'd seemed more sincere. Less shielded. And she'd found herself wondering whether what she'd taken as immaturity, as the aimlessness and shallowness of youth, was something else entirely.

"I kept thinking maybe he wasn't unformed at all, but opaque. Deliberately so." She adjusted the backs of her shoes until they were comfortable, bending from the waist instead of her knees. "Not shallow, but guarded. And if that's who he was, rather than a shiftless player who didn't care much about anything, maybe I could believe his interest in me was sincere."

She forced her lips to stretch into a smile as she slid her keycard into her pocket. "But now I know better, so don't worry. I won't let myself get hurt again. Especially since I don't have time for any complications right now, including those of the male persuasion. And that would be true even if I'd been right about Lucas."

"Babe…" Brown eyes troubled, Belle touched Tess's arm. "I'm sorry. Again."

Number eight. This conversation needed to end, stat.

Tess opened the heavy door to the hall. "I'm not. It's good to know where my weaknesses lie. Self-knowledge is important, as I always tell the kids."

"Maybe so." Belle didn't appear comforted by Tess's cheery tone. "You're not a kid, though."

"No, I'm not. But Lucas is."

Tess let the door swing shut behind her.

LUCAS WAS LEANING AGAINST THE CLUBHOUSE wall, his eyes on his sneaker-clad feet, when Tess approached the courts. Then he glanced up and saw her, and to her shock, he actually *rushed* toward her without an ounce of his characteristic indolence.

"Tess!" he called out, his gaze intent on her as he loped in her direction. "I'm glad you're early. Let's talk for a minute before we start the lesson."

On a scale from one to ten, her desire to discuss the young woman who'd visited him earlier that afternoon was negative infinity. But she supposed she couldn't escape at least a few seconds of postmortem conversation, much as she wished she could.

No matter. She was the adult in the room. Er, the court. She could handle this. She could handle him.

Moments later, he'd arrived within a step of her, and she held her ground. When he reached for her arm, though, she backed up a little. Not far. Just enough to make her point clear.

He watched her place herself out of his reach, his mouth compressed into a thin line. But he didn't protest or close the distance between them.

"Tess..." His throat bobbed as he swallowed. "I owe you an apology. I'd forgotten that my, uh"—his voice, low and quiet, faltered—"friend Karolina was arriving today. If I'd remembered, I—"

Oh, Jesus. Time to cut this off.

"No need to continue. I get it." She directed a bright smile somewhere over his left shoulder. "You wouldn't have asked me to lunch. I totally understand, and we don't need to talk about it anymore."

He shook his head, dipping his chin to bring his face closer to hers. "That's not what I was going to say. I wanted to have lunch with you. I'd still like to—"

"You know what?" She forced herself to make full-on eye contact with him. "Remember how you offered to keep things strictly professional two nights ago? No flirting, no innuendo?"

After a few seconds, he gave a small, slow nod.

"Let's do that today," she told him.

The shine in those olive-green eyes dulled, and his face seemed to sag.

"I should take better advantage of your tennis expertise. While we play, why don't you tell me more ways I can improve my game?" She gestured toward the clubhouse. "Do I need to pick out a racket again?"

His jaw worked. "No. I set yours aside for you. I have it in my bag."

His cheeks and chin appeared freshly shaven. He wasn't wearing the same clothing from their picnic, or even from his lesson before the picnic. The new outfit was dry and spot-lessly clean and unwrinkled, as if he'd changed just before her arrival. The skin beneath his eyes looked bruised and baggy, though, and those crags in his face—so odd for someone so young—seemed deeper somehow, the lines across his forehead more distinct.

Given the circumstances, what right did he have to look so...defeated? Resigned? What exactly was she seeing in his face?

God, she didn't even know. But she was fighting the impulse to grab his arm and apologize, even though she'd done nothing wrong and been nothing but polite to him.

No. This was the right call. She was doing the right thing.

"So are we ready to play?" Another moment of eye contact, and then she couldn't take it anymore. "Because I'd really like to get on the court. As soon as this lesson is done, I need to keep working."

A long pause. He opened his mouth, only to close it. Then

he gave another little nod, his lips quirking into a smile that didn't reach his eyes.

"Of course." His back straightened, and he hoisted his bag onto his right shoulder. "Whatever our guest wants."

NINE

COMPARED TO THEIR PREVIOUS CONVERSATION-filled lesson, this one felt more like a wake. Not a fun one either, filled with remembrances and love and music amidst the grief.

No, this was a wake attended only by quiet, emotionally constipated mourners. Possibly ones pissy about not getting more money in the will.

That was just fine with Tess. Better an impersonal and uncomfortable lesson than one that would leave her exposed and disappointed in both him and herself. Besides, she was getting lots of handy tips for her nonexistent future tennis matches back in Virginia. Those were certainly worth the stunningly large amount of money Belle had spent on the appointments.

She wasn't running for the ball, given the current state of her knee, so some of his shots whizzed past her, just out of reach. He didn't utter a word of complaint.

"Good job," he said whenever she hit the ball anywhere near him.

When she hit it into the net or to the side or—one memorable time—behind herself, he offered advice in a few brief words. Apparently, she should try using a two-handed grip for more power in her backhand and position herself next to the ball using smaller, more precise steps.

After a while, even those comments stopped, and they were playing in silence.

Compared to the other evenings she'd spent on the island, tonight seemed especially humid. Sticky and somehow electric, as if a storm were brewing. After only a few minutes, she grew uncomfortably sweaty from the heavy air and the endless rhythm of the rally, even without running.

Finally, she stopped and leaned on her racket. "Why don't you demonstrate some good serves while I rest for a moment?"

"I thought you didn't—" But he cut himself off. "Of course."

All the other tourists and employees had left the area for the evening, even Pat. The insects in the nearby trees were screeching and croaking, but they were the only disturbance other than a distant hum of faraway music from the shore.

She and Lucas were alone, but it didn't matter. She wouldn't let herself be vulnerable to him again.

At the baseline, he positioned himself just off-center, his front foot pointed toward the court, while his back foot stayed parallel to the line. After dropping one ball in his pocket, he bounced another on the ground a few times.

He didn't appear to be concentrating. The entire process seemed second-nature. Mindless, as if he'd done it a million times before, and maybe he had. She had no idea how long he'd been teaching, after all. And had he played in college?

Before he did anything else, he caught her eye as she stood at the side of the court and sipped from her water bottle. "Do you want me to do this slowly, or at full power?"

The humidity had molded his tee to his powerful shoulders, and under the court's lights, his thick, muscled thighs shone with sweat.

He was watching her, his jaw firm, his stare intent.

Oh, my. She took another gulp of water as she considered how to answer him.

Well, who was she to hold him back? "Full power."

"Okay." Another perfect bounce of the ball, without even a glance downward. "And do you want me to talk to you about what I'm doing and why, or just do it?"

"Just do it." God, she was thirsty. So thirsty. "No talking necessary."

If she'd blinked, she would have missed it. The ball tossed high in the air, his body coiled and then pouncing to strike, his racket swinging back and then smashing forward. She couldn't separate the process into individual movements, and the fluidity of it was...

Magnificent. Beautiful, in a way she hadn't anticipated.

When the strings of the racket slammed into the ball, the thwack echoed through the empty courts, and the ball flew like a missile across the net, landing just inside the service line before bouncing upward and hitting the back boards of the court with a thunderous rattle.

Holy fuck.

She'd never witnessed such grace and power twined and focused on a single action. Never. Not in her life, not in person.

He was an athlete. A talented athlete.

But it didn't change anything. She wasn't here to learn his story, even if he'd been willing to tell it to her—and from their previous conversations, she assumed he wasn't.

So she closed her open mouth and forced a casual tone. "How fast was that?"

"I'd say..." With his typical insouciance, he wandered over to his bag and grabbed a towel. "A bit under two-ten, maybe?"

He wiped his face and forearms, then his hands and the grip of his racket while she resumed gaping at him.

"Two hundred and ten miles per hour? Holy shit."

His lips quirked. "Sorry. Metric system. Two hundred and ten kilometers per hour. That's about one hundred and thirty miles per hour."

Still. That was almost inconceivably fast.

"No wonder I could barely follow the ball." Even though she knew—she *knew*—his ego didn't require any more stroking, she had to say it. "That was the single greatest athletic feat I've ever seen in my entire life, Lucas. And I once saw a student do over two-thousand sit-ups in our gym. She just missed the national record."

For the first time that evening, his dimples popped. "Poor kid."

"I know. She was shaking at the end. Nearly threw up, too." She couldn't help a grin. "Much like me, when I realized her parents hadn't signed a waiver beforehand. I'll be making sure that never happens again."

"The sit-ups?"

She shook her head. "The missing waiver."

He laughed, then leaned his head back for a sip of water, his throat bobbing as he swallowed. But he was still looking at her the whole time. And when he'd drained the bottle, he raised his thick brows. "Want me to do that again? Or break it down for you?"

The keenness of her desire to watch him serve a second time startled her. This go-round, she wanted to be closer, to study the flex and movements of his body.

Out of academic curiosity, naturally.

"Again." She cleared her throat, trying to remove the huskiness in her voice. "Please."

So he retrieved the ball from his pocket and demonstrated another serve. This time, she paid attention to the way the muscles in his arms and shoulders bunched and released, shifting beneath the thin fabric of his branded tee.

She still couldn't discern individual movements. The

85

whole act was one complicated, twisting motion, honed and perfect and lovely. After another ringing impact, the ball landed in a skid down the center line, near the point where all the lines converged. It rocketed into the boards with a clap of sound and bounced back toward them.

Licking her lips, she watched him amble toward his towel, his legs long and taut beneath his loose shorts. Those hard-muscled legs gleamed with a sheen of sweat, as did every other visible inch of his tall, honed body.

For the first time in her life, she understood sports groupies.

No wonder Lucas apparently had a coterie of young admirers. Why wouldn't he?

"Are you interested in learning to do that? I'd be happy to teach you, even if it makes the lesson go a little late. Consider the extra time another birthday present."

His voice startled her from her fugue state, and she flicked her eyes away from the tanned expanse of his bare skin. Maybe she should lean on the net for a little extra support?

"Um..." Focus. She needed to focus. "Thank you for the offer. But from what you just showed me, I don't think it's a good idea." She patted her knee and offered him a rueful smile. "Joint issues, remember?"

"Shit." He took a step toward her. "Did you hurt your knee climbing those steps at lunch?"

When she held up a hand, he stopped in place. "No. I'm fine. Just being cautious."

Technically, she really *hadn't* hurt her knee climbing those steps. The pain had come from the descent, as always.

"Okay, then. I don't expect you to hit like I do, Tess." Another swipe of the towel over his face. "Have you felt any pain from our lessons up to this point?"

"No." Not physical pain, not from the lessons themselves.

Or not too much, anyway, since he'd made certain she didn't have to work very hard.

"Good. Then tell me more about when and how your knee hurts. I'll accommodate any limitations you have and make certain the serve won't cause you pain. And if there's no way to do it without hurting you, we'll go back to an easy rally." He dumped the towel into his bag and braced his hands on his hips. "I won't injure you. Trust me that far, at least."

He expected her to trust *him*, of all people?

Arrogance. Sheer arrogance.

He had no idea. Give him another couple decades, and maybe he would. But not now.

She huffed out an unamused-sounding laugh. "I can't, Lucas. You're a kid, with a young, healthy body, and you wouldn't understand the sort of limitations I have."

"Then tell me, Assistant Principal Dunn." Across the net, he stalked closer to her. One step, then two. "What are they? Because I get the feeling there's a long, long list."

Thick sarcasm suffused every word from his mouth, and she almost slapped him.

Asshole. He had absolutely no right to look at her with those thick brows drawn together and those green eyes snapping with anger. No right to imply her limitations were more than physical. No right to dismiss her pain with such evident contempt.

He closed his eyes for a moment and let out a slow breath. "Tess, I shouldn't have—"

When she tossed her racket toward his bag, it clattered to the ground, and he fell silent.

Under normal circumstances, she'd be horrified at the prospect of potential damage to borrowed property, but this time, she didn't give a shit.

"You want to know my limitations? Fine. I'm more than happy to tell you." She ticked them off on her trembling fingers, rage burning in her cheeks. "Since my twenties, I've had arthritis in my neck from a bad car accident. Around that time, my knees began hurting too, for no specific reason. Starting in my thirties, I've had persistent lower back pain because my stupid breasts are too damn big." Her eyes met his, and she didn't flinch. "Bottom line: Most days I'm in pain *somewhere*. But usually my knees, especially when I have to descend a lot of stairs or run. So yes, my knee hurt some after our last lesson, and it's killing me after the steps today."

His expression had softened as she spoke, his shoulders dropping. "Tess—"

She didn't want to hear it.

"And before you tell me I should lose weight—"

He jolted. "I would *never*—"

"—yes, I know the knee problems might be due to my size, or at least exacerbated by it. But I promised myself I'd never be ruled by the scale ever again, knee pain or no knee pain. I won't invite that obsession back into my life, no matter what you or anyone else says."

He was watching her carefully, his eyes on her face.

She hated it. Her chest was heaving with each half-sobbing breath, and her eyes burned. Dammit, she'd lost control. Again.

"And don't bother telling me strength and flexibility training might help my joints, because no shit, Sherlock." She spat out the words. "But when I exercise on my own, I always manage to injure myself, and getting a trainer costs money I don't have. Besides that, I'd need time and energy to train, and I work all the time, Lucas. All. The. Time. And when I'm not working, I'd rather read and watch movies and hang out with my friends than go to a gym or physical therapy. Sue me."

"Okay." He inclined his head. "It's okay, Tess. Let's—"

When he reached across the net for her hand, she backed away. "So don't tell me to entrust myself to your care, Lucas.

You're a twenty-something athlete in the prime of his body and life, and you have no clue. No fucking clue."

At that, all the sympathy glowing warm in his eyes vanished.

Her pulse echoed in her ears, and it was the only sound on the court. At least until he spoke, his voice thick and loud.

"Well, that's some fucking irony right there." He bared his teeth in a faux-smile. "Since you don't know the first thing about me either."

And whose fault was that? The man didn't share *anything* of himself. Nothing real, anyway. "I just watched that display of serving machismo, so I think I have some id—"

"See these scars?" With a jerk, he raised his wrists to eye level. "Did you wonder how I got them?"

She had, actually, but she'd thought it both impolite and unwise to ask. They were both far beyond manners and wisdom now, though, so she figured she was about to hear the answer to her unasked question, like it or not.

To be honest, in her hurt and rage, she'd kind of forgotten about the scars. Shit.

She swallowed. "I thought—"

"Three surgeries. On my left wrist alone. It's basically held together with twine and a prayer." He rotated it for her inspection, his nostrils flared. "My backhand used to be a weapon. Now I can barely hit a seventy-mile-per-hour slice cross-court, and it hurts like a bitch every time that ball strikes the racket. The price of generating any power at all."

Why did a tennis instructor need to hit more than seventy miles an hour?

What was she missing here?

The other wrist began a slow spin for her perusal. "One operation on my right. After I finished rehab, that wrist didn't bother me anymore. Except when it did." When he'd made certain she'd seen every millimeter of that pinkish-white scar, he lowered his hands. "Maybe we should talk about my left knee. I had surgery there too. Or we could discuss the other places I hurt when I play too much or too hard. The commentators said I had joints of glass, and they weren't wrong."

Commentators? What the—

Oh. Oh, fuck.

He'd been a professional. A professional tennis player.

Now he was helping sunburned tourists determine the correct grip size for their borrowed rackets.

Remorse swamped her rage, drowning it in an instant. "Lucas, I'm so s—"

He was beyond her apologies. "I'm sorry the lesson and our date today hurt your knee. But don't tell me how I don't understand pain and how I'm in the prime of my body and life, lady. That's some condescending, ignorant bullshit."

Her face was burning for an entirely different reason now.

But he hadn't told her anything about his past. Also, she'd asked him several times why he'd come to the isl—

"And while we're having this enlightening discussion, let me add that I'm fucking *over* how you use your age as a weapon against me. Against us." He was leaning over the net now, a vein throbbing at his temple. "I get it. You're forty and have grey hairs and bad joints and grew up without the internet and probably listened to the Bee Gees or some shit on your record player. I don't *give a fuck*."

Of course it didn't matter to him, not given how little he wanted from her.

And she didn't want him to demand more. She *didn't*.

She met him nose-to-nose, relieved as anger and hurt roared to life once more and incinerated the shame. "Maybe you don't, since you're bored and just want to land me in bed for a week or two. But I don't have time for a fling."

"I never said I only wanted you for a week or two." He flung his hands in the air. "I wouldn't have said that, because it wouldn't be the truth. I don't know what I want from you. Not yet."

No. She wouldn't let that feel good. "Fine. But if we were together longer, you *would* care about my age at some point. Trust me on that. I know from personal experience."

His eyes narrowed on her. In curiosity? More anger?

"I see. So that experience tells you everything you need to know about me, a man you met two days ago." He waved a hand in insolent invitation. "Go ahead then, Assistant Principal Dunn. Enlighten me."

He was right. They were virtual strangers. Was she really going to tell him about her failed engagement?

Yes. If it helped her win this argument, which now felt like a mortal struggle for some reason, she'd do it. Happily.

"I was engaged for almost ten years to a history professor. A grown man in his mid-forties whose job included rules about ethics when it came to students. A grown man I found in our bed with a grad student." She tipped up her chin and pointed a finger at his hard chest. "So tell me, Lucas. If I couldn't trust my middle-aged fiancé not to fuck the nearest twenty-something, even when it might cost him his career and his wife-to-be, how can I trust an almost-stranger barely old enough to rent a goddamn car?"

When Lucas let out a slow breath, his expression softening, she thought he might...

Well, that was stupid. He wasn't going to reach for her. Not in the middle of an argument. Not when she'd just impugned his ability to remain honest and faithful.

Still, his jaw had unclenched, and she loathed the way he'd pressed his lips together in a sympathetic grimace. "Tess..."

"It's fine. I'm over it. I've learned my lesson and moved on."

One corner of his mouth quirked. "Clearly."

It shouldn't bother her, not amidst so many larger issues,

but… "All that said, the Bee Gees were mostly before my time." She paused. "Although I did own the *Saturday Night Fever* soundtrack on vinyl, I think. Also an album of ABBA's greatest hits."

He blinked at her.

This wasn't helping her cause. Back on point. "So there's no way I'd ever—"

Shaking his head, Lucas interrupted. "I'm sorry your ex was a cheating dickwad. But he's the one who committed himself to you and then fucked you over, not me." He grasped the finger still pointing at his chest. "He's not me. I cancelled my plans with Karolina. I would never sleep with someone else if we were together. You don't know me. You. Don't. *Know*. Me."

He gave her finger a gentle shake with every word.

Christ, she wanted to believe him. But how could she?

When she wrenched her finger free, he didn't try to hold on. "No, I don't. And you know why I don't?"

He dropped his head back and glowered at the night sky. "Oh, Jesus. Here we go."

"Because I may use my age as a weapon against you"— and damn him for noticing—"but you use your charm as a weapon against *everyone*. Me included." She drew his attention back to her with a finger under his chin. "Enough flirtation, enough lazy winks, enough innuendo, and no one notices you don't reveal anything about yourself. Ever. Not even your past as a professional tennis player, assuming people don't already know. Am I right, Lucas?"

One near-violent flinch, and then…nothing.

His indolent façade had vanished, but he was still unreadable, his eyes hard and blank.

So he wasn't unformed and devoid of life experience after all. But a man who wouldn't allow his true form to be known or share that life experience wasn't much better.

"You wouldn't even explain why you really came here to

work. The only reason you told me about your injuries is because I royally pissed you off." She gave his chin a light pinch and backed away. "If I said yes to you, maybe we'd be compatible in bed. Maybe we'd even be compatible outside bed, despite our age difference. But I can't make that determination if you don't let me see who you are. So either drop that careless-beach-dude shell of yours or don't expect me to trust you farther than I can throw you. Which, given my joint issues, isn't far."

No doubt he'd constructed his particular persona for a reason. She didn't know his full story, not yet, but she suspected it was painful and ugly, and she didn't want to hurt him. Didn't want to belabor his past. Didn't want to be the person who'd made him flinch like that, even for a moment.

She needed to make herself clear, though. Needed—for some unknown, no-doubt misguided reason—to give him one last chance to prove her wrong, to earn her trust by letting her peek beneath that playboy façade.

A glimpse. She just needed a glimpse, and then maybe…

Maybe she could try to believe in him. In the sincerity of his interest.

"Talk to me," she said. It was an invitation. A plea.

But he didn't say a word. He just stood there, gripping the net and staring at her.

His silence shouldn't sting. Shouldn't leave her raw and thick-throated.

"All right." She gathered her water bottle and started for the court entrance. "Fair enough."

"What about our next appointment? Do you plan to show?"

There was no emotion in that low voice. No indication he'd understood what she was asking of him or wanted her enough to risk it.

Just as well. She had a promotion to plan. "I don't think

I'll have time for another lesson before I leave. Consider yourself off the hook."

"There are no refunds," he reminded her.

Even stone-faced, he was damn handsome. Tall and strong and magnetic. Those tired-looking olive-green eyes bored into hers, and his shaggy brown hair rippled in the rising breeze. She wanted to smooth it.

A faint crack of distant thunder dissuaded her. The storm was almost upon them, and she needed to be safe inside before it hit.

"I remember the policy." One last good look, and then she'd go. "If I don't see you again, take care. I wish you good health and a good time and whatever else you want." She had to laugh, even though it hurt her throat and came out strangled and rough. "Not that I have any way of determining what that might be. God knows you won't tell me."

Then she walked into the roiling night, letting the wind whip away any trace of the foolish tears she refused to acknowledge. Even to herself.

TEN

Scrolling through Netflix options with fretful swipes of his thumb, Lucas attempted in vain to find a comfortable position on his couch.

It was a familiar exercise, doomed to failure. From the day he'd moved into his small, pre-furnished apartment, the generic sofa had defied his attempts at lounging. Its cushions were just a bit too hard for true relaxation, and they weren't deep enough for someone of his height. His calves and feet hung over one of the rolled arms if he tried to lay down. The nubby upholstery abraded any bare skin every time he shifted.

He could have bought a new one months ago.

He hadn't. Just as he hadn't replaced his mattress, which had a noticeable dip in the center, or contacted the appropriate person at the resort to ask if *they* might replace it. Just as he hadn't bothered to take any of the vacation days he'd accrued since his arrival.

The back of his neck itched, and it wasn't from sunburn or even the upholstery.

It was shame. Anger at himself. Frustration, because he knew what he wanted. He did. The only question was whether he was willing to commit, to put in the work, to risk himself emotionally and—

With a sigh, he put the remote down on the coffee table.

He should be honest, at least with himself. His inability to settle, his shame and frustration, weren't about a damn couch or his mattress. Inevitably, his traitorous brain had wended its way back to Tess. Again.

He knew what he wanted. Her.

But she'd made herself abundantly clear the previous night. She wouldn't seek him out again, not without some gesture of good faith on his part. More than flowers. More than a picnic.

Sex alone—sweat and tangled sheets and orgasms—wouldn't satisfy her either. Not unless he included a corner of his tattered soul with his body.

And over the past twenty-four hours, he'd begun to think maybe—maybe—he should give it to her.

Because yes, she was a serious pain in his ass. Yes, she was entirely too fond of hurling her age between them like an insurmountable barrier, when it was nothing of the sort. Yes, she appeared to be both a workaholic and a woman with trust issues.

But she wasn't wrong.

She saw him.

She saw beneath the Lucas he'd constructed over the past several years: shiftless, flirty, charming, and easygoing. A European playboy in search of a good time, a warm woman, and nothing more. All to compensate for the fact that he couldn't *have* more, at least not when it came to his career. All to ensure that even people who recognized him, who knew who and what he could have been without the endless parade of injuries, didn't pity him.

They might want him. They might envy him. They might marvel at how content he seemed in such a different lifestyle. But they didn't pity him, and they didn't see him.

Tess did.

He saw her in return. Under all that defensiveness and ambition lay a warm, funny, perceptive woman with her own unique charm. And he wasn't talking about her awe-inspiring breasts or her generous ass or her soft belly, although those were draws in their own right.

To be honest, he found her prickliness, that ambition, exciting too.

He was so tired of simple. He wanted complicated. He wanted a challenge. A battle, one-on-one, full of feints and openings and power moves and finesse and sheer, bloody tenacity. He'd always been able to endure pain to win a point, a game, a set, a match. Potential love, he figured, would be no different, and he didn't want it to be.

No, he just wanted her. He wanted to know what they could have together. And if having her meant he'd need to peel some layers of protection from himself, he could try to do it. First thing in the morning, before he lost his nerve, and before he wasted more of their scant time together on the island.

And in the meantime, to calm his nerves, he could check out the couch selection on the IKEA website.

***

LOATH TO WAKE TESS'S NEIGHBORS, LUCAS knocked softly on the door of Room 1249 the next morning.

Sure, a DO NOT DISTURB sign was hanging from the doorknob, but he knew she was an early riser from their topless ocean encounter. Hopefully she'd forgive him the dawn visit. Among other things.

He didn't think he'd ever knocked on a guestroom door before, not in all his months of working on the island. If he wanted to speak to a client—to confirm or change an appointment, or for personal reasons—he called the appropriate hotel extension. If a particular client wanted more than just a conversation, they met somewhere more private than the cool hallways of a luxury resort.

As always, however, Tess was an exception.

When she didn't answer the door after a minute, he knocked again. More loudly, this time.

The door swung open a few seconds later, revealing a very rumpled, aggrieved-looking woman wearing a silky, rose-colored robe. Not Tess.

That's when his fuzzy, sleep-deprived brain finally registered his mistake: Oh, yeah. She'd come to the island with a friend. Belle. The woman he'd met the other day under decidedly more auspicious circumstances, when she'd been smiling rather than scowling at him.

She and Tess were probably roommates. And he was guessing only one of them was an early riser.

Belle's brown eyes, already heavy with interrupted sleep, narrowed further on him.

This encounter was not starting well. No wonder he hadn't knocked on guestroom doors before.

"Umm…" He shifted his weight. "I'm sorry to bother you. I was hoping to speak to Tess."

"And you thought banging on her door shortly after sunrise during her well-earned vacation was the way to do it?" Belle cinched the waist of her robe tighter. "Especially after a disastrous late-night tennis lesson?"

Both women, it appeared, harbored serious doubts about his good judgment.

Whatever. He had his mission, and he was going to complete it, even if Tess and her outraged BFF roommate fought him the entire way.

"Evidently." He waited a moment, but she didn't move. "May I please talk to her?"

"Why?"

Oh, Lord. "You may, uh, have heard that we—"

"Were yelling at each other across a tennis court in public two nights ago?" She raised her brows. "Yeah, I heard. Trust me."

"Right." He scuffed his sneaker against the patterned carpet underfoot. "I, um, need to apologize to her for my unprofessionalism. As a resort employee."

"Not good enough." The door started to close. "Bye, Lucas."

"Wait!"

Operating on sheer instinct, he shoved his foot forward, and shit, that was a heavy door. Even though she wasn't trying to push it shut, the impact hurt like a mofo.

Belle opened the door a few more centimeters and eyed him like an insect. "Yes? Do you have something else to say?"

"I don't just want to speak to Tess as an employee." He dragged a hand through his hair and grasped the back of his neck. "I like her. I want to fix whatever I damaged on that tennis court and maybe see where we can go from here. If she's interested."

She swung the door wider. "That's more like it."

Thank Christ.

"Now can I talk to her?" He didn't crane his neck to look around Belle, but he was sorely tempted.

"Nope."

His stomach took another nosedive.

"Shit." He dropped his chin to his chest. "What did I do now?"

Belle laughed, completely unsympathetic to his torment. "Nothing. She's just not here. I'm guessing she got going before dawn, like she normally does. But if I know her, she's left me a..." Turning to scan the room, she gestured for him to hold the door. "Wait here."

A moment later, she returned from the coffee table with a small piece of paper in her hand, and he tried his best not to snatch it from her fingers.

"According to this note, she's on the far end of the island. The adults-only, swimsuit-mandatory beach. She says she'll be back within an hour or two, so if you want me to tell her you stopped by when she—"

"No." He could get to that spot within ten minutes, and it should offer them decent privacy. Perfect. "I'll go talk to her there. Thank you."

Belle grabbed his arm when he turned to go, her grip firm. "I don't think so, Sparky. Either you promise me you'll leave right away if she wants you to go, or I'm going with you. And I'll complain to management that you're harassing a guest after having yelled at her during her lesson."

Sparky? What the fuck? "If she tells me to leave her alone, I will. I promise."

He would, even though he was dying to talk to Tess. Because his desires weren't more important than hers. His parents had taught him that long before he'd gone on his first date.

"When she comes back, if she tells me you didn't keep that promise, I will rain hellfire upon you." Belle let go of his arm. "And I watched *Game of Thrones*, so you don't want that. Trust me."

He considered some of the plotlines he'd seen and shuddered. "Fair enough. Thanks."

Then, before she could threaten him more, he was jogging down the hall and toward the beach. Toward the most interesting woman he'd met in God knew how long. Toward the only woman who'd seen past his lazy-dude façade in months. Maybe years.

Toward a woman who might not want to talk to him at all.

Shit.

He put his head down and jogged faster.

Somehow, Tess had found his favorite place on the island.

The adults-only end of the resort was always quieter than the family beaches, not only because it was child-free, but also because reaching the area required a much longer walk from the hotel. Even by the adult-beaches standard, though, this spot was special. Peaceful and secluded.

At the very tip of the island, the resort had created a little pool of turquoise ocean water, protected by rocks about ten meters from shore. That line of rocks, a sort of homemade reef, absorbed the force of any waves before they reached the pool. More rocks marked the sides of the protected area.

While the pool constantly received a fresh influx of ocean water, that water moved only in tiny ripples, lapping like a gentle caress against the skin of anyone lucky enough to find the spot. Visitors could even see over the line of those dark rocks and into the stunning ocean beyond, with the mainland and other islands nowhere in sight.

If those visitors waded into the water and let it climb over their knees, their waists, their necks, and—briefly, if they were shorter than him—their heads, they'd find another hidden wonder. A sandbar rising beneath the sun-dappled surface of the pool, high enough in one spot to provide a seat. High enough for someone to sit comfortably on the silky sand, waist-deep in the water, surrounded by nothing but clear, beautiful ocean, and enjoy those caressing waves in solitude.

Sometimes, the sheer loveliness of the spot helped him forget everything he'd lost.

Other times, it helped reconcile him to that loss.

Today, Tess was there. Sitting in the middle of the water like a behatted mermaid, facing the ocean beyond as her hands swished in the water at her sides. Her dark hair lay loose around her upper arms, half-covering a blue...

What the hell was she wearing? Because that wasn't a swimsuit.

The water came up higher on her than it did on him, to her chest rather than her waist. But she clearly found the spot comfortable too, if the relaxed lines of her shoulders told him anything. And he hated to disturb her peace, he really did, but they didn't have much time.

Soon, some other early riser would find this spot, or he'd have to prepare for his first lesson of the day. He couldn't wait long.

"Tess?" he called out. "Do you mind if I join you?"

That hat-covered head turned, and she gazed at him for a long moment. Then she lifted a hand from the water and waved him toward her, and his heart uncramped in his chest just a tiny bit.

It took only seconds to tug off his tee and make his way through the warm water to her side. He sat beside her on the sandbar, the slight tug and sway of the blunted waves a comfort. When he tried to read her expression, she didn't look at him, only dug her fingers into the sand, gathered a handful, and let it sift and dissolve through her grasp.

That damn hat was getting in his way.

Taking a chance, he touched the edge of the brim, lifting it so he could see her face. "How did you manage to keep this dry?"

Finally, she turned those hazel eyes to him. Wary, tired eyes, with starbursts of lines at their corners. "I held it above my head with one hand while I paddled with the other. And the water was only deep for a couple of feet, so it wasn't hard."

Made sense. "This is my favorite place on the island."

"No wonder." She slid her hand through the water, just under the surface, as if riding the currents. "I can almost feel my blood pressure dropping each minute I'm here."

She needed to relax more, and he was interrupting her solitude. Dammit.

"I'm sorry to intrude." No more delaying. He needed to make his purpose clear, and he needed to reaffirm her consent to his company. "I came by your room to talk to you this morning. Belle told me where you were and made me promise I'd leave immediately if that's what you wanted. Which I would have done anyway, but she doesn't know me."

A faint snort from Tess.

He was pretty sure he could read her thoughts. *Of course she doesn't know you. Who does?*

She was right, of course. But he was trying to change that.

"If you want me to go, I will. But I'd really like to talk for a few minutes." He paused. "Is that okay?"

Her lips drew tight. "No arguing?"

"The last thing I want to do is argue with you, Tess." He didn't reach for her hand as it glinted like a fish beneath the water, but he wished he could. "I know you don't trust me, but please believe that."

She took a minute to answer.

Then she sighed and shifted her shoulders to face him. "Okay. You can stay. Say what you need to say, Lucas."

Yes. Hallelujah.

But also…

Oh, shit.

He'd hoped she would let him say his piece, but he hadn't let himself plan any further than the request. Hadn't thought about the exact words he'd use or the stories he'd tell. Hadn't visualized success, in the way his coach had always urged him to do.

Nevertheless, the moment had arrived, ready or not, and he was a battler. Always had been.

For this particular match, he wasn't walking out onto a court or waving to cheering crowds or hearing his name announced over loudspeakers. But the feeling was familiar. The anticipation. The nerves. The determination.

If he wanted a chance with her, he needed to concentrate, make his stand, and devote his time and wholehearted effort to that singular goal, now and for the rest of her visit. It was the sort of gut-level commitment he hadn't made in over a year. Something he hadn't pictured himself doing again in any context, professional or personal.

But right now, he was fighting for the promise of Tess Dunn.

And yeah, he was ready to admit it: For that, he'd do almost anything.

ELEVEN

Lucas took another moment to study the silent woman at his side.

Shoulders visibly bunched and raised high with tension. Tight jaw. Hands no longer slicing through the current in relaxed arcs, but instead fisted underwater in the sand by her hips.

Seeing Tess in that state because of him hurt worse than his post-match ice baths. And on a purely pragmatic level—Tess's preferred level—people under stress had trouble listening and taking in new information, much less coming to mutually agreeable decisions. As often as possible, his coach had waited for him to calm before discussing lost matches, and she'd told him that was why. He'd believed her. Still did.

Immediately tackling the fraught subjects from their last disastrous encounter wouldn't serve his purposes, then. Morning lessons or not, this conversation would require patience.

He'd ease into this conversation the same way he'd eased into those ice baths. Gingerly. Expecting discomfort. Hoping, in the end, the pain would help him move forward.

And speaking of pain... "This spot is a pretty long walk from the hotel. Is your knee feeling better?"

"Flat ground isn't a problem." One round shoulder lifted. "Ibuprofen helps too."

Which wasn't really an answer. "What does your doctor say about it?"

She was not responding well to his initial, get-Tess-more-relaxed topic. If anything, she'd become more tense beside him, her arms now crossed in front of her ample, glorious chest. "I'm at school before her office opens and working until after it's closed again. There's no time for non-emergency appointments."

A very practical reason not to go. But based on their argument two nights ago, he suspected practicality wasn't the only reason she'd been avoiding her doctor.

In fact, he was beginning to suspect practicality wasn't why Tess did much of anything.

He gave a noncommittal hum. "So you haven't told her."

"No."

Her chin had turned pugnacious again, and he waited. Let the silence spin out.

Finally, she swung on him. "I know what she's going to say, and I don't want to hear it."

"Okay," he said mildly.

"When you're fat, doctors propose weight loss as a solution to everything. Joint pain, strep throat, broken arms, spider bites, the bubonic plague, whatever." With a near-silent sigh, she dropped her arms back to her sides. "Since I have no intention of dieting, there's no point."

He looked down. Took a moment to think.

From what he could tell, she hadn't used the word *fat* as a pejorative. There had been no venom in the adjective, no bitterness or sadness, no implicit plea for his denial. It had served only as a descriptor, rather than a sign of self-loathing. Matter of fact. Value-neutral.

And he wasn't going to protest that she wasn't fat. They both knew better. Contradicting that would be patronizing as hell, insulting in its own way. More importantly, protesting might imply that being fat was somehow bad. Somehow the worst thing she could be, rather than merely one aspect of a complex, fascinating woman.

A wise man would probably change the topic. Immediately. Then again, if she'd wanted to chat with a wise man, she shouldn't have let Lucas sit next to her instead.

He'd spent years defined by his body, but not in the same way she had. He wanted to understand.

He met her eyes again. "Is that what your doctor usually does? She asks you to lose weight, no matter what the problem is?"

Another long silence.

"Not usually," she finally muttered. "If she did that, I'd have found another doctor."

Point made, he tugged lightly on the elbow-length sleeve of her garment and changed the subject. "This blue…" It was both bright and deep, like a jewel against the pale velvet of her skin. "It's pretty on you."

There. A less-fraught topic of conversation, served up nice and easy for her.

"Thanks." The hem was swirling around her thighs in the water, beneath the surface, and she pulled the fabric over her bent knees. "You're probably wondering why I'm wearing a cover-up in the water."

Honestly, he'd first thought maybe she was wearing it because she didn't feel entirely comfortable revealing herself in a swimsuit. His older sister had insisted on layering a t-shirt over her swimsuit for just that reason while they were growing up, and though he'd hated what it said about how she saw herself and disagreed with her reasoning, he'd understood the impulse.

That didn't make sense in Tess's case, though, not when

she'd already been running around the beach in a bikini. His conclusion: She probably just wanted an extra layer available in case another swimsuit went MIA. A disappointing but wise decision.

Since she might not appreciate a reminder of her topless state during their first meeting, he kept his answer neutral. "I figured maybe I'd missed out on a fashion trend. Wouldn't be the first time."

"I have a swimsuit beneath." She tugged the neckline of her dress to the side, revealing a thick, red strap over her shoulder. Then her lips lifted in a brief smile. "Not that damn bikini, though. Even if the top weren't sleeping with the fishes right now, I wouldn't have worn it again. Halter tops are not designed for women with my overflow of chesticular bounty."

She'd brought it up. She couldn't blame him for pursuing the topic.

He grinned at her. "I was very fond of that halter top."

"You never saw it."

"Exactly."

She gave him a companionable smack on his arm, and then they settled once more into silence. The hem of the dress swirled in the water again, dancing around her round thighs, and this time she let it.

"My parents didn't worry much about sunscreen when I was a kid, and the effects of that are showing up now." A quick sidelong glance his way. "That's not an attempt to use my age as a weapon against you. Just a fact."

Nope. Not commenting on that.

"Anyway, Belle was sleeping when I left this morning, and getting sunscreen on all the tough spots is even harder when you don't have anyone to help." She lifted a shoulder. "So I decided not to risk it. I figured I'd just wear my cover-up into the water. That way, I'd only have to slather sunblock on areas I could easily reach."

Watching her reaction carefully, he reached beneath the water and loosely interlaced their fingers. "That makes sense."

To his pleasure, she didn't pull away. In fact, her grip tightened, until their hands were locked together.

Her fingers were long and strong and warm between his. Perfect.

She chewed her lower lip for a moment. "In your profession, you probably have to be careful about sun exposure too."

Finally. She was seeing him, not some construct of her imagination or his. Thinking of ways they might be similar, rather than different.

"Yeah. My dermatologist is already looking pretty closely at a few places." He rubbed the hair—still thick, to his relief—covering his crown. "He wants me to wear a baseball cap when I play, but that's not something you can change after so many years. It just feels...wrong. I'll wear a sweatband during a match, but a hat? No way."

Her cute little ski-jump nose wrinkled. "Then how do you protect your scalp?"

"I mostly just spray a little sunscreen there in the mornings and call it good enough."

She shook her head. "I'm sure your dermatologist is thrilled when you dismiss his advice."

Lucas laughed. "He doesn't mince words. Every time I see him, he delights in telling me how much older I look than my actual age because of sun exposure. Then he tries to sell me some sort of laser treatment that would require way too much recovery time out of the sun for a man in my profession."

In his memory, he'd never discussed his sun damage with a woman who wasn't his mother or his sister. The sexiest of topics, it was not. But Tess wanted honesty, and he was trying to give it to her.

"You mentioned wearing sweatbands during a match." Her voice had turned soft. Tentative. "Do you still play? Competitively, I mean?"

He guessed they'd spent enough time dancing around the subject. "How much do you know about my history?"

"I spent some time Googling yesterday. So..." She shrugged. "A lot, I guess. The parts that played out in public, at least."

He'd figured as much. The woman was a former teacher, for God's sake. Discovering that he was a retired pro had taken her a while, but once she knew, she was going to do some research.

"Why don't you tell me what you discovered, and I'll fill in any missing pieces?" Stretching out his legs in front of them, he tried to keep his breathing even.

It probably wasn't fair to make her do most of the work, but they had to start somewhere, and he wasn't sure he could recite his entire professional history without humiliating himself.

Besides, if this morning progressed as he hoped, they'd eventually have time for other conversations. Time for him to explain the parts of his past no one could find online, because he'd never told them to a single soul. Time to get comfortable revealing themselves to one another in ways more intimate than physical nakedness.

Maybe she understood his reasoning, or maybe she didn't have the energy to argue. Either way, she took the conversational lead without protest.

As she spoke, she stroked the back of his hand with her thumb, the caress gentle. Soothing. "You went pro as a teenager and moved from the Stockholm area to Miami to train. Commentators considered you the biggest threat of your age cohort. Your serve and your backhand were your biggest weapons, although your forehand was consistent too. You won your first and only Grand Slam just before you turned twenty-one, defeating the top-ranked male player in the world in the finals. After that, you rose to number four in the world. Your highest ranking."

Over half a decade later, he could still recall every moment of that win with crystalline clarity. His backhand streaking down the line, Alvillar's forehand slamming into the net. The roar of the crowd. The disbelief that he'd done it. The glance at the umpire to confirm, and the smiling nod he'd received in return. Then a choked cry ripping from his throat as he fell to his knees on that blue court, buried his sweaty face in his sweaty hands, and sobbed in gratitude.

He'd climbed on some planters and jumped up to his box, where his coach, his physio, his hitting partner, and his family were waiting, and hugged them all while his father cried and the cheers and whistles from thousands of fans deafened him.

And then...and then...

"But you had to pull out of your next tournament after a bad fall, which left you with wrist and knee injuries. You had surgery." Tess's voice was soft. Barely audible. "When you returned to the Tour after a few months, you worked your way back up to the top ten."

The rehab had been excruciating, the return to form slow but satisfying. He hadn't won another major after that hiatus, but he'd taken a few tournament trophies home and kept working on his conditioning. Finaling in another Grand Slam was only a matter of time.

Until one day during practice, when he'd pounced on a drop shot from his hitting partner and hit a monster back-hand. Only to feel something go terribly, terribly wrong.

"Then came the next surgery on my left wrist. And some repairs on the right too, as long as I was already out of commission." Those procedures had required a longer recovery time. Afterward, he'd never been able to generate quite as much power on his backhand. Not even with two-handed strokes.

"You were ranked in the hundreds when you returned, but you worked your way back to the top thirty and reached the semifinals of a major. And then…" She trailed off, her thumb resting lightly on the T of his scar. "Your final surgery. At least the final one the public knows about."

Sometimes, the specialist still suggested another procedure, but Lucas told him to pay for his kid's college tuition some other way. He was done with wrist surgery, now and forever.

He filled in the rest of the story for Tess. "After that one, I couldn't put any topspin on my backhands, or any power behind them, without causing myself pain. Without risking another surgery. So I started relying on a cross-court slice. A shot to keep me in a point, but not one that would win the point. All my opponents knew they could exploit it."

His serve had still won him some free points. And his forehand had been passable, but even it had started to break down. Maybe for physical reasons, maybe mental. All the guys on the Tour had known if they rushed him, if they made it impossible for him to run around the ball to the forehand, they could keep hammering his backhand until they got him out of position and set up a winning shot.

His rank had dropped to the eighties. Then back into the hundreds.

Every time he'd played, commentators had lamented his promise. What could have been, if he hadn't injured himself so many times. If only he didn't have wrists of glass. Inevitably, they'd show footage of his lone Grand Slam win during interviews, and he'd watch himself on the monitor as he collapsed onto the coated asphalt, sobbing in thanks at his good fortune.

He'd grown so fucking sick of the same questions, the

same pitying looks, he'd wanted to scream at them. To rage. Him, of all people.

But how many times could he reiterate how it felt not to have his backhand as a weapon anymore? How it felt to enter majors as a wild card, solely because of his previous win? How it felt to watch the other guys in his generation, men whom he'd left in his wake once upon a time, reach semifinals and finals while he languished in the early rounds?

And how long could he keep pretending he still had any glimmer of a real career? A plausible shot at another title?

"I'm sorry, Lucas." Tess lifted their entwined hands, rubbing her cheek against the backs of his knuckles. She dropped a soft kiss on his scar, and then let their hands fall into the water once more. "I know this must be hard to talk about."

He took a deep breath and finished the story. "There was no point anymore. So I left."

Late last year, he'd retired from professional tennis. Quietly, without some grandiose fucking announcement, because if he had to hear about his vanished potential again, he didn't know what he might do, to himself and to everyone around him.

"You've asked me several times why I chose to work here, and the answer isn't especially impressive. I accepted the first job offer with decent pay and benefits." He shrugged. "The island isn't far from where I used to live, and this position lets me make a living from tennis. The only thing I do well."

But not well enough. Not anymore.

He gestured at the endless ocean and sand surrounding them. "It's a private island. Not much media finds its way here, so I don't have to answer pointless questions all the time."

She raised that skeptical brow of hers. "Not even from tourists?"

"It happens. But I can usually distract them."

One side of her generous mouth quirked. "With flirting."

He'd picked a sharp one, all right. Good thing he found intelligence sexy in a woman. "Or by playing dumb and changing the subject."

She exhaled slowly. "So that's your story."

"Yeah. That's my story."

The bare outlines of it, anyway. Again, if she wanted to know, if their relationship went somewhere, he'd tell her the rest someday. The details. But right now, neither of them had time for it, and he didn't have the wherewithal.

Still, he'd told her more than he'd told anyone in the past six months. Maybe longer.

It felt...exposed.

But Tess was still holding his hand tight in hers and watching him with such softness in those hazel eyes. Not pity, but sympathy. Affection.

"Thank you for telling me." Her voice was as sweet as a strawberry lemonade cupcake, as certain as the sunrise. "Sometime soon, we'll have to discuss how you could possibly think tennis is the only thing you do well, because that's just stunningly inaccurate. Not now, though. Your lessons must be starting soon."

Then she leaned over, gently cupped his cheek with her free hand, and kissed him.

Such warmth. Her lips courted his with a sweet nuzzle, and even that light pressure jolted him like a clap of thunder. Her fruity scent, something like apricots or peaches, filled his lungs, and he was dizzy with the promise of her.

She pulled back for a moment. "Is this okay?"

In answer, he let go of her hand and slid both arms around her. She filled them. She filled him, when he'd been empty for what seemed like years.

When he lowered his mouth to hers, he supported her neck with one hand. The other he slid around to her back, smoothing it up her spine while he teased her lips open with his tongue.

God, she was minty and sweet, and she pressed close to him with a low murmur in her throat as the tip of her tongue touched his. Her fingers traced the line of his collarbone, the swell of his shoulder, and every spot she touched bloomed with heat.

The kiss grew hotter. Wetter. And when he worked his way beneath that floating hem and found her bare back, stroking the soft flesh there, she clutched at his arm and gasped into his mouth.

Her nails dug into his skin, and it felt like a benediction. A victory, the likes of which he hadn't known for years.

He tore his mouth from hers, keeping eye contact as he slid his hand around to her front, still under her cover-up. His thumb stroked the side of her breast in a sweeping arc as he waited for permission. For a sign he wasn't taking more than she was offering.

She rested both palms on his chest, but not in refusal. In exploration. They slid up and over his shoulders, down his arms. Then she covered his hand with hers and moved it over her breast. Positioned it so he was cupping the heavy, warm weight of her, her tight nipple pressing into his palm through the swimsuit.

Suddenly, not enough oxygen was making its way into his lungs.

"Tess..." He licked his lips. "Älskling, I can't—"

Voices. In the distance, but too close to continue.

He dipped his head for one last taste of her, for one last feel of her plush lips parting for him. Open. Vulnerable. Exquisitely soft. And then he slid his hand out from under her cover-up and straightened it around her suit.

But he couldn't stop entirely without making sure she understood what he wanted from her. Not just sex and bodies and careless pleasure, easily dismissed. More than that.

How much more, he didn't yet know. But he couldn't wait to find out.

So he brushed his lips across her temple, where fine threads of her dark hair had dried in the sun. Then across her eyelids, that fragile skin traced by tiny blue veins. Then her cheeks, velvety and hot. Finally, he rubbed his nose lightly against hers and hoped she grasped what he was attempting to communicate.

She rested quiescent beneath his attention, her fingers curled once more against his chest as her mouth curved in a soft, private smile.

"We have company." He whispered the words into her ear, his nose nuzzling the plump lobe. "And you're right. I need to get prepared for my early lesson. I should go."

When he began to pull away, though, she laid a hand on his arm. "Wait."

That single word was satisfyingly breathy, and he smiled at her and obeyed.

"Lucas…" Her thumb swept over his cheekbone and dipped into his dimple. Then she caught his eye, her gaze steady. "I'm sorry I was thoughtless and harsh when we argued. I have no good excuse, and I swear I'll do better from now on."

Sincerity shone from every word, and he owed her the same respect. The same honesty.

"I owe you an apology too. I was unkind." He took her hand. Kissed her fingers. "And we both have our reasons, but you're right. Neither one of us has an excuse. I'll act differently in the future, I promise."

Dammit. He really had to go.

Relinquishing her touch caused a literal, physical ache in his chest, but he somehow managed to pull away. To stand by her side and look down at that floppy hat, the swirling blue dress, the pale curves of her legs and feet shining beneath the water. To memorize the near-perfection of her in this moment.

She tipped her head back, and her round, sweet face came into view below the hat's brim. Perfection achieved.

"See you tonight?" she asked.

"For our lesson?" This close, he could spot an adorable freckle dotting her right cheekbone. He wanted to taste it. "Or dinner?"

He'd take anything and everything she was willing to give him. Especially since they had so little time before she left the island and him behind.

"Both." Then, to his pleasant shock, she raised her hand and gave his butt a light pinch. "Now get going before I lose control and ravish you in full view of other guests."

Her grin was wide and confident, her eyes assessing as they scanned him from the top of his tousled hair to the insistent bulge pushing against the cool, damp material of his trunks.

"You never told me that was an option." He frowned down at her. "I feel misled."

Another, harder pinch. "Go, Karlsson. I need to get to work too."

Several tourists came into view around a stand of palms, and he reluctantly moved a step away from her and turned his back to them, the water lapping around his knees.

"You'll pay for that pinch," he told her.

She clapped her hand onto her hat, making sure it wouldn't fall off as she dropped back her head and—

Did she *wink* at him? Really?

Her teasing grin grew even more wicked. "I certainly hope so."

TWELVE

"They called him the Sweet Swede, Belle." Tess brushed yet more sand from her tablet, which she'd been using to unearth yet more information about Lucas. Clips from his matches; articles lauding his talent and lamenting his physical deterioration; accounts from fans who'd met their favorite, doomed tennis star. "He was famous for being soft-spoken with reporters. Well-liked in the locker room. A bit goofy at times on the court, but mostly quiet and hard-working. Not someone to scream at an umpire or posture or..."

Belle sat up and dipped her chin until she could see Tess over the top of her oversized sunglasses. "Or what?"

"Or act like a player. Off the court, anyway."

Despite Karolina. The woman who'd shown up at the overlook, clearly anticipating and accustomed to a certain amount of intimacy with the island's tennis pro.

Dammit. Was Tess fooling herself?

"Here's the thing. For all his talk of sun and relaxation and lounging in the sand with various willing women, he *doesn't* lounge. He works from early in the morning until late at night." Tess hadn't put the pieces together until she'd seen him at dawn for the second time in a week. "When he doesn't hide behind that beach-bum-Casanova façade, he's quite thoughtful. Sweet, like they said."

Belle gave a neutral nod. "And the women?"

"I definitely think he gets around." Tess shifted on the lounger, the towel bunching beneath her. "Although, to be fair, I imagine he's less the chaser and more the chasee. I'm sure women are all over him because of how he looks and because he was famous."

"He's certainly chasing after you." Belle set her book on the little wooden table between the loungers, lips pursed. "I don't know whether to congratulate him for his excellent taste or start worrying."

"Because if he's chasing me, he might be chasing other women too?"

Belle let out a slow breath. "All this is beginning to sound less like a potential fling and more like the start of a potential relationship. I just don't want you to get hurt."

A roundabout, kind way of saying *yes*.

"When it comes to woman-chasing, I'm hoping he made an exception for me because I'm so freaking awesome." Oh, Lord, was she letting herself believe what she wanted to, regardless of the evidence? "I know I could be wrong about him. But he seems sincere, Belle. And you know I have a top-of-the-line bullshit detector after what happened with Jeremy."

Belle took off her sunglasses entirely, meeting Tess's gaze with concern pleating her brow. "I don't mean to be unsupportive. Whatever you decide to do, I'll be here for you. It's just..."

Tess waited.

"If he hurts you, I'll feel responsible, since I basically threw you in his path." Belle reached for Tess's hand. Squeezed. "Please be careful. Even smart women make mistakes sometimes."

That sounded...personal. More so than seemed reasonable under the circumstances.

"Honey? Did something happen with Brian?"

Belle was silent for a long moment. "Yes and no. But give me a little time before we talk about it." Another pause, and then her fingers slipped away from Tess's. "Maybe you shouldn't listen to me when it comes to Lucas. I'm feeling kind of anti-men at the moment."

She'd crossed one leg over the other, and her top foot was jiggling. Definitely agitated.

"Are you sure you don't want to talk?" At her friend's immediate nod, Tess persisted. "I'm happy to be your sounding board or your soft shoulder, if that's what you need. Or your angel of vengeance, I suppose."

At that, Belle snorted. "You? An angel? Please."

"A vengeful one, like I said. The standards are a bit more lax." Tess grinned. "So is that what you need? A flappy-winged bringer of doom?"

Belle raised her paperback in front of her face once more. "Weren't you supposed to be working?"

A clear attempt at distraction, but she was right. Tess's morning was almost gone, passed in a blur of Lucas and exactly zero new work-related ideas.

She tucked the tablet into her beach tote and got out her notebook. "Yes, ma'am. I'll get back to work."

Maybe, instead of fooling around with a twenty-something former tennis pro, she should do the same that night too.

DESPITE THE DOUBTS NIPPING AT HER CONFIDENCE —*Was* she being played? Shouldn't she spend this time working instead? Given the circumstances, where could any relationship with Lucas actually go, anyway?—Tess made her way to the clubhouse that night in her sexiest oversized tee.

Which seemed like a contradiction in terms, she knew.

But she wasn't sure how she wanted this evening to end yet, so hedging her bets and pretending she might be there for a lesson instead of lovemaking made sense. Besides, if he really did intend to pursue a relationship with her, he should know she prioritized comfort over all else in her non-professional clothing. If he wanted a woman who'd squeeze herself into Spanx and put on spike heels for a normal night out, he needed to keep on looking.

Somewhere in her late thirties, her supply of fucks had become extremely limited. Some might even say nonexistent, except when it came to her work and her friends.

And, it appeared, Lucas. Because she did indeed give a fuck about how he saw her. Whether he wanted her. So she might have pulled on a comfy tee, but she'd made certain the garnet color flattered her skin and the vee neckline dipped low. Given how much he enjoyed her boobs, he'd appreciate the amount of cleavage it displayed.

Speaking of which...

She tugged the neckline a little lower as she neared the clubhouse, her heart skittering.

Once more, Lucas was waiting for her. This time with his head up and alert, not pointed at his toes. Once more, as soon as he spotted her, he jogged her way, eating up massive amounts of ground with each long stride.

No wonder he always looked so indolent. He only had to take a single step where a normal mortal might need three. His big body had exacted a price for that advantage, though, paid in pain and surgery and a disappointing end to a promising career.

He didn't appear worried about any of that right now.

No, he was smiling at her. Not the facile grin of a flirt, but a beam that popped his dimples and warmed his eyes. When he got close, he immediately dipped his head for a gentle press of his lips against hers, brief and sweet.

"Hey, älskling." His arms slid around her, and he cuddled her neck with that big, warm palm of his as his fingers laced into her hair, and she almost melted on the spot. "What do you want to do tonight?"

Älskling. Again.

Determining the correct spelling of that Swedish word had taken some time earlier that day—umlauts were not her friend—but she'd finally managed to locate the translation.

Darling. Honey. Or...beloved.

He'd asked her a question, but she couldn't seem to form coherent words. "Uh..."

A touch of that flirty grin returned as he backed up a bare inch and looked down at her. "The tee says *let's play tennis,* but the neckline of that tee..." He shook his head. "It says *if I run toward a ball, I may experience another wardrobe malfunction.*"

The teasing unlocked her tongue. "No fear. I wore my most sturdy sports bra tonight. It's basically a straitjacket for my breasts, only more uncomfortable and with less opportunity for escape."

He laughed. "Who said anything about fear? I'm half agony, half hope." At her questioning look, he shrugged. "My coach was a Brit. She made us listen to Austen during long car trips. Sue me."

She had to ask. "So what's the hope?"

"Your breasts might be too powerful for containment."

She couldn't help a snicker. "So you're praying they'll break out of sports-bra jail at any moment and make their daring escape, and you'll be around to witness the whole thing?"

"Can you elaborate a little? Add a few more details?" A faraway look had appeared in his eyes. "Maybe stage a dramatic reenactment of the event?"

"Perv." She flicked his arm, ignoring his little yelp. "It

can't be a reenactment if it hasn't happened yet. Anyway, what about the agony?"

"All those hooks, of course." His smile faded a little. "And that undecided look on your face when you saw me just now. I figure you're reconsidering our dinner tonight."

Note to self: Don't play poker with Lucas. Unless it's strip poker and you want to flash the goods.

She wouldn't lie to him. Even if she tried, it evidently wouldn't work. So she told him the truth, flat out: "I have doubts. But I'm here, and I brought a change of clothing and a toothbrush in my bag."

He stopped breathing. "Really?"

At her nod, that dimpled smile returned. Turned blinding with the sort of joy she hadn't seen since a freak snowstorm caused an early dismissal from school the Friday before spring break. Rasheed Millman, a first-year teacher from the science department, had literally tackle-hugged her, and Frau Kauffman had almost mowed down several sophomores as she sprinted, cackling in Germanic glee, to the parking lot.

All students believed they loved snow days more than teachers. All students were wrong.

"I have big plans for tonight." She nodded toward the chain-link fence. "Let's hit the court and get this evening started."

He didn't move toward the concrete expanse in the near distance. Instead, his forefinger followed the edge of her hairline and traced the outer rim of her ear, a taunting, shivery tease of a touch. "Sounds perfect. Unless your knee is hurting too much for a tennis lesson?"

He didn't sound impatient or disappointed by that possibility. Just matter-of-fact in a way that eased her instinctive defensiveness.

"I've been babying it the last couple of days. As long as I don't run too much, descend a bunch of stairs, or twist in an odd way, I'm not in any pain," she told him honestly.

"If that changes, let me know. We'll stop right away." His hand lowered to splay on her back, and he gently guided her toward the court. "As long as you're not hurting, though, I'm glad we're doing this. I've found…"

He trailed off as they walked, his mouth drawing tight. When they arrived on the court, he stepped away from her to lower his huge bag. Bending over, he dug inside, emerging with an armful of towels, a can of balls, two water bottles, and two rackets.

She accepted the racket he handed her. "You've found what?"

Another long silence.

Then he met her eyes and gave an apologetic wince. "Sorry. I don't mean to be obstructive. I just haven't talked about certain things for a while now."

Part of her wanted to let him off the hook and tell him to forget it, if that would erase those deep brackets on either side of his mouth. But if this morning had been an exception, if he couldn't make himself reveal more of his past and his thoughts to her, she needed to know that. Now, before they became any more entangled.

"Understood. That said…" Gesturing to the court around them, she smiled at him. "What better place for a little practice?"

One corner of his mouth rose. "An excellent point."

"I thought so."

He snorted. Then, after dropping another quick, dizzying kiss on her mouth, he hopped over the net and shook a couple balls loose from the can.

"I was just going to say…" A long pause as he gathered his words and forced them out. "Back when I was on the Tour, time on the court often clarified things for me. If I was worried, an hour with my hitting partner did me a world of good. Even though, toward the end, sustaining a rally hurt me physically as much as it helped me mentally."

She let out a slow breath. He hadn't avoided her question or hid himself behind that shell he'd constructed. This was...

This was good. It could be really, really good.

Which was, in its own way, really, really bad.

In a practiced gesture, he slid one of the balls into his pocket and palmed the other. Clearly, he was done with his story and ready to play.

But she needed to clarify something first. "When we were arguing, you said your left wrist still hurt sometimes. Is that true?"

As he bounced the ball against the blue concrete, he nodded.

"Is that only when you go full-force? Or does it hurt all the time? With every backhand you hit?"

The thought of that—his greatest joy and comfort twined with inescapable pain—tore a hole through her heart, and damned if she didn't need to blink back tears.

Bounce, bounce, bounce.

He wasn't looking at her. "Not every backhand." A pause. "Some."

Screw her doubts. She wouldn't make him suffer because of her dithering. "Would you rather do something else, then? We could go to dinner right away, if you wanted."

"I said I wanted to play a little tennis with you, and I do." He didn't sound impressed by her offer or concerned about his own pain. "And you said your knee is fine, so we're both good to go."

She couldn't stand the thought of him hurting. "But if you're—"

"This is one of the reasons I don't talk to people about my injuries." When he glanced up at her, a wry smile had split his face. "They tend to question my own judgment about what I can and can't handle. About how I should treat my body."

She winced. Was that what she'd just done to him?

Yeah. Yeah, she kinda had.

"I'm sorry. I'll try not to do it again." God knew, she'd received enough unsolicited advice about her own body over the years. "That said, if I saw you obviously hurting, I'd say something. If that's a deal-breaker for you, you should let me know."

He thought for a minute before answering, and then gave a little nod.

"I would do the same, so it's not a deal-breaker. Besides, I know I can push myself a bit too hard at times." When she began to speak, he sent her a quelling look. "Although now isn't one of those times, so you can close that sweet mouth of yours."

"I can." She smirked. "But I probably won't."

His eyes rolled to the darkening sky above. "Quelle surprise."

"So you want us to hit the ball back and forth?" Lifting her racket, she mimed hitting a forehand.

He raised his own racket in a salute. "Yes. And while we do, we can play a game other than tennis. What do you think?"

When she raised a brow, he glanced at it and huffed out an amused breath.

"I think you're overestimating my ability to multitask," she told him.

That wink of his. It made her want to smack him *and* screw him. "Truth or dare on the tennis court, Tess. A few rallies, a few secrets, a few risks. What do you say?"

She flipped her hair over her shoulder and tilted her chin high. "I say bring it on, Lucas. Bring. It. On."

THIRTEEN

Lucas began bouncing the ball in readiness to take a shot, and Tess shifted her stance, setting her feet shoulder-width apart. For a moment, she was tempted to sway in place like she'd seen his opponents do when he served to them in those YouTube videos, but...no. Unlike them, she wouldn't look ready for her return. She'd look like she'd been drinking too much.

Instead, she braced the racket in front of her. "Who's going to start?"

"I will." One more bounce, and then the ball was flying over the net toward her. "Truth or dare, Tess?"

As always, the ball landed near her, and she hit it over the net and into the back corner of his court by sheer accident. "A gentleman would let me go first."

"I can be gentle. If and when that's what you want." Irritatingly, he reached the ball without seeming to hurry in any appreciable way. "As far as your going first—"

Another easy shot for her to reach. "Oh, Jesus. I set myself up for a *coming first* joke, didn't I?"

"You really did. Although I consider it less a joke and more a promise." With two giant strides, he reached the spot where she'd barely managed to get the ball over the net. "Assuming you decide to spend the night with me. If not, no problem. I'd be happy if we just—"

He cut himself off as she lined up her return shot.

"Just what?"

Wait. Were his cheeks becoming a little pink? "Went out to dinner and talked. Held hands, maybe."

Oh, my goodness. They were. He was *blushing*.

His mention of hand-holding had embarrassed him. *Him.* The same man who could cheerfully, shamelessly discuss for hours how her boobs might flee the harsh confines of her sports bra and roam free, crushing small towns in their wake.

For him, she supposed, a suggestion of holding hands might be more intimate—more revealing of who and what he really was—than any amount of sexual banter. And now he'd turned shy, his cheeks flushed and his gaze landing anywhere but on her.

The Sweet Swede had arrived for a visit.

"Holding hands should definitely be doable." She smiled at him as they kept hitting the ball back and forth. "Depending on how our game of Truth or Dare goes. If you make me run around the court naked, you should anticipate a lonely evening ahead with only your own hand for holding. And I mean that in every possible way."

His rumble of laughter crossed the court. "I promise I won't make you run."

"I notice you made no promises about nakedness." Lord, Florida was an armpit in the summer. Tess was starting to sweat already. "An accidental oversight, I'm sure."

He only grinned in response. "I repeat: Truth or dare, Tess?"

Another of Lucas's perfectly placed shots. He didn't even look like he needed to pay attention. Maybe she should try to hit a little harder?

The next time he sent the ball her way, she put more

power behind her swing, and the ball promptly sailed into the net.

Good enough. That would buy her a moment to rest. "Truth."

His question came immediately. "Why are you working so hard during your vacation?"

Leaning on her racket, she raised the hem of her tee to wipe her forehead. When she lowered it again, Lucas had frozen in place, and his eyes appeared glued to an area just north of her belly.

"My principal announced she was retiring at the end of this upcoming school year, and you already know I want her job. If Gary Enders gets it instead, the consequences will be disastrous for our school." It was wrong of her to tease him, and she knew it. But she still lifted her shirt a second time and dabbed at her upper lip, pretending not to hear the faint groan from the other side of the net. "So I need to spend all my time for the foreseeable future proving myself. Working overtime, suggesting initiatives, spearheading committees."

She frowned. "Also attending carnivals, where I'll get dunked by the entire girls' softball team. They're vicious, they hold a grudge, and their pitches are pinpoint-accurate."

He'd tilted his head, his brow creased.

"Why would the softball—" He shook his head. "You know what? Never mind. Forget about teenage softball-playing mafiosos, and tell me about an initiative you plan to suggest."

She bit her lip, picturing the list she'd created in her notebook. "I want to break down our suspension statistics and analyze how they differ by race. I have a feeling our students of color get hit with suspensions, rather than verbal warnings or detention, much more frequently, much more rapidly, and with much less cause than our white kids. So I want to look at the data to confirm my suspicions. If I'm right, that needs to be addressed school-wide, pronto,

129

because it's not right, and I won't allow it to keep happening."

"That's an important topic. I'm glad you're tackling it." He sounded sincere, and he was looking at her with such warmth in those olive-green eyes. Such patient concentration. "It'll be a lot of extra work for you, I imagine."

"Definitely." She started ticking off other priorities. "Then there's this initiative I want to propose that involves the school nurse. We have free and reduced-price meals, of course, but kids still come to her with headaches and stomachaches because they're hungry, and I'd like to give her enough money to stock food for—"

"Wait a minute." He held up a hand. "Your initiatives are great. And at some point, I want to listen to every single one of your ideas in detail. But maybe not right this second."

She offered him a sheepish smile. "Sorry. I get a little carried away sometimes."

"For good reason." There wasn't an ounce of impatience in his voice. Just calmness and interest. "I still want to know why you're working on those initiatives now, instead of when you return home."

"That's easy. Because there's no time for anything but triage once the school year starts. Big ideas are best incubated during the summer." She waggled a chiding finger at him. "Also, don't think I didn't notice what just happened here. You got two questions answered, maybe three. Get ready for payback, Karlsson."

Tucking his racket beneath his arm, he strode to the net and leaned into it with both hands. "To quote a true visionary: Bring it on, Dunn."

"Truth or dare?" She didn't care which he chose. Either option sounded as delicious as those strawberry-lemonade cupcakes.

He paused to think. "Truth."

"Hmmm." After a moment of consideration, she decided

to start serious and shift to sexy later, as desired. "How many long-term relationships have you had?"

"Uh…" His brow pinched, and all hints of mirth disappeared. "Are we including familial relationships? Or friendships?"

After laying her racket carefully on the court, she propped her fists on her hips. "Nope."

"Would a month count as long-term? If you and your partner were only in the same place for a week during that month, because of your conflicting schedules?"

Her eyebrow did the talking for her.

His shoulders drooped in response. "I joined the ATP Tour as a teenager, Tess. And here's the thing: When you're a professional tennis player, you're on the road almost continually. If you tend to make it far in tournaments, you may not get home for weeks or even months at a time."

"Why not date a fellow player, then?"

She tried not to picture it. Two athletes, young and toned and capable, arms around one another as they celebrated their victories and shared secrets only other tennis pros would understand.

"If I'd dated a WTA player, we'd still have had trouble connecting. A lot of tournaments are at venues too small for men and women to play at the same time. And when you're not competing, you're practicing. Or, in my case, recovering from injuries and doing constant, intensive physical therapy." In a seemingly absent gesture, he looked down and rotated his wrists, as if testing whether they still hurt. "There was no time to nurture anything more serious than a casual arrangement, and it got lonely sometimes. *I* got lonely sometimes, even though I had my team around me almost constantly."

His voice was low. Vulnerable, in a way she wanted to honor.

"I'm sorry, Lucas." She came to the net and laid her hand on his. "That sounds like a hard, unforgiving life."

He acknowledged that with a slight jerk of his head. "Don't get me wrong. I loved tennis. Loved my team. Loved seeing so much of the world. But I didn't feel good about starting anything serious with anyone when I had so little time and energy to give to a relationship. So the answer to your question is zero. I've had zero serious romantic relationships. To this point."

The last phrase, he stated with emphasis. Eye contact. Determination.

He wanted her. She doubted everything else, but not that.

Still. He'd never committed to a woman. Not once. And she was supposed to believe that he wouldn't hurt her? That a woman like her could keep a man like him happy long-term?

A fling, Tess. This doesn't need to be more than a fling.

If she believed everything he was telling her, though, he wanted more than that. Not just her body, but her trust. Maybe her heart.

She needed some outlet for all the emotion roiling within her. Picking up her racket again, she pointed it toward him. "I'm ready to keep playing."

He looked at her for a long moment before backing up from the net and hitting the ball in a gentle arc to her side.

"So…" She hit it back. Hard. This time, it whizzed over the net, and he had to rush to get it. "I think we're even. I asked you two questions. Your turn."

"All right, then," he said, slightly breathless. "Truth or dare?"

He'd still managed to hit the ball directly to her, and she sent it back with an easy swing from her shoulder. "Truth."

The more, the better. Maybe a few additional truths would help them make wiser decisions about one another.

Once more, he didn't have to pause to formulate his question. "What did you think of me when we met?"

Easy-peasy.

"I thought you were a cocky bro, too handsome and flirty for your own good." Her lips curved, despite her best efforts. "I also thought you felt amazing between my thighs."

He promptly shanked his shot, and the ball bounced into another court.

She watched the ball roll into a dark corner. "Maybe I shouldn't share how my nipples reacted to your back. I don't want to endanger tourists on the other side of the island."

A sort of choked cough racked his tall frame. "I assumed you were cold."

"Pressed up against you? Please." A laughable idea, particularly given the amount of heat his big body gave off. "Truth or dare?"

"Dare." His voice had turned raspy. Hot.

She tilted her head. Considered him. Considered what he'd told her earlier. "I dare you to tell me five things you're good at other than tennis."

He stared at her for a moment before heaving an exaggerated sigh.

"I was hoping for something more sexual," he said.

"I'll bet."

When she didn't back down and change her dare, he eventually began fiddling with the strings on his racket, speaking without looking at her. "Uh...I'm decent at basketball, I guess."

Yeah, he still wasn't getting her point, but he would. Eventually.

His eyes flicked up, and those dimples appeared alongside his flirty, concealing grin. "And of course, you wouldn't *believe* how good I am with my tongue."

"Yes, yes, you're a sexual dynamo. I look forward to experiencing the wonder of it all later tonight." She waved her free hand dismissively. "But right now, I want to know what you're good at that doesn't involve your body, and I want you to tell me."

His grin promptly disappeared. "You didn't specify that in your dare."

"You're going to make me use another turn to get what I want?" Once more, she employed her single-brow intimidation technique, which had served her well throughout her teaching and administrative career. "Interesting."

He tapped his racket against his outer thigh, agitation in every movement. "No, of course not. I just…"

Dammit. The way he saw himself was slowly becoming clear to her. Too clear. And in her sorrow and frustration— her innate desire to fix everything, *now*—she was pushing him too hard.

She walked up to the net again. Gentled her voice. "Lucas, I've had two and a half tennis lessons with you, at least one of which actually involved tennis, rather than shouting or service motions demonstrated solely for my sexual gratification."

There. That got a half-smile out of him.

"I also observed you with that couple the other day," she continued. "So I know at least some of your non-physical strengths. I'm just wondering if you know them too."

His chin dropped to his chest, which rose and fell once. Again.

Then he backed away, retrieved a ball from his pocket, and bounced it on the court. "Let's play as I answer your question. It'll make thinking easier for me."

"Sure." She stepped back a few feet and waited.

After an easy shot to her forehand, he cleared his throat. Started speaking, his cadence calm and even once more. "I know a lot about tennis. Proper form. Match strategies. Training techniques. My clients seem to think I do a decent job explaining those things to them."

"That's two strengths." When he hit the ball to her again, this time to her backhand, she connected at a weird angle. The shot flew high but not far, landing only inches past the net. "And as one of your clients, I can confirm how knowledgeable you are and how well you explain and share that knowledge. What else? I need three more strengths."

With a flick of his wrist, he directed the ball back to her forehand. "I'm never late for a lesson. I always have a plan in place to maximize our given time."

"So you're prompt and organized. I observed that too." She was falling into the rhythm of the rally, hitting without much thought involved. "One more thing."

He remained silent for another few hits, his brow furrowed in thought.

"I work hard," he finally said. "I've always worked hard. And—"

When he cut himself off and didn't finish his sentence, she waved her racket at him between shots. "And what?"

Another swing of his racket. Another *ping* as the ball landed on the racket's sweet spot and sailed over the net. "I'm friendly. I know how to put people at ease."

"You're also funny and intelligent and well educated." She lunged to return his forehand. "At some point, I want to talk to you about the Swedish educational system, by the way."

Jesus, she wasn't getting a hint of the ocean breeze on the court, and she hadn't bothered to invest in a moisture-wicking top. Her t-shirt was soaked.

He didn't even seem to look at the ball as he hit it, damn him. "No problem. I'm all yours."

She swallowed over a dry throat at that declaration.

Maybe he'd meant it as a generic turn of phrase, but it sounded like a vow. And the way he was watching her now, tracking her every movement, gaze somehow both soft and hot—

Her next shot went wild, landing far off to the side, and he sprinted for the ball.

"Sorry," she whispered.

After he got off his shot, his gaze met hers from across the court.

The ball whizzed past her, and she didn't even move.

He didn't spare that ball a single glance.

"Truth or dare, Tess." The words were firm. Rumbly. Laden with promise.

She didn't know which to choose. Which was safer. Whether she wanted to be safe in the first place.

Deep breath. In through the nose, out through the mouth.

"Dare," she said.

His nostrils flared.

"I'm hot, Lucas." She smiled at him, slow and easy. "Dare me to take off my shirt."

He was starting to sweat. Striding to his bag, he snatched up his bottle of water and drained it in one gulp. Then he returned to his side of the court, but positioned himself close to the net. Close to her.

His eyes never left hers. "Take off your shirt, Tess. I dare you."

Normally, she'd yank the tee over her head and be done with it. This time, she made it a tease. A flirtatious reveal of inches as she wiggled and swayed just the tiniest bit. And then the t-shirt was off. Clutched in her hand as she melted beneath the heat of his stare.

All sound from the other side of the court had ceased, even the faint shush of his breathing. When she strode toward his bag and tossed her tee on top of it, her breasts bouncing despite the support of her sports bra, he made a weird choking noise.

Even after she positioned herself for a return, he didn't move until she snapped her fingers in front of her cleavage. "Time to stop staring at my boobs and keep playing, Lucas."

"Sorry." He shook his head hard, as if trying to clear it. "I

136

just…wasn't prepared for the full glory of…" His eyes dropped again. "Those."

"You sweet summer child." She had to snicker. "What you can see right now is nothing. My boobs are like an iceberg."

"I don't—" His olive-green eyes, slightly unfocused, lifted to hers. "I don't understand."

She flicked a hand in front of her substantial cleavage. "Ninety percent is still below the surface."

"Wow." His throat bobbed as he swallowed. "Oh, wow."

He didn't lift his racket, even when she waved hers back and forth.

Maybe another snap of the fingers in front of her chest would do the job. "Hit the ball, Lucas."

His expression still dazed, he did. Her return arced over the net, and she watched it land in the far corner.

He ran for the ball. "Nice shot."

"Thanks. I have a great teacher." She experimented with a bit more force, and the racket responded, sending the ball within inches of the baseline.

"You should know that this is the best time I've ever had on a tennis court, bar none." He was hustling, but she could still hear the smile in his voice.

"Bullshit. You won a Grand Slam."

"Yes. But Alvillar's cleavage was much less impressive than yours."

His return shot wasn't as controlled as usual. Its trajectory meant she'd need to run a few feet to get it. So she did, even though her knee twinged and the jiggling of her breasts wasn't entirely comfortable.

Then there was the ball, bouncing only a foot away, within perfect reach of her racket.

What the hell? Why not see what she could do if she bludgeoned the thing full-force?

She hit through it, just as he'd told her, using her shoulders and every ounce of her strength. The ball slammed against the sweet spot of the strings with a satisfying little *ping* and whipped across the net.

Where, she saw an instant too late, Lucas was standing frozen.

The jiggle. Oh, Jesus, her boobs had immobilized him yet again.

And before she could finish shouting his name, before he could tear his stare from her admittedly ginormous rack, the ball whacked him directly in the face.

FOURTEEN

Lucas collapsed to his knees on the concrete, clutching his nose.

Fuck, that hurt. Although he supposed it served him right for ogling Tess's astounding cleavage—again—when he should have been paying attention to the rally.

Rapid footsteps echoed through the court, and she appeared by his side. "Oh, shit, Lucas. Are you all right? Can you move your hands so I can see your nose?"

"Uh…" Jesus, his face was throbbing. "I'm not sure."

She was kneeling beside him, her arm around his shoulders to offer support, and he could feel her trembling as she nudged the fingers covering his nose. He moved them a fraction and peered down at them to check for blood.

None. And when he scrunched his nose, it didn't feel broken, just sore. It appeared Acute Breast Paralysis had bruised him, but not severely injured him. Not yet, anyway.

Her voice was hushed as she repeated her question. "Are you all right?"

He really shouldn't tease her. But how could he resist?

"My face!" he howled, anguish in every syllable. "Oh, God, my beautiful face!"

Her patting hand on his shoulder stilled. "Are you fucking with me?"

"How can you ask me that?" He lowered his hands to his sides so she could get a good look at his total lack of serious injury. "How can you question the severity of my wound, when my distinguished nose and razor-sharp cheekbones have been desecrated, my stunning good looks ruined forever?"

She pursed her lips and gave a little nod. "You're fucking with me."

"I'm hurt you would say that." He blinked at her soulfully. "You should take pity on a poor man whose handsome visage has been ravaged by your errant ball."

"*Your* balls are going to be errant if you don't stop teasing me." But she couldn't suppress a small smile. "And that tennis ball went exactly where I wanted it to. You just weren't paying attention because you were too busy staring at my jiggling rack."

He gazed down into her magnificent cleavage. "Can you blame me?"

"I guess I should consider it a compliment." She raised her voice to an announcer's boom. "Behold! The power of boobs."

"*Your* boobs," he corrected. "Your boobs are the only ones that cause my vital life functions to cease."

It was the simple truth. He'd seen plenty of breasts before, large and small. But something about hers brought him to his knees. Literally, in this instance.

They were hers. Tess Dunn's breasts. And that was enough to stop him in his tracks.

As was her insistence that he acknowledge his abilities, his potential, in arenas that had nothing to do with how much topspin he could put on his backhand.

"How flattering." She touched a gentle fingertip to the bridge of his nose. "Are you sure you're okay?"

He brought that fingertip to his mouth for a quick kiss. "I'm fine, älskling. Don't worry."

She glanced up at the floodlights surrounding the court. "Maybe we should check the injury under some decent light, just in case."

They'd never been alone in private. Not once. He wanted that privacy, that opportunity for real intimacy, more than he could express. More than was wise, most likely.

But not like this. "I know you brought an overnight bag, but you said you have doubts. If that's still true, if you haven't made up your mind about me yet, let's keep things public. In private, I have a feeling everything could get—"

"Combustible?" Her hazel eyes seared through him.

He inclined his head. "Yeah. Quickly. If that's not what you want, we shouldn't put ourselves in that position. I mean, I can obviously control myself, and so can you. But maybe it's better to avoid temptation until you know how you're playing this."

She laid a palm against his cheek, and he leaned into it. "I'm not playing."

Tennis. Truth or Dare. Both had served as inroads toward intimacy, rather than simply lighthearted games. He'd understood that almost from the beginning, and apparently she had too.

"I know." He closed his eyes. "I know. But—"

"I like you, Lucas Karlsson." Her words were soft but matter-of-fact. "I like you flirty, and I like you shy. You're thoughtful and funny and smart and gentle. I trust that you wouldn't deliberately hurt me. So I don't have any more doubts about whether I want to spend the night with you, or whether one night will be enough. I do, and it won't."

Turned out, her breasts weren't the only things that could make his world screech to a halt. Because those words, the affection and hope in them, stole his ability to do anything but gape at her and confirm the truth of what she'd said.

"Are you sure?" he whispered.

"I'm sure." She rubbed her lips against his in a teasing caress. "Now why don't you show me where you live, at long last?"

"I'd love—"

Wait. Was that…?

Shit. So much for romance.

"You'd love what?" She sounded confused.

He turned his face away from her, pinching the bridge of his nose. "Going to my apartment is a fantastic idea."

She took a moment to answer. "Then why aren't you looking at me?"

Nope. Pinching his nose wasn't going to take care of the problem.

"Because…" Springing to his feet, he ran for a towel. "My nose just started bleeding."

SOMEHOW, LUCAS HAD NEVER PICTURED USHERING Tess into his apartment for the first time with a bloody tissue shoved up each of his nostrils.

On the walk to the dark clubhouse, she'd started giggling several times at the sight of his *nose tampons*, as she preferred to call them. But she'd also slung an arm around his waist and bumped hips with him as they walked, so he was still considering this the greatest night ever.

He unlocked the door to the clubhouse and deactivated the alarm, flipping the deadbolt back into place once they were both inside. Then he guided her around the racks of tennis equipment and toward a discreet door across the room, the whooshing of the fan overhead the only sound.

"You're rushing me past the rackets." She squeezed his waist. "I'd hoped we could talk more about my various string choices."

It didn't seem likely, but… "If that's what you want to do, I can speak at length about the various advantages of natural gut versus polyester versus a combination thereof."

Even in the dim nighttime lights, he could see her lip curl. "Natural gut?"

"Also known as catgut, although it's not made from kittens." He grinned at her. "At least, not the nice ones."

She shuddered, which was a rather pleasant sensation with her pressed to his side. "Never mind. I hereby retract my teasing and request that you never, ever mention kitten intestines to me again during a date."

"This is a date?" He liked the sound of that. "I should have brought you more flowers."

As they climbed the stairs to his apartment, she scanned his face and started giggling again. "You gifted me with the sight of you sporting nose tampons. That's good enough for me."

In retaliation, he tickled her ribs until she gasped with laughter. Then he unlocked the door to his apartment and stepped aside to let her enter first.

In hopes she might visit, he'd spent a few minutes earlier that afternoon straightening up the kitchen, where he'd left some dishes soaking the night before. The rest of the apartment hadn't needed help, since he didn't tend to spread out much. The consequence of too many years spent living out of suitcases, he supposed.

Even tidy, the apartment wasn't much to brag about. She could see most of it from the doorway, and she took a moment to scan the area before moving inside.

She made a noncommittal noise. "Utilitarian, but cozy."

After setting down their bags, he tried to evaluate the space through her eyes. The small galley kitchen, the clean beige carpet, the white walls, the nubby blueish upholstery on the couch. The huge TV dominating the living room. The shiny oak coffee table.

All generic. Reflective of exactly nothing about him or his interests and tastes.

That wasn't good enough for him anymore. Once Tess left, he'd—

No. He wouldn't think about that now. They had tonight and more nights to come, and he was hoping they could make the most of their time together.

He swallowed back a twinge of panic and nodded toward the narrow hallway leading off from the living area. "The first door on the right is a half-bath. The other one is for the master bedroom and bathroom." *Master bathroom* was a grandiose name for the tiny space with its claustrophobia-inducing shower, but technically correct. "And that's about it. The apartment came with the job, completely furnished, and I don't need much room for my stuff. All those years on tour, I never accumulated a lot of furniture or knickknacks or whatever. I know it's not much, but—"

"Lucas." She tugged his arm until he faced her. "You don't have to defend your apartment to me. I understand why it looks like a hotel room. It doesn't reflect who you are, because you *chose* not to have it reflect who you are."

She got it. The deliberation with which he'd failed to insert himself into this space. Into this half-life he'd created on the island. Perceptive as hell, as always.

He let out a slow breath. "Yeah."

"So...what now?" She was watching him, her hazel eyes bright.

Raising a hand, he smoothed the fine hairs at her temple. "Are you hungry?"

"Nope. Are you?" She tapped the bridge of his nose, her finger light as a whisper. "And is your nose still bleeding?"

"I'm not hungry either. But give me a minute in the bath-room to figure out whether I can remove my..." Her eyes brightened even more in anticipation, and he sighed. Whatever. He could use that damn name if it made her happy. "Whether I can remove my *nose tampons* yet."

He started for the hall. "Make yourself at home in the meantime. The remote's on the table, and it's pretty straightforward to use. There's juice in the fridge. A few snacks too, in case you change your mind about being hungry."

He could really use a quick shower. If this evening progressed how he hoped it would, he didn't want to subject Tess to Eau de Sweaty Balls.

As he opened the door to his bedroom, though, her hand on his arm brought him to a halt. He jumped a little, startled.

"Uh-uh." She shook her forefinger at him. "I still want to see your injury in decent lighting. And if you think I'm getting naked with you before I wash off some of this sweat, you're vastly mistaken."

At the confirmation of all his most fervent hopes, his heart seized in his chest. "You said you were spending the night, but I didn't want to assume…"

"Oh, come on." She rolled her eyes. "I told you I liked you, and I'm a grown woman who enjoys sex. It's not as if we're going to spend the evening alone in your apartment together and do nothing but watch baseball." Her grin plumped those cute cheeks of hers. "Although I do intend to round a lot of bases."

"Tess." He covered her hand with his. "I don't want you to think this is casual for me. We can wait a few days."

Her smile didn't falter, and not an ounce of wariness clouded her gaze. "*Is* this casual for you?"

"No." His hand squeezed hers. "Not in the slightest."

"And you want to sleep with me?"

"You're the sexiest woman on the face of the earth, and I honestly think my penis will spontaneously combust if we don't have sex soon." He aimed an apologetic grimace at his groin. "But I want to earn your trust first."

She didn't hesitate. "You already have it, Lucas. Let's do this."

He was pretty sure he was going to die if he didn't start breathing again.

Tilting her head in thought, she added, "If you want me to spend the night, you'll have to get up early. Belle and I booked a tour at the Inglethorpe Mansion tomorrow morning, so we need to leave on the first ferry to the mainland."

"That's..." He cleared his throat. "That's doable."

A light tap on his butt made him jump again. "And so are you. Let's peek at your nose, get clean, and then get dirty again."

He led her into the tiny, white-tiled bathroom, and they squeezed into the space between the vanity and the shower. Squinting in the overhead light, he studied his reflection.

Bags under his eyes from another sleepless night spent fixating on Tess. Shiny forehead from the heat. Sweat-darkened clothing. Blood-spattered tissue twists shoved up his swollen nose.

He started laughing. "This is literally the least seductive I've ever looked in my entire adult life."

"This may not be your finest hour." Her lips twitched as she scanned him in the mirror. "But rest assured, *you're* still fine."

"Are you sure you want to have sex with...this?" He waved a hand at his reflection.

Now she was laughing too, her head leaning against his chest as her mirth echoed in the small room. "Well, I didn't plan to make tender love to your nose, Lucas. Or your sweaty workout clothes. So yeah, I think I'm good."

Surrounding her shoulders with one arm, he pulled her closer. "Okay, then. Let's survey the damage."

With his free hand, he yanked the tissues from his nose, tossed them in the trash, and waited for the flood. And waited.

"Well, this is anticlimactic. I'd hoped for something reminiscent of The Shining. Or Carrie, at the very least." Her brows furrowed, that adorable trident appearing between them. "Now that I consider the matter, Stephen King really has a thing about floods of blood."

He gave his nose an experimental wiggle. Still nothing. "Sorry to disappoint you."

"Apology accepted." She lightly rubbed the bridge of his nose. "Does that hurt?"

When he shook his head, her eyes met his in the mirror. "Then, from what I can tell, you might get a bruise, but you didn't sustain any major damage. Do you think that handsome face of yours can survive some contact?"

He wanted his face in a variety of enticing locations on her body, all of which would involve extensive skin-to-skin contact. As long as he wasn't actively bleeding, there was only one answer to give. "Definitely."

At her wicked grin, he had to support himself with a hand on the vanity.

"Good. Then let me call Belle and confirm I'll be out tonight. I don't want her to worry." She headed back into the hallway. "Commence your manly sexytimes preparations, Lucas."

He blinked after her. "Is that your former-teacher way of telling me to shower?"

"And whatever else you guys do before a woman spends the night." Without turning around, she flicked her wrist in a dismissive gesture. "But make it fast, because I'm getting impatient, and I need a shower too."

Tess, wet and naked in his apartment. Mere meters away from him.

That really seemed like a lost opportunity.

"We could shower together." He cleared his throat. "For efficiency's sake."

She looked at him over her shoulder, her phone already at her ear. "I like the way you think."

This seemed way too good to be true. "You'll do it?"

"Brace yourself, Lucas. The Boobening is almost upon you." Then she spoke into her cell, her eyes locked to his as he sagged against the bathroom doorway. "Belle, honey? Don't expect me back at our room tonight. I have big plans for our tennis pro. If you don't hear from him again, assume he died as he wanted to live: smothered by my ginormous rack."

What a way to go, he thought. *What a way to go.*

FIFTEEN

TESS CAST A DOUBTFUL LOOK AT HIS SHOWER. "ON second thought, I'm not sure we're both going to fit inside there. I think the stall started its life as a coffin."

"Oh, we'll fit." He reached for the top hook of her sports bra and paused a moment. When she didn't protest, he carefully tugged the fabric until the hook popped free from the eye, and then moved on to the next one. And the next. "Although I suspect our exit from its confines will look clown car-esque."

His knuckles were brushing warm, slightly sticky skin. Soft. So soft. More cleavage was coming into view as the vee between her breasts deepened. Soon, he was going to strip off her leggings too, and witness the glory of her ample butt and round belly. Then feel her against him, length to length. Flesh to flesh.

"Clown car-esque?" She snorted. "If you honk my boob or spray me in the face with your flower, I'll make sure your balloon animal never fully inflates again."

He paused on the last hook. "Have I told you how much I admire the creativity of your genital-maiming threats?"

When she laughed, her bra's final hook strained at its epic

task. "Discussing potential injury to your date's dick and balls is the key to an effective seduction, I've found."

He smiled at her. "Well, it clearly worked on me."

After pressing a quick kiss to that cute ski-jump nose of hers, he released the final hook and tugged the sports bra off her shoulders and down her arms. But he only let himself sneak a quick glance at her breasts before raising his eyes back to her face.

He had to have *some* class, after all. Or at least the pretense thereof.

Just that one glance was more than enough. The vision of her topless had seared itself onto his brain forever.

Because of their size, her breasts rested low against her ribcage, her areolas large and brown, her nipples tight. They were generous and plush and more beautiful than he'd imagined, and God knew he'd imagined them countless times since she'd plastered them against his back four days ago.

He wanted them in his hands, against his tongue. But more than that, he wanted her entirely naked in front of him for the first time. So he could wait a few more minutes. Maybe.

She stretched a little, and his mouth became the Sahara. "Oh, God, that feels good. Bras are the work of the devil."

"Feel free never to wear one, then. I'll fully support your decision." He flexed his fingers. "Really. However you need support, I'm there."

"How kind of you." Her fingers grasped the hem of his shirt, her knuckles brushing his lower stomach, and he drew in a harsh breath. "Raise your arms."

Lifting his arms and lowering his head, he let her remove the damp tee. He stood stock-still as she traced the lines of his abs and drew circles around his chest.

Her swallow was audible. "I'm...not sure I've ever been with someone like you before. If I have, it's been a crapload of years. Maybe decades."

She wasn't meeting his gaze, and her voice had turned subdued.

Nope. He wasn't letting her go down that particular road again.

"Someone like me?" He pressed his lips against her forehead. "Do you mean a guy with a bum wrist who occasionally hits his head against light fixtures?"

"You're an athlete. And so—" Another pass of her hand down his chest, to his belly. "So young. Guys my age, most of them look a little different. And women your age don't look like me. Gravity's a real bitch, Lucas."

He took a moment to consider the best way to respond.

"Maybe you don't look twenty-six. But you look like you." Covering her hand with his, he drew it down further. Lower and lower, until her palm rested against his eager dick. "You can feel what that does to me."

When she pressed a little harder, he bit off a groan.

He stared at her downturned head. "I want you, Tess. Will you please let me take off the rest of your clothes so I can show you how much?"

After a moment, she gave a little nod. "Yeah. But first, let's get that big body of yours bare. I've seen you without your shirt, but never without those shorts. I have a strong suspicion your ass will ruin me for all other men's posteriors, forever and ever."

Her chin tipped up, and she was smiling at him again, her fingers playing at his waistband. All doubts evidently banished once more, at least for the moment.

He nuzzled his nose against hers. "One can only hope."

She tugged his shorts and boxer-briefs down in one quick movement, and he stepped out of them. His erection hot against his stomach, he turned in a circle for her perusal.

Never, not once in his life, had he appreciated his training so much. If all those burpees and lunges and sprints and lifts meant Tess Dunn got that dazed look on her sweet face and kept staring at his ass with the sort of longing usually reserved for, say, the crown jewels, he'd do thousands more of them. Millions.

"You have that line," she whispered. "I didn't know that was possible in real life."

He frowned, confused. "What line?"

"I mean, your cock is impressive too, which I kind of expected. But this..." She touched a spot above his hip, then traced a path down and to the center, just short of where his dick was eager to meet her touch. "Wow."

"That?" Her finger lingered, and he attempted to keep breathing. "My physio called it the iliac furrow."

"And those dimples on your ass..." She caressed a spot on each cheek. "I want to bite them later. Is that okay?"

Red alert. Time to deploy baseball statistics. Like numbers of home runs or strikeouts or touchdowns or field goals or—

Wait, he didn't know any baseball statistics. He didn't even *watch* baseball.

Shit.

"Uh..." Deep breaths. Those might work. "Yeah. Please."

"Really?" Her face brightened to near-incandescence. "In that case, hurry up. Let's get me naked."

Thank Christ.

Before anything could delay him further, he yanked those damn leggings down as she obligingly lifted each foot in turn. Within the next heartbeat, he'd whipped off her panties too.

Someday, he'd take his time appreciating the sight of her in her underwear, but not tonight. Not while he was awash with this sort of desperation.

He clambered to his feet, but didn't let himself stare until he'd reached into the shower and turned on the water. Then, as it began to heat, he clasped her upper arms and gave a gentle squeeze. "Hold still, älskling. I want to take a good look at you."

Her body was lush and round, not a straight line to be

seen. He skimmed a palm over the curve of her belly, the swell of her hip, the abundance of her dimpled ass.

He understood her desire to bite, in a way he hadn't mere moments ago. More than that, though, he wanted to sink into her and never emerge.

The shower was steaming now. So was he.

He raised his gaze to hers, and she wasn't quite smiling. But her eyes were soft and warm and direct. Not shy or, God forbid, ashamed.

"Let's get in the shower." He opened the door, stroking a hand down her bare back as he ushered her inside. "If it's too hot or too cold for you, just turn the handle."

He squeezed in beside her, and they stood naked, only a bare centimeter away from one another. The water streamed over her shoulders and down the extravagant arcs of her body, the rivulets gleaming in the light overhead. Her hair turned inky beneath the flood, a rosy flush blooming on her pale skin at the heat of the spray.

"I love how you have dimples everywhere. Here." She rose up on tiptoes and pressed a kiss to both his cheeks. "Your butt, of course. Even your knees, kind of."

He glanced down. "Those are just my kneecaps. They're knobby."

"They're perfect, so hush." She shook a disapproving finger at him. When he caught it in his mouth, her breathing hitched. "None of that until we're clean, mister."

They took turns washing each other. She went first, soaping her hands and gliding them over his skin, leaving slippery trails along his arms and inner thighs and across his belly. Then she was sliding her hand up and down his cock and cupping his testicles, and the bubbles tickled while his flesh tightened and surged beneath her attention.

Much more of that, and they'd be done before they began.

"Enough," he told her, and gently moved her aside so he

could quickly shampoo his hair, finish soaping himself, and rinse away all the suds.

Her lower lip poked out a tad, and he could see for a moment the sulky teenager she might once have been. But she sounded more amused than disgruntled when she spoke. "I'd just gotten to the good bits, spoilsport."

There. He was clean, and now it was her turn.

"Oh, the good bits are still coming." He winked at her. "So to speak."

A handful of his shampoo later, and he was tunneling his fingers through her hair, letting them massage her scalp as he worked up some lather. "Does this feel good?"

He interpreted her inarticulate mumble as a *yes*. Tilting her head back, he supported her neck with his palm as he rinsed away the shampoo beneath the spray.

When he was done, her eyes blinked open again, water droplets shining from her lashes like diamonds. "That felt amazing, but we've waited long enough. Take me to bed, Lucas."

He slapped a hand against the side of the shower stall to steady himself.

No. No, he wouldn't rush this first time. "I was told we had to get clean first. And that's what we're going to do."

"But I—"

So he lowered his head and kissed her while he turned the soap between his palms. His tongue played with hers, the wet heat of their mouths echoed in the steamy bathroom. While she was too busy to protest further, he began running his hands across her soft shoulders, down her long arms, and over her back. Along the way, he dug in his fingers as he'd felt his physio do millions of times, in hopes he could help ease any soreness.

She made a noise in her throat, a kind of strangled moan, and he smiled against her mouth. As he took her lower lip between his and suckled it, he soaped his hands again.

Under her arms and along her sides, she was a little ticklish, and he made a mental note of specific spots for future torment. Then he finally got to cup that bountiful, beautiful ass of hers, and it slipped beneath his hands like silk. When he squeezed her there possessively, her thighs parted, and he nestled his leg between them.

Given his height and the small stall, soaping her strong, curvy legs proved a challenge, but he did it half-kneeling on the floor, the drain digging into his knee.

It hurt. But at his current level, he had possibly the world's best view. Amazing breasts above, lovely legs below, and just in front of him, peeking out pink and slick beneath her dark curls—

Her hand lowered to cover those curls. "I appreciate the thought, Lucas, believe me. But my knee won't let me do anything too acrobatic in here. Also, if I fell, I'm pretty sure I'd kill us both."

No matter. They'd have plenty of time in bed for him to get his mouth on her, and in the meantime...

"No need for anything complicated." He managed to rise to his feet without jostling her too much. "Just lean against the wall and relax."

The lines between her brows smoothed. "If I'm reading your expression correctly, please know I'm completely on board with what you have planned."

"You're reading my expression correctly," he told her.

Her lips yielded beneath his, and he sucked her tongue into his mouth while he soaped up his hands again. Then he was nudging her legs a little further apart. Not enough to cause her discomfort while holding the position, but enough to give him room to work.

She was slick and hot and smooth, and her clit swelled beneath his touch as she arched against his hand. He toyed with her folds, letting the water, the soap, and her own wetness make the movements easy and light. Then, with two fingers, he opened her to the spray of the water, and she gasped and trembled as he rinsed her clean.

No soap left to irritate her delicate skin. Now he could really play.

He'd washed away her natural moisture, but he had no problem working to bring it back. While he scattered little bites down the side of her neck, he rounded her clit in a steady, slow circle. Again and again, until she was moaning and grinding against his hand.

She'd become slick again, and he sank two fingers inside her, rubbing and trying to find the angle that made her whimper.

There. She was clutching him now, her short nails digging into his back as he braced her against the shower wall with his weight. After one last slide of his fingers inside her, he returned to her clit, and she cried out.

With one hand, he found her nipple, brushing his thumb back and forth over the beaded tip. With the other, he kept up that same easy glide, around and around her clit, letting her rub herself against him for more pressure as she tensed and began to pant.

Not too long now. He lifted his head and watched her face, the way her delicate eyelids drifted shut and her lips parted and her breath came in little puffs. The way she lost herself in pleasure at his touch.

He pinched her nipple lightly. And with a high, loud keen, she came against his hand, her head falling back as her thighs shook and her fingers bit deep into his skin. Her sex quivered, pulsing as her body sagged against the wall.

A good partner would wait for her to recover before dragging her to bed and fucking her into twelve more orgasms. He gave it about a minute, coaxing the last few tremors from her flesh and rubbing her back soothingly.

Finally, she sighed and rested her forehead against his shoulder, her body still and lax. And he was done waiting.

Flipping off the water, he shoved open the shower door, took her hand, and marched her to his bed, the two of them dripping all over that generic carpet.

At his bedside, he paused, his chest heaving with each desperate breath. "How can I make this good for you? I don't want to hurt your neck or knee or back or—"

"If I start hurting, I'll let you know. You do the same if your wrist bothers you. Until then"—she climbed onto the bed and sprawled across his comforter, arms and legs open for him—"let's not worry."

A condom. He needed a condom.

A quick search of his bedside table produced a small package, and he rolled the condom over his cock while he enjoyed the view of her spread wide and gleaming in the light from the bathroom. God, she was hot enough to burn this fucking island to cinders.

Without another word, he crawled between her thighs and buried his face in her sweet, swollen pussy, starving for the taste of her. And yeah, it hurt his nose, and yeah, he was grinding his stiff-to-bursting dick into the comforter as he licked her, but it was worth it to have her push herself against his face as he circled her clit and feel her legs shake as he sucked that small bit of flesh into his mouth and rubbed it with his tongue.

"Let me..." She tugged at his hair. "Let me move my knee a little."

He waited until she'd resettled, then lowered his head again.

When she was clutching his hair and grinding against his mouth, whimpering with every stroke of his tongue, he pulled away, knelt between her legs, and rested a hand on her belly.

"Do you want me to do this slowly, or at full power?"

His eyes held hers as he echoed words he'd used once before. As he invoked the memory of how she'd watched

157

him serve, her eyes narrowed and hot on his arms, his thighs.

Both times, he'd hit the ball much harder than necessary, much harder than was wise, for one reason and one reason only. To see that look on her face.

He wanted to see it again, at intimately close range, as he used his power for her pleasure.

Just like last time, her words emerged with a slight slur. Lust. "Full power."

Rising up, he urged her long legs around his hips. Then he was pushing inside her, feeling her quiver and stretch around him as he slid balls-deep.

He didn't give either of them time to recover or think. Rearing back, he withdrew almost all the way before sinking his cock deep again. And again.

She might have doubts about dating a twenty-something athlete, but if there was one thing a man like him could offer, it was stamina. He could do this for hours, if that's what she needed. And if he came too quickly, he knew the mere sight of her would make him hard and hot soon enough, and he could get back to work between her thighs.

This first time, though, he was determined to wait until she climaxed again, because he needed to feel her tighten and spasm around his dick. He needed to know he'd satisfied her. Most of all, he needed her to understand what exactly she'd be giving up if she let her fears and that shield of pragmatism drive him from her life and her bed after her vacation ended.

Supporting himself on his elbows, he cupped her sweet face in his hands and kissed her as he buried himself deep inside her pussy with steady pushes. Within minutes, they were both sweating, and she was making little sounds into his mouth each time he bottomed out and ground against her. His balls were aching, and a warning tingle had started at the base of his spine.

He was coming soon, like it or not. Lifting himself higher,

he slid one hand down between them and found her clit, and when he tapped it with his fingertips, she tore her mouth from his and gasped. He did it again, a little more firmly, and her legs spread even wider, her hips raised high in silent plea.

But silent wasn't good enough. Not for this.

He raised his head, a drowning man in sight of land. "Harder?"

"Yeah." Her eyes closed tight, she gritted out one more word. *"Now."*

One last rub of her clit as she twisted and moaned, and then he gave that stiff, hot bit of flesh a little slap, and God help him, she nearly snapped off his dick with the force of her orgasm. She arched beneath him, her pussy spasming again and again, and her cry was nearly soundless.

With a sense of profound relief, quickly drowned by the sort of intense, blinding pleasure he'd never, not once in his life, experienced before, he pushed inside her one last time and came until he couldn't remember his own name—and was hoarse from shouting hers.

SIXTEEN

THE BLARE OF AN UNFAMILIAR ALARM WOKE TESS the next morning, and she rolled over to see what the hell was happening. Only to find herself face to face with Lucas, who was just blinking open sleepy olive-green eyes.

He reached for her right away, and she let him draw her close, the hair on his chest tickling her nose. His skin was warm, his limbs long as they wrapped around her.

He'd wanted to cuddle as they slept too, telling her with his inimitable charm how romantic it would be to nod off while spooning or with her head on his chest. But she knew herself too well for even his particular brand of sweet talk to work. If they attempted to sleep intertwined, she'd never even doze. And if by some miracle she did, she'd either awaken sore or drown them both in a lake of her sweat.

She'd always run hot at night. A fact to which he'd responded with a certain amount of delightful innuendo.

In compensation for her refusal to sleep cuddling, she'd offered another round or two of lovemaking. And Jesus, sex with a twenty-six-year-old had its definite perks. As in, a perky penis with very little refractory time necessary—which meant a little bit of chafing but a *lot* of orgasms for her. Mind-blowing, multiple, and memorable.

She'd never believed that *forty-year-old women are in their sexual prime* bullshit, but she was starting to think she'd been way too cynical about way too many things for way too long.

"This is nice," he murmured, nuzzling the crown of her head.

It really was. She tightened her arm around his chest and wedged her leg deeper between his. With a pleased rumble, he stroked her bare back, his indefatigable cock stirring against her thigh.

Mmmm. She wouldn't mind starting every morning like this.

But the damn alarm kept getting louder as they failed to heed its call, and she needed to get moving, like it or not.

"You'll have to address Mr. Perky on your own today, hon. Sorry about that."

She pressed one final kiss below his jaw, where bristly whiskers had begun to emerge, inhaling as deeply as she could. That heady lungful of Lucas needed to last until evening.

His grip tightened for a moment before he let her slide out of his arms. "Mr. Perky?"

"I've given your penis its own adorable nickname." Spying her pile of discarded, sweaty clothing just inside the bathroom door, she grimaced. "I don't want to put any of that stuff back on, not even for the walk to my hotel room, and I don't want to put clean clothes on a dirty body. Can I shower here? Or do you need the bathroom to get ready for your morning lessons?"

Without a word, he lumbered out of bed and into the living room. Hoisting her overnight bag over his shoulder, he brought it to the bathroom, set it on the tiled floor, and sat beside her on the edge of the bed again.

She smiled at him. "Thanks."

"My pleasure." The words were low. Intimate. Accompanied by his own devastating smile.

Holy Moses. Those dimples made her hotter than the last time the school's HVAC system had malfunctioned. Which was saying something, since she figured she'd gotten a preview of menopause that late-July week.

When he reached for her again, though, she sprang up. "Nice thought. But I need to pee and brush my teeth before you get any closer. And I have"—she glanced at the alarm clock—"an hour to get clean and ready for the ferry trip to the mainland. There's no time for any shenanigans."

As she ran for the bathroom, he sighed. "And you call *me* a spoilsport."

"I'm saving you from morning breath!" she called back before closing the door.

When she emerged twenty minutes later, he gave her a lingering pat on her bare butt and took her place. While he conducted his business, she opened up her overnight bag. Only to realize she'd somehow packed one of Belle's shirts instead of her own.

In theory, the two of them were roughly the same size, but the same could not be said for their breasts. Still, that tee was all she had, since Lucas's clothing wouldn't fit. Good enough.

A couple minutes later, the door to the bathroom opened, and then he was studying her, his lips twitching in an altogether annoying fashion. "That shirt is—"

"Can it." She tugged at the chest of the t-shirt again, hoping the material might abruptly loosen and decide to stretch more over her breasts. "I may be too much woman for this shirt, but I consider that a flaw in its design, not mine."

He took a step forward and tucked a runaway strand of hair behind her ear with gentle fingers. "I was about to say that the shirt looks amazing on you. It emphasizes some of my favorite bits. And if you wore *just* the shirt..."

His eyes grew cloudy, and Mr. Perky sprang to life once more.

After one more futile tug at the chest of the tee, she gave up and laughed. "I should have known you'd love me in a too-tight top."

"Yup." He grinned at her, shameless. "You really should have."

After slipping on her socks and sneakers, she slid her keycard into the pocket of her yoga pants. "I need to get to my room and pack for the outing today. Change shirts, too." She hesitated. "Do you want to come with me, or would you rather—"

"Are you kidding? Of course I'm coming with you." He hurriedly donned his usual work clothing and shoved his feet into a pair of flip-flops. "I intend to spend as much time as possible looking at you in that shirt. And while I was in the shower, I realized I don't even have your contact information. I need to get that before you leave for the day, just in case."

His stride toward the door stuttered. "Um, assuming you want to see me again?"

Why did his particular combination of lasciviousness, sweetness, and vulnerability knock her already-problematic knees out from under her?

"I want to see you again," she told him, and the tense lines across his forehead vanished.

His kiss, gentle and warm and devastatingly affectionate, made her even later than she already was, and she simply couldn't bring herself to care. Not even a little.

When they finally exited his apartment, they walked to her room holding hands, making their way along a sidewalk already crowded with early-bird beachcombers and through a lobby teeming with loudly chattering families headed to and from the breakfast buffets. His secure grip didn't falter. Not when several of his coworkers glanced at her with raised eyebrows after greeting him. Not even when one of the twenty-something female guests, a woman who'd apparently taken tennis lessons during her vacation, did the same.

Tess didn't fret about those sidelong stares either. Maybe people were simply surprised to see Lucas claiming a girl-friend so publicly. Even if she was wrong about that, even if their reaction was specific to her, a forty-year-old male tennis instructor sleeping with a twenty-something ingénue wouldn't raise a single brow. And she wasn't ashamed of her size. Not one bit. Not at this point in her life.

No, her Lucas-centered worries had nothing to do with the opinions of outsiders. Just a hard-eyed assessment of two disparate lives that had, however improbably, intersected for two weeks. Which didn't mean those lives would or should intersect again, outside of these specific circumstances.

Those were concerns for later, though. For now, she would ignore her looming departure in favor of thinking about the light brush of his thumb over her knuckles. The casual way he immediately pushed the call button for the elevator instead of suggesting she take the stairs. The sly satisfaction in his grin as he crowded her into the corner of that empty elevator and claimed her mouth once more, his tongue demanding and hot.

By the time they reached her room, she was lightheaded with the rush of his proximity and single-minded attention but trying not to show it. The man already looked entirely too self-satisfied for her liking.

Unsure whether Belle would be in any state to greet guests, Tess knocked on the door with an unsteady hand instead of using her keycard. Belle responded right away, swinging open the door and regarding them both with a smirk.

"Couldn't drag yourself out of bed any sooner, huh?" Belle stepped aside and let them enter the room. "I was starting to wonder whether we'd miss our ferry."

"An early-morning tour of the mansion was a terrible

idea." Tess grinned at her friend as the door shut behind them. "Why didn't you plan our day better, Belle?"

Belle tipped her face toward the ceiling, as if beseeching the heavens for patience. "Get everything you need into your backpack, Ms. Come-On-Belle-We-Should-Get-Up-Early-To-Beat-the-Heat-and-Have-More-Time-On-the-Mainland Dunn."

"You can see why I changed my first name to Tess," Tess told Lucas.

At Lucas's huff of laughter, Belle's baleful stare lowered to Tess. "Because of you, I rose before the actual sun while on vacation, which I consider a violation of my constitutional rights."

"She probably hasn't had coffee yet." Tess let go of Lucas's hand, located her backpack in a corner of the room's little closet, and dumped the bag onto her double bed. "Without caffeine, you could say she's not a morning person. Much the same way Joan Crawford was not a wire hangers person."

Belle bit back a smile. "Less flirting with Sparky. More packing."

Lucas emitted a small, pained sound.

As Tess dropped sunblock, a hat, and the guidebook into her backpack, she considered his nickname. "Sparky? I like it."

"Thank you. I thought it had a certain ring." Belle donned her own sun hat and adjusted it in the closet mirror, tipping the floppy brim up a smidge.

"I call him Mr. Perky," Tess said to Belle. "Well, part of him, anyway."

This time, Lucas groaned loudly.

So did Belle. "I don't want to know."

"Interesting." Tess added a bottle of water to the back-pack. "I'm pretty sure that's not what you'll be saying once we're alone, Ms. Give-Me-All-the-Details-the-More-Salacious-the-Better-and-Maybe-Draw-Some-Stick-Figures-Too-So-I-Can-Picture-Everything-More-Clearly Cantner."

"Tattletale." Her friend flapped a hand in the direction of the closet. "*Pack*, woman."

So Tess did, throwing everything else into her backpack with much less care than usual while Lucas and Belle sat on the edges of the beds and watched. As soon as she changed her shirt in the bathroom, all three hurried out of the room, the door swinging shut behind them with a bang that made Tess wince.

Despite both women's protests, Lucas carried their backpacks on one shoulder. On his other side, he promptly reclaimed Tess's hand, squeezing it gently whenever she glanced his way. Which she did, often. Too often.

Together, they hustled to the dock, fast enough that Tess and Belle became breathless.

Then…silence. They'd arrived with five minutes to spare, and the woman who coordinated the ferry's arrivals and departures was off talking to someone on her cell a few feet away. No other guests seemed to be leaving on this particular ferry, maybe because they'd chosen later activities and flights home.

"I'm going to wait"—Belle reclaimed her backpack and pointed to a weathered wooden bench—"over there. Have fun, but try not to get arrested for public indecency before the ferry arrives, okay?"

With a shake of her head, Tess watched her friend's retreat. Only to discover she suddenly had no idea what to say to Lucas. *See you later, and thanks for all the great sex* seemed flippant. *Hope you didn't hurt your wrist rubbing my clit with such talented industriousness last night* seemed a bit too graphic for an early-morning conversation. *Holy Christ, I think I could fall in love with you way too easily* seemed…well, ill-advised at best.

Desperate, she turned toward the water instead of him.

The ocean, sparkling and aquamarine, lapped against the

dock's pilings and tumbled in gentle waves onto the white sands of the shore. It was beautiful and pristine, and a good place to fix her gaze while she figured out what to say.

After setting her backpack on the dock, his free hand squeezing hers the whole time, he broke the silence. "We should exchange information."

Oh, yeah. At the moment, she had no way of contacting him except through the hotel, and he had no way of contacting her at all once she left.

The realization struck home. They'd known each other for a total of five days. Five. Days. Yet somehow they were already entangled, and—damn her doubts—she ached for even more ties binding him to her.

For now, acquiring his contact information would have to suffice.

"I always have a stash of pens and sticky notes in my purse, just in case." She unzipped the middle compartment. "Do you want me to write down everything for you, instead of dictating it?"

He paused, his brows drawn together, before directing an odd, amused glance her way. "Sure. I can scrawl my contact information for you too, if you have an extra pen."

He let her hand go, and she dug into the depths of her purse and emerged with the supplies they needed. A block of sticky notes for him, another for her, and two pens. They both used the dock's rail as a writing surface.

She bit her lip and looked up. "I gave you my cell number and my e-mail address."

"I did the same." He carefully peeled the note from her pad and passed her the one he'd written. "There you go."

After dropping her pens and sticky-note blocks back into the middle compartment of her purse, she tucked his information within the same zippered side pocket where she stored all essentials. Tampons. Her lip balm. Her lucky piece of jade. And now him.

He folded her sticky note into a small, neat square and deposited it deep within the pocket of his athletic shorts, then looked at her.

He was still smiling. "You realize we could have just used our cell phones for all that."

"Oh." Damn, she was old. "Yeah, but electronics malfunction or go missing. I don't want to risk losing your information."

That teasing smile died, his eyes turning soft and warm as he gazed at her. "Same here. But let me text you my information, just in case."

They exchanged information the modern way too, and once he was safely stored in her contacts list and he'd saved her data in his own cell, he took her hand again.

"So…" His fingers, warm and strong, played with hers as she watched. "Are you free tonight?"

She'd known. She'd known. Only a fool would consider his actions that morning—the near-constant physical contact, his company on the dock, his flirting, his request for her contact information—the polite gestures of a man ready to scrape off an unwanted one-night stand. But the confirmation of his continued interest steadied her anyway.

In the distance, a horn tooted. The small ferry boat, nearing the dock.

"Belle and I will be gone most of the day, and we have dinner reservations, but after that…" She lifted a shoulder. Smiled at him. "I'm available."

The furrows in his forehead eased. "Good."

The dock manager was exchanging shouted greetings with the captain of the ferry, and Belle had risen to her feet and stepped closer to the boarding area of the dock. The ferry hadn't officially arrived yet, though, so Tess didn't move.

"Do you want me to text you when I get back to the hotel tonight?" she asked.

He inclined his head. "Yeah. And if you want to spend the night, pack a bag."

"Is that what *you* want?"

It was a challenge, a request for him to declare himself. Also a sign of her lingering worries, whether he knew it or not.

He didn't hesitate before bending forward, his bristly cheek a tantalizing scrape against her skin. "I want back inside you," he whispered into her ear. "I want your taste on my tongue. I want to watch you come so hard around my cock you can't breathe, and I want to do that as often as possible."

Fuck, she couldn't breathe *now*. "None of that requires spending the night."

His head raised an inch, and his eyes closed for a moment. When he reopened them, they were soft. Vulnerable enough to disorient her. "I want to reach out and touch your hair on my pillow, Tess. I want to see you as soon as I open my eyes in the morning."

Yes, she could definitely fall in love with him way too easily.

"Okay." She could barely hear her own words over the sound of her tripping heart. "I'll spend the night."

The dock shuddered as the ferry bumped against the tire-protected pilings, and she rose up on tiptoe. He met her halfway, his mouth hard and insistent against hers. No teasing. No finesse. Just desperation and need.

Dimly, she could hear conversation and laughter as several employees debarked from the ferry and began the short trek to the resort. But her sole focus was on the man clutching her tight and claiming her tongue like a battle prize.

Another blast of the horn, this one a warning.

"Time to board!" the dock manager called.

Belle had already climbed onto the ferry's deck, and there

was no one else traveling to the mainland on this particular trip.

The dock manager was speaking to Tess.

It was time to leave.

With one last rub of her lips against his, Tess ended the kiss, and Lucas didn't fight it. He cupped her face in both hands and looked at her, his gaze intent.

Whatever he saw seemed to satisfy him.

His thumbs stroked her cheeks. "Please call or text me when you get back from dinner. If I'm in the middle of a lesson, leave a message, älskling. I'll respond as soon as I can."

She nodded, and he nuzzled his nose against hers.

Then he let her go and hoisted her backpack. "Let me get this on board for you."

He deposited it in the storage area on the ferry and held her arm as she stepped onto the swaying deck. One last squeeze, and he retreated back onto the dock, his mouth pressed tight.

The dock manager unlooped the ferry's ropes from around the pilings and tossed them aboard, and the boat began to drift away from the tires. Another toot of the horn to mark their departure, and the engine thrummed to life, vibrating the deck under her feet.

She wiggled her fingers in a wave. He returned the gesture, and then patted his pocket, as if checking to make sure her note was still there.

With a jerk, the boat began its journey to the mainland.

"I'll text you," she called out, the wind whipping her words away almost before she could utter them.

His deep voice, calm with certainty, carried over the widening water between them.

"That's good," he said, his fists on his hips and his eyes on her. "Because I have plans for you, Tess Dunn."

SEVENTEEN

After one of his early-afternoon lessons, Lucas checked his phone again, as he'd been doing all day. A ridiculous tic, and he knew it. Tess wouldn't return to the island for hours yet, and during her busy day on the mainland, she wouldn't be thinking of him, much less texting him.

This time, though, his foolishness had been rewarded. Tess had left a voicemail at some point during the lesson. Not a text. Which was another generational marker, he figured, and one he appreciated.

He wanted to hear her voice. Missed her voice.

More foolishness.

Sadly, when he played the message, covering his other ear with his palm to limit background noise, he found he'd been mistaken. His foolishness hadn't been rewarded. Not at all.

Her voice was crackly. Tired-sounding. "Lucas, this is Tess. I'm sorry to bother you while you're working, and this is incredibly awkward, but I figured you should know."

His chin dropped to his suddenly-aching chest.

She'd changed her mind. Allowed the distance between

them to resurrect all her doubts. Reconsidered another night together.

"I got my period today," she continued. "I should have remembered it was coming, but I've been kind of distracted the last few days."

At that, his head jerked up, and he blinked at the clubhouse a few times.

"I also should have talked to my gynecologist before the trip about avoiding this sort of situation, but to be fair, I hadn't anticipated plastering my naked, wet boobs against a random bro's back, finding out he's actually the resort's very talented and appealing tennis pro, and then boning him until my vagina raised a tiny white flag this morning."

He snorted.

Also: very talented and appealing? Nice.

"I know you said you had plans for me, but..." Her sigh whispered into his ear. "I'm sorry. I'm crampy and achy and not feeling particularly sexual at the moment."

It was true. He'd had plans. Lots of them.

Plans formulated over an endless, sunny day without Tess. Plans created with her sexual preferences and physical limitations in mind. Plans incorporating both his greatest talents and the vibrator he'd managed to buy on the mainland over an extended lunch break.

Most of all, plans to make certain the next time he accompanied her to the dock—in just over a week, a stretch of time that now felt like the snap of his fingers—watching her leave wouldn't mean watching her leave *forever*, because this goodbye had been hard enough.

Plans he now had to scuttle.

But that was okay. He could take or leave sex, even the sort of transcendent sex he'd had with Tess last night. As long as he still had the woman herself at his side, he wouldn't ask for more.

Her voice lowered even further. Turned tentative in a way

that made him frown. "So..." A hesitation. "I'm not sure what that means as far as tonight. Whether we're still getting together." Another pause. "Call or text me when you get a chance, okay? Hope you're having a good day."

That was it. The end of her message.

He glared at his phone, battling the urge to throw it in frustration. Did she think he only wanted her for sex? What the fuck?

Or, worse, did she only want *him* for sex?

A quick glance at the screen revealed he still had five minutes before his next lesson began. His clients, a mother and daughter, were already waiting just outside the chain-link fence surrounding the courts, their eyes on him. He forced a smile in their direction, then turned his back to them to make the call.

Tess answered after the first ring. "Hi, Lucas."

"Hey, Tess." He didn't have time to ease into the conversation. More than that, he couldn't tolerate this level of uncertainty, not when it came to her. "I just listened to your message, and I get it. We can't have sex tonight. Do you still want to see me? Or not?"

With his free hand, he pinched the bridge of his nose and squeezed his eyes shut.

Dammit. That had come out a bit too blunt. A bit too demanding.

Her long silence in response seemed to indicate her agreement.

"Wow," she finally said. "No flirty charm there, Karlsson. You're losing your touch."

He pinched harder and managed to grind out two words. "Tess. Please."

"Tell me first." The words were a challenge, their aggressive bravado only a little undermined by their shakiness. "Do *you* still want to get together tonight?"

She had to ask? To repeat himself: What the fuck?

"Of course I do." The words emerged in a whisper, more pained than he'd anticipated. "When have I ever given you any indication I only want you for sex?"

Over the line, he could hear the rapid rush of her breath. "You haven't. But we've known each other for less than a week, Lucas. How could I be sure?"

His frustration died at the reminder of how little time they'd actually spent in each other's company. How little, in the end, they actually knew about one another, for all that she made him feel naked in every conceivable way when they were together.

"I guess you couldn't. Which brings us back to my question." His hand wasn't entirely steady, and he tightened his grip on the phone. "Do you still want to see me?"

Yes, his greatest talents all involved his body and its capabilities. On the tennis court. In the bedroom. But the things she'd said to him on that overlook and during their night together...

For the first time in a while, he'd begun to believe he might have more to offer.

Maybe she'd been humoring him, though. Maybe she hadn't meant a word. Maybe he'd been fooling himself.

"Yes." Her answer was firm. Definite. "Yes. I do."

As he finally exhaled, that ache in his chest disappeared.

She added, "Even though I'm kind of bloated. Also exhausted, since Mr. Perky didn't let either of us get much sleep. When Belle said she wanted to do the guided tour of the blazing-hot gardens, I told her I would take a self-guided tour of this bench in the shade."

Poor thing. His older sister, from what he remembered, had complained about bloating and cramps and tiredness the first couple days of her period too.

What had Annika done about that, anyway?

Turning back to his next clients—now visibly restless, shifting from foot to foot and staring at him—he held up a forefinger, tacitly requesting patience as he tried to remember Annika's monthly rituals and their accompanying supplies.

Tampons. Over-the-counter painkillers. He couldn't remember anything else.

"I'm sorry you're hurting." He kept his voice soft. "Do you have everything you need?"

She huffed out a small laugh. "Are you offering to buy me tampons? Real ones, not the nose variety?"

"Yeah." Wouldn't be the first time. Annika had assigned him that particular task more than once. "If you want tampons, I'll get tampons. Or pads, or whatever. Do you need ibuprofen or acetaminophen?"

Another long silence.

When she finally spoke again, her voice was equally soft. "That's such a sweet offer, Lucas. Thank you. I have what I need on the tampon front, and I always carry a bottle of ibuprofen in my purse. You don't happen to own a heating pad, though, do you?"

Now he remembered. Annika had used one of those too.

Until last year, he'd owned several of them, and they'd seen him through recovery from his surgeries. But they'd gotten lost during the move to the resort, and since he hadn't injured himself since, he hadn't bothered to replace them.

"I'm sorry." He was, genuinely. "I don't have one anymore."

"It's okay. I'll be fine without it." For a moment, he could only hear the chirp of birds from her end of the line, along with the distant murmur of strangers' conversations. "You need to go, don't you? Isn't it time for another lesson?"

Past time, actually. By a minute.

"Yeah. I should probably go." He bent down to pick up his racket. "But you'll let me know when you're done with dinner, like we planned?"

"I will." The simple sentence was warm. Sweet. A caress. "See you tonight."

175

"See you tonight. Take care of yourself, älskling."

Then the call was over, and he placed his phone back in his bag and strode over to his clients. Smiled at them and apologized. Started his lesson.

All the while he made plans. New ones.

Ones that had absolutely nothing to do with his body.

———————

THE DOOR TO THE SPA ENTRANCE CLOSED BEHIND Lucas with a muffled whoosh. Suddenly, he was breathing scented air, herbal and pleasantly woodsy, as his eyes adjusted to the decreased light in the expansive space. Despite the candles burning in the enormous stone fireplace, various recessed light fixtures, and the large picture window behind the check-in counter, the wood-paneled walls kept the area surprisingly dim.

A half-dozen people—all clad in snowy-white robes, all seated in cushioned, solid-wood couches and chairs—glanced up at him. He nodded at them, and then took stock of his surroundings, searching for what he needed or help getting it.

Wooden racks of beautifully packaged merchandise. Framed photos of the Matterhorn and other snowy peaks against vivid blue skies. Delicate paintings of edelweiss and asters.

And piped in through hidden speakers, almost too low to hear, was that…?

Yes. Yes, indeed. It was.

Although no one would call him an expert identifier of musical instruments, he remembered the commercials of his early youth. This particular sound he associated quite strongly with Swiss herbal cough drops and lederhosen-clad men on mountaintops, rather than tropical beaches.

The resort's island only possessed one hill, but apparently

that hill was alive with the sound of music. Alphorn music, to be precise. Also yodeling.

Weird. Oddly charming, but weird.

Behind the counter stood two of his dirndl-clad colleagues, one of them a familiar sight. Heather, a woman roughly his age who often attended gatherings at Brendan's mainland apartment, was stationed behind the computer. Standing beside her was an unfamiliar woman, slightly older than Heather, her pale skin poreless, her tawny hair tucked into a braided crown, frowning in concentration as she ticked items off a printed list. Fiona, the spa manager, according to the engraved name badge pinned to her bodice.

"Lucas." Heather looked up from her computer with a bright, professional smile, her warm brown skin smooth and glowing and impeccably accented by discreet makeup. "How may I help you today? Are you here to book a peel?"

A peel? Like a banana peel? Did this have something to do with the apple-scented oil for sale on the counter?

"Or an Extreme Edelweiss Microdermabrasion session?" Her arched eyebrows rose in query. "You can reserve a series of sessions at a slight savings, which can be used along with your employee discount. We actually have a last-minute cancellation for this evening, if you'd like."

Ah. *That* kind of peel.

"Uh, no." He scrubbed a hand over his bristly, sun-damaged cheek. "That's not why I'm here."

She appeared to be staring at his nose and forehead, her own brow creased. "We also have a line of Cocoa Corrective repair masks with exclusive Toblerone—"

"Thank you, Heather," he interrupted. "But I don't need anything for my face. I asked Brendan and Pat whether the resort sold heating pads or hot water bottles anywhere, and they thought the spa might have something I could use."

"Oh." After one last glance at his forehead, Heather heaved an almost imperceptible sigh and let it go. "We don't

177

have heating pads or hot water bottles, but we do offer heatable aromatherapy booties that could work. Our microwaveable Alpine Aromatherapy eye masks might suffice too, depending on how much area you want to cover."

"Perfect." He smiled at her, pleased. "Just point me in the right direction."

"They're in the far left corner. Second shelf from the top. Do you want me to show you?"

He shook his head. "I'm fine."

"If you have any trouble finding them, just let me know." Another entirely professional smile, almost blinding in its shine. "And if you change your mind, I'd be delighted to help you book an appointment. We have a variety of special packages available this week."

Fiona left for the other end of the spa's welcome area, her list still clutched in her hand, and disappeared through a semi-hidden doorway.

They both watched her leave and waited several seconds.

Then Heather leaned in close and lowered her voice to a bare whisper. "So what do you think? Was I right?"

He nodded. "Like a Swiss chalet vomited over a Pottery Barn showroom."

"Exactly." She glanced around before continuing. "The café donated a bottle of génépy liqueur so I could get Fiona drunk last week and find out what the hell happened to this place. Turns out, the resort owner's then-wife found out he was cheating a couple years ago. After pretending to forgive him, she asked to be in charge of the latest spa renovation and said she wanted it to be a surprise. He agreed."

A mistake, that. And not the resort owner's first or most grievous, clearly.

"The day after the reno ended, she invited him inside the new spa, where she served him divorce papers in an alphorn and told him to go blow himself." Her brown eyes dancing with glee, Heather kissed her fingertips in homage to that particular choice.

"Ingenious." He considered the matter further. "But now the spa is essentially one big advertisement for an Alpine ski resort, rather than an island getaway. Wasn't she sabotaging her own alimony?"

"Airtight prenup. No alimony."

"Ah." That explained it.

Heather indulged in a subtle eyeroll. "At our last staff meeting, I tried to suggest a different, less chilly theme for the next renovation, but Fiona's gotten into the cosplay aspect. Apparently that dirndl is getting her a lot of frauleinon-fraulein action. LaTanya agreed we should choose another theme, but then she started discussing the northern lights and fjords, and I gave up."

He gave her a fist-bump. "Keep fighting the good fight."

"When I manage this place, it'll be different," she vowed, her voice firm. "The spa won't serve raclette and rösti potatoes and Toblerone fondue in the café anymore. Or sell decorative cowbells."

"You want to manage the spa?" He'd had no idea. Then again, Brendan's gatherings weren't always conducive to serious discussions of professional aspirations. More to beer pong, really.

"Not just the spa." She grinned at him. "I plan to manage the entire resort."

For that, he gave her another fist-bump. "Nice."

Then he headed for the booties and eye masks, almost immediately spotting the best option for his purposes. The fluffy white booties, whose microwaveable inserts were filled with various grains, along with thyme and—of course—"natural edelweiss scent," would cover more of poor Tess's lower belly than a standard eye mask.

He held the sample pair up to his own belly, considering the surface area issue. After a moment of thought, he repositioned the booties, arranging them like puzzle pieces, with the feet at opposite ends. Better, although he supposed he could always visit the first aid station to see whether it stocked—

"I think you may have misunderstood the purpose of the product." A familiar, amused voice came from behind him. "Unless you've sprouted abdominal growths I didn't notice during my last visit, those booties go about three feet lower."

When he swung around, Karolina was standing there in her robe and matching slippers, her blond hair piled into a loose knot on top of her head, her ivory skin glowing from whatever treatment she'd just experienced. Something involving Gruyère cheese, probably.

He didn't have much time to chat, but he also didn't intend to treat her like a hindrance or a nuisance or anything but what she was: a woman he liked and with whom he'd once had a casual relationship.

Still, this was a bit of a tricky conversation, given the context. "They're, uh, not for me."

At that, her husky laugh rippled through the spa. "Yes, I somehow thought that might be the case." Her gaze lowered to the booties pressed against his belly, and she gave a little nod of understanding. "If your Tess is dealing with discomfort in that area, those should help. Or if you'd like, when I make a trip to the mainland tomorrow, I can pick up something better."

It was a kind offer. Surprisingly kind, under the circumstances.

And he liked the sound of *your Tess*. Maybe more than he should.

"I think the booties will work for now. Thank you for the offer, though." He tucked an unopened package beneath his arm. Then, upon further thought, added a second package, in hopes of covering more surface area. "When I was on the Tour, we had basic medical supplies around us at all times, including heating pads and cold packs. Now I basically only have bandages and ibuprofen in my apartment. Which is probably a good sign, considering the reason I retired, but rather inconvenient at the moment."

Karo's lips parted, and she didn't say anything for a few seconds. Her study of him sharpened.

"You know," she said slowly, "that may be the most personal information I've ever gotten from you. It's definitely the first time you've talked about your past on the Tour."

That couldn't be true. Could it?

When he thought back, though, he couldn't remember a conversation with Karo about anything of actual import. Just interludes of flirting and innuendo and small talk as a prelude to sex.

"I'm sorry." What else could he say, really? At the time, he hadn't had more to offer, and she'd never given any indication she actually wanted more. And now there was no room in his head or his bed—maybe not even in his heart—for anyone but Tess.

Oddly enough, it hadn't hurt to talk about his past. Hadn't left him uncomfortably exposed or tempted to deploy flirtation as a distraction.

Huh.

"No need to be sorry." Karo smiled at him, the expression seemingly sincere. "I'm just...startled, I guess. If I'd met the man who talked to me on that overlook, or the man who's currently shopping for cramp-relief supplies in booty form, before this trip—"

When she gave a little shake of her head, loose tendrils of hair danced around her face. "Well, I might have played things a bit differently. That's all." Her bright smile dimmed a bit. "But that never would have happened, right? No matter how long you and I were involved. Because she's the reason you've finally opened up."

The conversation had turned from ill-timed to uncomfortable. "I don't know what to say, Karo."

"You don't have to say anything, Lucas. You haven't done anything wrong." She glanced toward the treatment rooms. "I'm due for a Kirsch-cherry blossom scrub, so I'd better go. Take care of yourself and your Tess."

"I will. Thank you again, Karo." He pressed his lips together, holding his hands awkwardly at his sides. Under normal circumstances, he'd hug her before she left, but...

Before he could make up his mind, she was already gliding away, graceful as ever despite the oversized slippers.

"One more thing, Lucas," she tossed over her shoulder, her smile restored to its normal wattage. "In Tess's position, I live by one simple motto: When in doubt, eat chocolate."

He saluted her with a package of booties, and then she was gone.

Beside the register, there was a basket of giant Toblerone bars. He bought two. One for Tess. One to hold behind the counter for Karo as an additional silent apology, even though she'd said apologies weren't necessary.

Admitting it, even in his own thoughts, made him wince.

It was harsh. It was also true.

Karo was right. One hundred percent correct.

Even if the two of them had conducted their idle, monthly affair for another decade, he would never have let down his guard for her. Because she wasn't Tess. And Tess, as he was beginning to discover, was at the center of everything for him.

Absolutely everything. Which was, to be frank, absolutely terrifying.

When in doubt, eat chocolate.

Before he left the spa, he bought one of those Toblerone bars for himself too.

EIGHTEEN

Tess stared down at the booties in her lap. "So these are, uh, supposed to keep my feet warm?"

In her peripheral vision, she could have sworn Lucas's dimples appeared for a fleeting moment. But when she looked directly at him, he was staring at her solemnly.

He inclined his head. "Yes. Just like it says on the package."

"And you got me two sets?"

"Evidently."

Don't say what the fuck. Don't say what the fuck.

She offered him a weak smile. "Um, thank you so much."

"You're more than welcome," he told her graciously.

Another smile, this one hopefully more convincing. "They're very pretty. Very fuzzy. Very...warm-looking."

As soon as she and Belle had returned to the hotel from a day spent outdoors, they'd lowered their room temperature to sixty degrees and turned the fan on full blast. Then they'd decided to flip a coin to determine who got first shower.

Poor Belle. She'd never suspected treachery, although she should have. Once she'd turned away to find a coin in her wallet, Tess had dashed into the bathroom, locked the door, and flipped on the shower.

Belle might never forgive her—even through a closed door and over the sound of water, Tess had distinctly heard the words *dracarys* and *queen of the ashes*—but so be it. She had her period, and thus deserved first crack at the bathroom. That was just basic justice, or maybe an unquestionable scientific fact.

Either way, she'd shamelessly reveled in every moment of that shower, her second of the day, this one ice-cold and meant to sluice away the sweat of hours and hours spent in Satan's jockstrap. Otherwise known as the Gulf Coast of Florida in August.

Somehow, though, she was still sweating. She figured it was carryover heat at work, like when the temperature of her Thanksgiving turkey kept rising for a while even after it emerged from the oven. Or maybe it was simply Belle's curse in effect already. Hard to say, really.

Which was why, once again, she was only barely restraining herself from asking Lucas what unholy impulse had made him look at heated booties and think, "Yes, if there's one thing Tess needs right now, it's hot feet."

Still, the booties were a sweet—if decidedly odd—gift. One she might be able to use in, say, three or four months. Assuming she ever cooled off again.

"I'm sure these will be very effective at keeping my feet toasty." She reread the label. What exactly did edelweiss smell like, anyway? "Thank you again."

He blinked innocently at her. "Why don't you try them on?"

Fuck, no.

"Uh…" She hesitated, searching for a courteous way to refuse.

Which was when he started laughing. Loudly.

"Th-the look on your face," he choked out. "Oh, God, Tess, it's amazing."

He was fucking with her. Again. But how?

"Are these…" She poked the booties with her forefinger. "Are these not a gift?"

"They are." He managed to pull himself together after one last snort. "But they're not for your feet."

She glanced down at herself. There were four booties. Was she supposed to have one on each boob and the others on her hands? Or—

"I'm sorry. I shouldn't tease you when you're not feeling well." His arm circled her shoulders, and he gently tugged her close and kissed the top of her head. "Wow, you're kind of sweaty."

"Which is only one of many reasons you're not getting another hug or kiss from me anytime soon." She pulled away and narrowed her eyes at him. "Explain my sudden bounty of fuzzy booties, Karlsson."

His smile was soft. Affectionate. "You asked me if I had a heating pad, älskling. This was the closest thing I could find on short notice."

All at once, the Mystery of the Unseasonable Booties was solved, and in the sweetest way she could have imagined.

Yeah, he'd been fucking with her. But only after venturing into that weird Alpine spa and locating the nearest equivalent to a heating pad on the island. And he'd done all that sometime during a full day of lessons. Because she had her period and was hurting, and he wanted to help.

All was forgiven.

More than forgiven, actually. So much more than forgiven, she turned her face away from him for a moment.

"Thank you," she told the back cushion on his couch, swallowing past the thickness in her throat. "This time, I really mean it."

His knuckles stroked her cheek, but he didn't urge her to

look at him. Instead, he gave her time to regain her composure in semi-privacy. "You're welcome."

This surge of emotion in her chest hurt her. Frightened her. But maybe it was her hormones rioting, another transient inconvenience imposed by her menstrual cycle, rather than something meaningful enough to last beyond this hiatus from daily reality. Maybe the barriers around her heart weren't eroding beneath the steady tide of his attention.

Maybe she could still escape this interlude unscathed.

As a former teacher and current assistant principal, she knew bullshit when she heard it. Even in her own thoughts. She might as well be a student explaining how word-for-word transcriptions from Wikipedia weren't really plagiarism.

Unlike with her students, however, she was letting the bullshit stand. At least for now.

A few deep breaths, and she'd gotten herself somewhat together. When she finally faced Lucas again, she offered a wobbly curve of her lips. "So what are our revised plans for tonight?"

"Well..." The pad of his thumb lightly skimmed her cheek. "That depends."

"On what?"

"A lot of things." He scratched his jaw thoughtfully. "Did you have dessert with dinner? If you didn't, I might or might not have convinced the pastry chef at The Sands to let me have a lemon chess meringue pie today. Or if you'd prefer dessert in mountain-shaped-chocolate-bar form instead, I have that too."

He'd remembered the pie. Not only remembered, but taken action to get her what she wanted. Interrupted an already very-busy day in yet another way, all on her behalf. Considered the likelihood that she might want chocolate, given her hormonal state. Further indicated his total disinclination to police her eating without having to say more on the subject.

He was trying. He was trying so hard, and she wasn't sure she remembered that sort of effort from Jeremy. Not even in the beginning, and definitely not by the end of their engagement.

With her ex, if something needed remembering, she remembered. If errands needed to be run, she ran them. If someone needed care, she cared for them.

Even when the person who needed caring was herself.

More near-tears, and this time she didn't turn away.

"Tess, no. Please don't—" He gently swiped away a renegade tear, one that had survived her most committed blinking attempts.

"I'm not crying about pie and chocolate," she told him.

He inspected his wet thumb, then looked at her through his lashes with a sweet smile. "That seems, uh, less than accurate, älskling."

Dammit. "Okay, I'm crying about pie and chocolate."

He spoke in his most soothing voice. "If they're upsetting you, there's a family of raccoons behind one of the cafés, and if I set everything near the trash bins—"

She pointed an authoritative, if slightly shaky, forefinger at him. "Don't even joke about that."

Holding up his hands, he nudged her foot with his. "I promise to stop joking if you promise to stop crying." He paused. "Or if you want to keep crying, go ahead, but please let me hold you. I'd be doing it already, but you said you were sweaty and didn't want hugs."

Normally, this degree of overheatedness would make her eschew all physical contact for hours. Maybe days. But even more than a reasonable core temperature, she needed—

Oh, Jesus.

She needed Lucas.

And he was right by her side, waiting for her.

She launched herself into his arms, and he hit the back of the sofa with a distinct *ooof*.

They waited for him to catch his breath before she spoke again. "Sorry. I probably should have warned you first. And made sure my knee landed in a better spot."

"I very much appreciate your enthusiasm," he wheezed. "Just...give me a moment."

God, she was about to combust with their combined body heat, but it didn't matter. The way he gathered her to him, cuddling her close even as he recovered from her errant knee, soothed something inside her she hadn't even known was raw, and that rawness had nothing—absolutely nothing—to do with her period.

She needed to tell him. He needed to know.

"I was crying because you're so thoughtful," she whispered in his ear. "Because you work so hard, but you still put in time and effort to make me happy and make me feel better. So I was crying about the pie and the chocolate, sure, but I was also crying about the booties, and about our picnic and the tulips, and about how you wanted to see me tonight, no matter what."

He gave her a fierce squeeze before his hold turned gentle once more. "You deserve effort."

She wasn't done. "I was crying because you're a good man, and I'm so sad you don't live anywhere near me."

His palm skimmed along her spine, the steady movement both combatting and eliciting another wave of tears. "That's nothing that needs to be solved tonight, Tess."

"And I was crying because I'm hormonal as fuck." She sniffed, hard. "I can't wait to be a crone with withered ovaries."

"Okay," he said neutrally.

"When I'm cranky, I'll whack people with my cane, and no one will say anything."

"I think that's still assault, älskling. Even if you're post-menopausal."

She let out a sigh against his shoulder and slumped into

him. "Dammit. I was looking forward to cane-related carnage."

"I'm certain you can find legal ways to torment your enemies." He pressed a kiss to the crown of her head. "I have great faith in your creativity."

"Thanks."

Slowly, her breathing evened, and the urge to cry diminished.

"You never told me." His voice surrounded her, vibrating against her chest. "Do you want some pie?"

She shook her head. "Big dinner. I had guava and cream cheese empanadas for dessert. When I tasted that filling, I almost cried then too. It was amazing." Tipping back her chin, she caught his eye. "I'm sorry I'm too full for the pie."

"There's always tomorrow." He didn't sound or look concerned. "How are you feeling?"

She lifted a shoulder. "About the same as when I called. Tired. Bloated. Crampy."

"I could heat up the booties." Shifting her in his arms, he leaned over to retrieve the packages from where they'd fallen on the floor. "Doctors always say that Alpine-themed booties provide the most effective cramp relief available over the counter."

She stifled a snort. "No doctor has ever said that, not once, in the entire history of the medical profession."

"Are you sure?" His dimples popped. "I was certain I'd heard that somewhere."

"Just microwave the damn booties, Karlsson."

After one last kiss on her forehead, he let her go and got to his feet in one graceful motion. "I will. But first, I'm going to lower the AC to arctic-tundra levels. Hopefully that'll keep the rest of you cool while you're using the booties. Otherwise, you may simply melt into the couch." Heading for the thermostat near the entry door, he tossed the next words over his shoulder. "I'm afraid for my security deposit."

He didn't seem to hurry through any of the tasks he kept setting himself in pursuit of her comfort. Somehow, though, a mere five minutes later, she was stretched out along his couch, her head resting on a pillow in his lap, an icy glass of fresh strawberry lemonade within easy reach, four floral-scented booties tucked inside her shirt and warming her belly as the rest of her finally cooled to tolerable levels.

He, on the other hand, had donned a faded blue sweatshirt with three yellow crowns on it. "Because the temperature in here is beginning to remind me of a Stockholm winter," he'd told her. "Polar bears should come strolling by any minute now. Don't worry, though, Tess. Swedes are taught to defend themselves from polar bear attacks as toddlers, lest our population dwindle to one old dude named Sven Svensson living in an ice cave. I'll protect you."

More bullshit she was going to let slide, simply because she was so damn comfortable.

He placed the remote in her hand and waved toward the wide-screen television in clear invitation. "I have lots of cable and streaming options. Pick whatever you'd like."

Well, he'd asked for it.

She flipped through the choices in one of his streaming services until she found what she wanted. A few moments later, the black-and-white RKO logo appeared, and she snuggled her cheek into the pillow and waited for Cary Grant and Katharine Hepburn to appear onscreen.

"*Bringing Up Baby*?" He stroked a hand down her arm. "Interesting choice. Why do I feel as if I'm Susan in this particular scenario, despite my disappointing lack of a pet leopard?"

After a jaw-cracking yawn, she smiled at the screen and modified one of her favorite lines. "Now it isn't that I don't like you, Lucas, because, after all, in moments of quiet, I'm strangely drawn toward you, but—well, there haven't been any quiet moments."

His body shifted beneath her as he laughed softly. "This is a quiet moment."

"Fair enough," she said, and then yawned again. "Thank you again. For everything."

"You're more than welcome."

His fingers threaded through her hair, sifting gently, and she raised a hand to rest on his hard thigh. It turned to granite beneath her touch, and his fingers stilled for a moment before he kept playing with her hair.

The two of them watched the movie.

Well, one of them, mainly, since she lasted only a few minutes before falling asleep.

NINETEEN

When Tess's eyes blinked open again, the picture on the television had turned to full, vivid color, and screwball dialogue had transformed into grunts of effort and intermittent commentary about second serve percentages.

She could barely hear any of it. Lucas had set the volume very, very low.

"I didn't know if you still watched professional tennis." She blinked blearily at the screen, trying to gather her fuzzy thoughts. "I thought it might be an unwelcome reminder."

His response was quiet. "I love the game. Despite everything. And I like to support my friends on the Tour."

Her hand was still resting on his thigh, and she gave it a gentle, consoling squeeze.

As she shifted, something atop her moved, and she suddenly realized they were both covered in light blankets. She twitched a corner of hers. "I thought you were worried about my melting on your couch."

"After about half an hour, you got goosebumps and kept cuddling closer and closer." He leaned down and pressed a kiss on her temple. "I was afraid for my virtue."

"Your virtue is in no danger." She shifted to her back

and looked up at his handsome, craggy face. "Largely because it's already dead. I suspect you murdered it long ago."

"There's always the possibility of zombie virtue."

Her laugh jarred the booties, and the faintly warm weights slid to her side. "How long was I asleep?"

"About an hour, I think." His brow creased. "Do you want to sleep more? Maybe make an early night of it? You can stay here, or I can walk you back to your room, if that would be more comfortable for you."

Actually, she was beginning to feel more alert than she had all day. "I'm fine. Let's watch tennis."

His body relaxed beneath her, and his lazy smile made the warm blanket entirely unnecessary. "Not *Bringing Up Baby*? I can restart it where you fell asleep. In other words, five minutes into the movie."

"Sorry about that." She scrunched her face in apology. "It was a long afternoon, and I'm always tired the first day of my period."

"I understand, älskling. Don't worry." His forefinger smoothed the lines between her eyebrows. "How's your belly feeling?"

Tentatively, she levered herself up with one arm. "Better, actually. Much better."

"Alpine-themed booties." He nodded, his expression suspiciously solemn. "The choice of medical professionals everywhere."

Ignoring his nonsense, she answered his earlier question. "We can watch *Bringing Up Baby* another night. I'd like to hear your perspective on the matches we see."

Wait. Had she been too presumptuous?

She was assuming there *would* be another night, and maybe—

"Sounds good." His tone was pleased, not affronted. "But if you get bored, just let me know. We can watch anything you like, or have a snack, or go to bed, or..." He lifted a shoulder. "Whatever you want to do is fine by me."

When she sat up all the way, they weren't touching anymore. She rectified that immediately, scooting until her hip pressed against his and she could rest her head against his solid chest. His arm encircled her, cuddling her close, and he began fiddling with her hair again.

Her scalp tingled, and her spine seemed to melt.

He smelled good. Felt better.

Yeah. She could get used to this, too easily.

Not going to think about that now. "Tell me about the players. This match is just about to start, right?"

The women on court were warming up, from what she could tell, hitting balls to one another and practicing their serves while various graphics flashed on the screen, listing their head-to-head record, ages, prize money totals, and other information.

"Within a minute or two, yeah," Lucas said. "The player on the right is Danielle Forrester, an up-and-coming American. The player on the left is Lilly Tulu."

At Tess's inquiring look, he elaborated. "Tulu is a former top-ten player. Swedish. The most accomplished female tennis pro my country has seen for a long time. She's still all over the tabloids there, even though she's been recovering from a hip injury for almost a year. We've met a few times over the years, but only in passing."

"What about Forrester?"

He shook his head. "Never met her."

Forrester had her long, sandy-colored hair bound into a ponytail, and a red sweatband striped her tanned forehead. She bounced around the baseline and called out an occasional laughing comment to some spectators near her side of the court. Her family or coaching staff, Tess presumed.

Tulu, on the other hand, concentrated on her shots with a fierce frown, her black braids bouncing against her slim, impressively sculpted back with every movement. She didn't glance toward the crowd once, but Tess got the sense Tulu—older than Forrester by four years, according to the graphics—didn't miss much.

When the chair umpire called time, the women walked back to their benches and took several final gulps of their drinks before the start of the match.

"So your Swedish compatriot is the favorite to win, I assume?"

"Normally." His brow furrowed as the players took their positions for the opening game. "But her injury may make this a more competitive match than she'd prefer."

Forrester tossed the first ball in the air and served wide, and Tess and Lucas settled back to watch the close, hard-fought contest. Tulu won the first set, but only barely. The tiebreak ended when her opponent double-faulted, and the Swedish player retreated to her chair by the side of the court, mouth pinched, and downed another bottle of sports drink.

After the coaches finished brief visits with their players, Lucas turned to Tess. "What did you think of the set?"

"They're incredibly talented." The honest truth. "Both of them. I can't even imagine being able to move that way, or hit with that much accuracy."

"Practice." Lucas shot her a quick smile. "Lots of training and practice."

She had nothing more to contribute, despite her enjoyment of what she'd seen. "What are *your* thoughts about their play so far?"

Eventually, she wanted to hear some behind-the-scenes stories and gossip. But right now, she was more curious about what Lucas had noticed on that screen. How his experience informed and changed his perspective on the match. What she'd missed in her ignorance.

As the women left their benches for the start of the second set, Lucas shook his head. "If I were Lilly's coach, I'd have used that visit to discuss a few specific fixes, instead of just encouraging her to focus. Her ball toss is too far behind her, and she's ceding too much ground when Forrester serves. She needs to get closer to the baseline."

Fascinated by the concentration creasing his forehead, the sharp intelligence in his gaze as he studied the two women, she nudged his shoulder with a forefinger and tried not to press her thighs together. "What would you tell Forrester?"

"Her coach was dead on. She has to work on her movement. Instead of lunging for the ball, she needs to get her legs going and take smaller steps. If she did, she'd have much more control over her shots." He blew out a breath. "But a lot of that will come in time. After this tournament, I'd also suggest some doubles matches to improve her play at the net. Maybe—"

After glancing at Tess, he paused. "Why are you looking at me like that?"

"Competent men murder my vagina. In the best possible way."

Instantly, he turned away from the television, his head bowing so their eyes could meet. "Is that so?"

His voice had deepened. Turned gravelly in a way that shivered down her back.

"Yes. Which makes my current state unfortunate." She sighed. "I know sex is possible right now, but I'm just not a fan of mess."

His arm around her shoulders drew her closer to his heat. "You know, I've heard—"

"So let's change the subject and discuss whether you ever considered coaching after you left the Tour." Tilting her head, she studied him. "Maybe the idea doesn't interest you, but with your knowledge and communication skills, you'd clearly be amazing at it."

His mouth opened. Closed.

It took him a while to answer. "I didn't really consider the possibility, no."

In one way, she hated to say all this, since becoming a professional tennis coach would require him to traverse the globe once more. It would literally and figuratively distance him from any possibility of a future together, however slim that possibility might be in the first place.

But he needed to understand. Needed to acknowledge the gifts he had and the options that lay before him.

In the end, their time together might be brief—and for all he'd given her, she had so little to offer him in return. As her ex always said, she was no good at emotions, just pragmatics. But this...this, she could do. This, she could give him.

"The other night, I was thinking what an incredible tennis commentator you'd be too." Funny. Charming. Handsome. Reliable. Sharp as the paper cutter in the school's copy room. "But I'm sure you must have weighed that option before."

His chest rose beneath her in a hitching breath, then fell again.

"No," he finally said. "I can't say I have."

That had to be enough of a nudge for the moment. They had other issues to discuss, unfortunately.

"Lucas, I need to talk to you about something." Flattening her hand over his heart in mute apology, she looked up at him. "I want to spend some time with Belle in the evenings. We don't live in the same place anymore, and she's my best friend. It's not right to leave her alone every night during a trip we planned to spend together."

His mouth pressed tight for a moment, but he nodded. "I understand."

"I also need to start working again. Not as much as I was"—and if that was a mistake, it was hers to make—"but sometimes. Maybe for an hour or two every other night."

"Okay." His tone was neutral. Unusually so.

Shit.

Her fingers curled, folding into her palm. "Not that you necessarily want to spend every night with me. I'm sure you have other pl—"

"Tess." He squeezed her shoulder. "I want to spend every night with you. I want to spend as much time with you as I can before you leave."

"Oh." She let out a relieved breath. "Then I'm sorry that time will be somewhat limited."

His smile was wry. "That was always going to be true, no matter what. And like I said, I understand."

"Speaking of work..." Her hand flattened on his chest again. "I have a favor to ask."

He didn't even hesitate. "Whatever you need."

"I was hoping you might keep me company while I'm working," she said. "I'd love to have someone I could brainstorm and discuss ideas with, and Belle's already given her opinion on everything. Can you be my new sounding board? Please?"

He simply stared at her for a moment, face blank.

"I haven't talked to anyone else about my plans. Just her, and"—she flashed him a tentative smile—"you, that other night on the tennis court. I'd like to tell you more."

"Why—" After clearing his throat, he started again. "Why me?"

"You're smart. Perceptive about people. I think you'd help me see possibilities and drawbacks I haven't considered." But she wasn't going to pressure him if he wasn't interested. "If that doesn't sound like a good time, though, I completely get it. I can work from my hotel room like I've been doing before now."

"No." The word was abrupt. Loud. "No, I'll help. I *want* to help."

His hand covered hers, pressing both over his heart. And he was looking at her...

Well, she didn't quite know how he was looking at her.

But she'd never seen such naked emotion in a man's eyes before, not directed her way.

"I'm glad," she whispered, and licked lips that had abruptly turned dry.

His eyes followed the movement. He swallowed, the effort visible, and hectic color washed over his cheekbones as he studied her mouth.

That look, she recognized. She'd seen it several times over the course of a long night spent with him around her, above her, inside her.

She still didn't like mess. But she wasn't aching or exhausted anymore, and she hadn't lied. Competence turned her on. If he had some creative suggestions as to how they should spend their night together, she was more than willing to listen.

"Tess." It was a near-rasp, one that did nothing to diffuse the heat suddenly billowing between them. "I bought a vibrator today."

Wow. He'd had an *extraordinarily* busy day. Pies and vibrators and booties, oh my.

"Someday," he said, "when my face is buried between your legs, I want to slide that vibrator inside you and feel your thighs tremble as you come."

Her breath hitched. Hitched again.

"But not tonight. Tonight, if you'd like, we can find out how it feels against your clit. What intensity you like. Which settings you prefer." He leaned forward. Ducked down. Nuzzled that sensitive spot at the base of her throat as she gasped and squirmed. "And I have very good hands, as I've told you before. Let me remind you how good. No mess necessary."

His fingers gently fisted in her hair, and he turned her head away from him. When he licked a slow line up the back of her neck, she shuddered.

"I've heard that orgasms help with cramps," he whispered

in her ear, and the sensation sharpened an ache between her legs that had nothing to do with her period. "What do you say?"

What *could* she say, really?

Her lips curved in an anticipatory smile. "Let's find out."

TWENTY

AS SOON AS TESS EMERGED FROM THE BATHROOM, Lucas tugged her into his arms. "If you decide you'd rather just sleep, or you're too uncomfortable doing this, let me know. Tonight doesn't have to be about sex at all, like we said earlier."

It was an ongoing, earth-shifting revelation for him.

She liked his body, sure. She enjoyed the way he could please her in bed.

But she also wanted to hear his thoughts. About tennis, but also about her professional plans. Because she thought he had something to offer.

Her faith in his judgment disoriented him. It swept his feet from beneath him, like that dangerous riptide at the rocky, visitor-prohibited stretch of beach beneath the overlook. It bore him inexorably away from the only land he'd known for years.

He might drown in the end, of course. Suddenly, though, because of Tess's inescapable pull, he could see other destinations. Other welcoming shores, waiting patiently in the distance.

One fresh discovery he'd already made: The way she

valued him for non-physical reasons made him want to give her more orgasms. As many as she could handle. Ironic, that.

"I'll tell you," she promised. "Where do you want me?"

Everywhere. In his life. Within touching distance as often as humanly possible.

"You've cooled off a bit, right?" When she nodded, he guided her toward the bed. "Then let's cuddle for a minute or two first."

Her eyes rolled to his shadowed ceiling. "Men. Always with the cuddling."

"We can't help it." Taking his time about it, he located the hem of her flowing turquoise t-shirt and began to raise it. "Your cuddle-ability levels are just that high. Off the charts."

She lifted her arms, and he tossed her shirt onto his nightstand, then took a moment to study her newest sports bra. This one didn't offer much support and boasted zero hooks. Instead, it slipped on and off over her head and clearly showed her nipples through the soft cotton fabric.

He approved.

Cuddling suddenly a distant second in priorities, he sat on the edge of the bed and positioned her between his legs.

"This is only a bra in the loosest sense. It's mostly there to absorb under-boob sweat." Her feet shuffled a bit. "I would have worn something sexier, but I didn't think we—"

Ducking his head, he licked the fabric over her left nipple. Licked again, as she gasped and fell silent. Once the cotton was wet, he played with her there. Circled the tight nub now pushing against his tongue. Nuzzled it with his nose. Bit gently through the fabric and watched her reaction carefully, since she might be especially sensitive at this time of the month.

His hold on her hips kept her steady when he switched to her other breast.

"Take off my bra. Take off your shirt." It was a murmur. A husky plea couched as an order, even as she arched her back and offered herself to him. "I want to feel your skin against mine."

She could have whatever she wanted. She could have everything.

He reached back to strip off his tee, but her hand closed over his.

"I changed my mind," she said. "Let me."

In her fist, the fabric crumpled and rose. Every inch of flesh she exposed, she stroked with her free hand. His belly. His chest. His nipples, which she rubbed with her thumb. His collarbones and shoulders and neck, which she traced with her tongue.

He shuddered, again and again.

When the shirt lay on the floor, she lightly tugged the hair at the back of his head, and he cursed at the jagged bolt of sensation to his groin. Helplessly, he fell forward into her. Rested his face against her shoulder. Wallowed in her softness and heat for a moment before recovering himself and remembering what this was about.

Not him. Only her.

No hurry. Just lazy pleasure, a gift freely given.

Her sports bra was tricky to maneuver over her head, but he managed. Then he moved her further in between his legs, pressed their torsos together, and went exploring, the loose waist of her cotton shorts and her generously sized panties allowing him plenty of room to maneuver.

"Easy access." One hand he slid down over her ass, cupping an ample, soft-skinned cheek. The other stroked her warm belly, the crisp hair between her legs. "Nice."

She kissed him then, her lips urgent, her tongue demanding entry. As she swept inside his mouth and claimed it as her own, he lightly rubbed his forefinger over her clit.

The small sound she made, he breathed in. Her knees sagged as he circled the hardening nub of flesh, and he tightened his hold on her ass.

With a tampon inside her, she wasn't going to get wet. He'd have to supply his own moisture. Breaking the kiss, he switched their positions, easing her back onto the mattress as he stood between her legs. Then he licked his fingers and got back to the most pleasurable work he'd ever known.

There was something unexpectedly erotic about watching his hand move beneath the fabric, the contrast between what was hidden from view and her very visible reaction. The way her thighs convulsively opened and closed on his forearm, her lips parted and wet and her breath fast.

He leaned down and sucked that glorious curve of flesh between neck and shoulder, teasing her puckered nipple with his free hand. "Still feel good?"

She was swollen and twitching beneath his fingers now, raising her hips for more pressure. But he didn't make his touch any firmer. No, he intended to make this feeling last and last for her.

"Oh, yes. Lucas...oh, God." Her eyes drifted closed, and her chin tipped back as she squirmed on the bed.

Fuck, Tess on the verge of orgasm was the most glorious thing he'd ever seen.

Gentle, gentle.

The shush of skin against fabric was the only sound other than her panting breaths. He kept circling, lightly rubbing, glorying in the occasional spasms that told him she was close.

Then she moaned, her brow pleated, her flesh pulsing beneath his touch as she bucked and trembled and came. He bent down to kiss her, to take those whimpers of reaction into his mouth, and kept stroking her until her body relaxed and subsided into the mattress.

When he raised his head, her eyes were still closed.

"Want to sleep now?" he whispered.

Given the rampant state of his body, he wasn't sure he

could drop off anytime soon, and he'd had other ideas for their evening together, but she needed her rest.

She blinked open heavy-lidded eyes. "No."

"Good." Urging her to lift her hips, he stripped away her shorts. "Because I want to test out the vibrator tonight, if you're willing. You know, for scientific reasons. To find out whether using it helps your cramps."

Her lips curved in a sudden, wicked grin. "I don't know if my orgasm helped my cramps, but it certainly did a lot for my mood."

"Noted for future purposes." He mimed scribbling the information on his palm. "Now for our next experiment. Let me get the vibrator from my—"

"Let's save that for morning." She caught his hand and tugged him down beside her. "Right now, I have other priorities."

"Cuddling, I hope." He frowned at her. "You deliberately distracted me earlier, and I didn't get my promised allotment. It was all very unfair."

She gaped at him for a moment, then closed her mouth with a snap. "I mentioned under-boob sweat, which is possibly the least sexy thing in the world, and the next thing I knew, your hands were in my panties. How on earth can you blame me for that?"

The sweep of his hand encompassed all of her, from her rumpled hair to her cute pink toes. "You were standing there in just a sports bra and shorts. So the better question is: How was I supposed to resist that sort of temptation? It was entrapment, really."

Despite his best efforts to stifle a grin, she gently poked a fingertip into his dimple. "It was a faded cotton sports bra and baggy shorts, smartass. Not to mention my period panties, which are enormous."

"It was you," he said simply.

She faltered for a moment, swallowing hard. "You're the one who took off my shirt."

"Then I hereby accept the blame for the offending orgasm." He inclined his head, his tone lofty and gracious. "And now claim the cuddling time due to me."

When he tried to tip them both back onto the mattress, her hand on his bare chest stopped him. "Not so fast."

"Don't tell me you're reneging on your cuddle-related promises." His stare was mournful, even as his lips twitched. "I may cry."

She wasn't even trying to hold back her own grin anymore. "Strip, Karlsson."

"Naked cuddling, I'll accept." Quickly, he shucked his shorts and boxer-briefs, then urged Tess back against the pillows at the head of the bed and wrapped her in his arms. "Sorry about, uh—"

"Mr. Perky isn't a problem." Her hand closed over him. "Mr. Perky is a bonus."

He'd been prodding her soft thigh, despite his best efforts, but now...

Fuck. Her hand was strong and agile, the pressure on the sensitive underside of his cockhead perfect, and this wasn't what he'd intended. At all.

He rocked his hips against her touch, helpless. "Älskling, I didn't mean—"

"Hush," she said, and licked her palm before gripping him once more. Then her fingers paused. "Unless you don't want to do this? It's okay if you're not in the mood, or—"

"Oh, I'm in the mood. Trust me." He blew out a breath. "I just wanted tonight to be all about you. Not me."

Her brows rose in emphasis. "And what I want is to make you come, just like you made me come. Giving you pleasure makes me feel..."

Her grip tightened as she trailed off, and the wash of pleasure stole his breath. "Makes you feel what?"

"Connected to you. Powerful. The way you look at me right before you have an orgasm…" She bit her lip. "I want that. Again. But only if you do too."

They both looked down then, and the sight of her long fingers wrapped around his ruddy cock, her pale, plump thigh gleaming in the light of his bedside lamp, the swollen wetness of her lower lip…

The urge to rut into her hand, against her giving flesh, overwhelmed him. He had to close his eyes for a moment to regain even a sliver of control.

When he opened them again, she asked, "Do you want me to stop?"

Silently, he shook his head. Closing his fingers over hers, he tightened her clasp.

She didn't move a millimeter. "I need words."

"Don't stop. Please."

His voice was hoarse, and maybe he would have been embarrassed by that, by his pleading, another time, or with another woman. But not now, and not with Tess. Not with the way she immediately responded.

Her smile, the slow slide of her hand along his aching flesh, were his rewards, and they were more than enough. He helped her find the rhythm, then let go and lay back, helpless before her.

"You never have to beg." She leaned over him, arching her back until her breasts were within reach of his mouth, and God, he didn't deserve her. "Unless begging turns you on."

The edges of his vision were already turning white, and he couldn't deny the truth. "It does. With you."

Her silky hair fell around their faces, hiding them from the outside world. He smelled sweat and peachy apricots and edelweiss, and it was yet more enticement to buck his hips, to pump into her hand and groan in exultant agony.

Raising his head, he sucked her nipple into his mouth, licking it and taking it carefully between his teeth. Then fell back when he couldn't concentrate anymore, couldn't moderate the pressure of the bite.

He wouldn't hurt her. He wouldn't.

Her rhythm never sped up. Each stroke of her hand remained slow and excruciating, even as he threw back his head and made low, rough noises and panted.

"Look at you," she murmured. "You're so swollen and thick now. So wet. Gorgeous."

With her thumb, she gathered more moisture from the tip of his cock and spread it, adding a slight twist of her hand until everything was slick and unbearable.

He was delirious with need, thrusting jerkily into her grip, against her lush thigh. Her breasts swayed with his near-violent movements, but she still didn't speed up. Didn't take him over the edge into glorious nothingness.

Then he understood.

"Please," he said, his voice strangled.

Her hand paused. "Say it again."

"Please make me come." He heaved upward and captured her mouth in a brief, desperate kiss. "I need you."

Her slow smile was gorgeous. Befitting a benevolent goddess bestowing her favor on a worthy mortal.

Her fingers tightened on his cock, and suddenly she was pumping him without pause, her pace magnificent and unforgiving. He shouted, the ecstasy of it like lightning forking up his spine.

In seconds, he was moaning and heaving and spurting all over her belly and thighs and hand, his mind absolutely, wonderfully blank. She nursed him through it, her grip turning gentler, her lips on his sweet and coaxing. Then she sat back and let him recover, stroking his chest with one hand.

He was jelly on the mattress. Incapable of movement. At least until he caught her subtle squirming, the way she was rubbing her thighs together the tiniest bit.

"Did that turn you on?" he managed to rasp out.

"That"—she lifted her slick hand with a rueful smile —"has never made me hot before. But...yeah. This time, it did. You did."

Somehow, that felt almost as good as his orgasm.

With a fingertip, he traced the edge of her panties along her belly. "You want me to take care of it? Take care of you?"

Her head dipped in a little nod.

"Words," he reminded her.

She swayed toward him, above him. "Yes. I want your hand between my legs again."

"Can these come off?" He tugged at the elastic of the waistband. "And do you want us to wash up first? I know you don't like mess."

"I think these can safely go," she said, and wrestled her panties down her body and onto the floor. "If I'm wrong, so be it. I don't care about mess right now."

Her hand guided his between her parted thighs. Then he was stroking the softest, hottest flesh imaginable, her vulva puffy, her clit still swollen and stiff from her earlier orgasm. She was already near the edge, so near that after only a minute of playing and circling and rubbing, she was grinding against his fingers and trembling, her flesh pulsing into his hand as she moaned loudly and came again.

Later, when he was soaping her sticky belly in the shower, she suddenly laughed.

He looked up from his task, smiling at the sight of her cute scrunched-up nose. "What?"

"My cramps are totally gone." She grinned and patted his hand. "Doctors should prescribe your fingers, Lucas. Women everywhere would be lining up for a monthly dose."

"I'm afraid the supply is exclusively yours." Angling her into the spray, he rinsed off the soap. "Sorry, pharmaceutical companies."

When she stepped closer, her wet breasts pressed into his

side, and he had to work hard to concentrate on the conversation.

Her grin had disappeared. "Really? Just mine?"

Those hazel eyes of hers slayed him. All that tentative hope, all that fear.

"Just yours," he told her, each word firm. Decisive.

"Good." Her palm cupped his cheek and urged him down for a kiss, which he gladly gave her. "Good."

THE NEXT MORNING, SHE WENT DOWN ON HIM AS he fisted his hands in her soft hair and called her name like an invocation. A plea and prayer of gratitude both, wrenched from a heart fit to burst from everything she was doing, everything she was.

After they'd both washed up and she took care of tampon business by herself in the bathroom, he produced the new vibrator with a courtly flourish that made her snicker. When he eased her down onto her back in bed, though, making certain her neck was supported by a pillow, she stopped laughing.

He stretched out along her side and settled down to play.

The right side of her clit, he discovered, was more sensitive than the left, and she liked little circles in that area, her hips rocking against the insistent buzz. Her hand clutched at his arm, his shoulder, the sheets, while her sex grew swollen and flushed. When she got close, a rosy stain spread across her face and chest as her knees drew up high.

Her head tossed on the pillow, and he cupped her hot cheek. Kissed her softly.

When he raised his head, she was panting. Squirming. "Lucas…"

"Higher intensity?" he murmured.

At her nod, he twisted the base of the vibrator, and the buzz grew louder. She moaned.

Her dazed hazel eyes squeezed shut, but he coaxed them open again, willing her to see him. See them. Associate the sight of him with her pleasure.

The orgasm shuddered through her as she gasped and made rough little sounds. He noted every twitch, every whimper, with satisfaction sharp enough to cut, even as he tenderly stroked the soft, damp skin of her belly with his free hand and gentled the pressure of the vibrator.

You'll miss this. You'll miss me. *Before you leave, I'll make sure of that.*

In that moment, he felt almost savage in his desperation. But he kissed her sweetly, lightly, as she lay trembling beside him, and he held her carefully as they both recovered.

When her breath steadied again, she eased away from him, sat up, and heaved a dramatic sigh. "Now I'm all sweaty and need another shower. Your insistence on giving me really intense orgasms is probably causing water shortages all along the Florida coastline."

Her hair was sticking up around her head, rumpled by the pillow and his hands. She was, in fact, a bit sweaty and red-faced, as if she'd just completed an epic tennis match.

She was a mess. *His* mess, and he loved it.

She patted his chest. "Lucas Karlsson: One-Man Environmental Catastrophe."

Offering a gracious bow from a prone position wasn't easy, but he tried. "At your service, milady."

She grinned at him. Then, smile fading, she turned toward the lone window in his bedroom. Normally, it offered a better-than-average view of a few palms, some sand, and a small wedge of blue ocean. This morning, the blinds were still shut, so he had no clue why she kept blinking in that direction.

"I guess..." After a hesitation, she looked down at him again. "I guess last night wasn't typical for you."

Landmines. In her voice, he could almost hear her edging closer to them, reluctant but determined to know whether she could survive the blast. Whether they could survive.

He sat up. "What do you mean?"

Her lips compressed before she spoke again, each word careful. "You must have gone to a lot of social events when you played on the Tour. And I get the sense you visit the mainland a lot now, for parties or dinners or...whatever."

The wall behind his back was cool from the air conditioning, slightly damp from the humidity. He pressed himself tighter against it, forcing himself to stay silent and let her say whatever she needed to say.

"During the school year—" Abruptly, she raised her knees toward her chest, resting her unsteady hands on them. "At work, I spend all day surrounded by people, kids and teachers and administrators and parents. When I leave school, I don't..."

Her gaze lowered to those clasped hands. "I don't want to go to bars or parties, really. Last night was more typical of how I like to spend my free time, even when I don't have my period. I eat. I watch movies or TV. I chat with Belle. I might get together with a friend for dinner, but it's usually one-on-one, and most nights I don't want to leave the house again once I'm there."

He understood now, and his shoulders slumped against that damp wall in relief.

Ducking his head, he tried unsuccessfully to catch her eye. "You're wondering if your life would bore me."

"Yeah." It was an exhalation as much as a word.

Now that his heart had restarted, her decision to broach such a fraught topic heartened him. No, downright *delighted* him. If she was worrying about how he'd fit into her daily life, she was picturing a possible future together. Considering how it would work.

Even better: He had a good answer for those worries. An honest answer, too.

With one scoot to the side, he had his hip pressed against hers. "Älskling, I didn't want to leave professional tennis the way I did. But even at my most bitter, I loved the amount of unscheduled time I had after my retirement. I still do."

Suddenly, he had eye contact again, and her fingers were no longer bone-white from tension. Which meant he could cover them with his own.

"The public saw my matches." As she relaxed, he turned her hand over and held it. "They didn't see me with my coach, reviewing endless tapes of my play and my opponents' matches. They didn't see me on the court, practicing with a hitting partner. They didn't see me with doctors and physical therapists as I recovered from my injuries and surgeries. They didn't see me with a trainer, doing strength and endurance and flexibility training, or see me signing autographs at an event, or see me traveling with my team. My coach, my hitting partner, my physio...."

He trailed off, shaking his head. "So many commitments. So many people. Good people, but an endless stream of them. Always. I miss them sometimes, but I'm glad to have more quiet time and more time to myself now."

She was listening intently, that familiar trident between her brows. "Were you ever alone?"

"Late at night. Then I was pretty much always by myself in an unfamiliar, cold hotel room, trying my best to get enough sleep." Somehow, he'd almost forgotten that part.

"So it was all or nothing." The squeeze of her hand was gentle. Warm. "People you saw for work or no one at all."

He considered that. "A lot of the time, I guess."

Odd how many places loneliness could find him. In a crowded arena. Alone in a too-hard, silent bed. In the aftermath of casual sex, emotional isolation chasing hard on the heels of momentary physical satisfaction.

The latter had been a recent discovery, and not a welcome one. He'd been trying his best to ignore the realization, to bury it in yet more work, yet more sex, but no longer. Not after Tess had showed him what the alternative felt like.

Connection. He wanted more of it. More of her.

Lifting their hands, he kissed her knuckles. "What I'm trying to say is, yes, I had lots of people around me and attended public events before, and I occasionally travel to the mainland and get together with coworkers now. They're good people, and I enjoy their company. No matter what I end up doing with my life, I would want that life to include friends, and sometimes I'd want to see those friends. With or without my partner. But last night was—"

Blisteringly hot. Heart-wrenching. Companionable.

"—perfect." He rested his cheek against the back of her hand. "That's what I want, Tess. That's who I am, on a daily basis. Your life wouldn't bore me. *You* wouldn't bore me."

Her eyes were wide. Cautious. "You're sure?"

"Yes." One word. The only one necessary, stark and uncompromising and honest.

Even Tess couldn't misinterpret that answer, though she'd most likely try.

She was staring at him, unblinking, her lips parted.

Those lips barely moved as she spoke, her whisper almost inaudible. "How the hell can a twenty-six-year-old athlete be the perfect boyfriend for me? In what universe is that even possible?"

Boyfriend? *Perfect* boyfriend?

This was the greatest morning ever, bar none.

He straightened against the wall and beamed at her. "I'm your boyfriend?"

"Shit." Her eyes squeezed shut, her brow wrinkling as she

cringed. "Yes. No. Well, kind of. I mean, at least for now. I leave in a week, and—"

He was taking that as a *yes* in wary-Tess-speak. At least for now, as she'd said. And if that was the wrong interpretation, she'd no doubt tell him. Loudly, with one eyebrow raised to the heavens.

Changing *for now* into something more long-term might prove challenging, but he still had a week to convince her. A lot could happen in seven days, as recent experience had taught him.

He planted a smacking kiss on her scrunched-up nose. "I accept the change in my status. Gladly." Another kiss on her furrowed brow. "Wow. Boyfriend status: achieved. And after only a week of effort!"

Slowly, she began to uncurl from the human ball she'd made of herself.

Letting go of her hand, he adjusted an imaginary microphone. "This is an unexpected honor, but I'd like to thank my entire team—"

"Lucas," she groaned. "Oh, my God."

But her lips were twitching, and she was peeking at him through her lashes.

He raised an invisible trophy above his head with both hands. "And of course, I never anticipated reaching a *perfect* ranking, but I can only bow to the judgment of others and accept the designation as accurate. My gratitude to—"

"Oh, my *God*," she repeated, full-on laughing now, her feigned ire entirely unconvincing. "Lucas, if you don't shut up—"

This time, he kissed her mouth.

"Make me," he said.

So she did.

TWENTY-ONE

When Tess returned to her hotel room later that morning, she found Belle's suitcases splayed open on both beds, already half-packed.

"Belle…" Letting the door shut behind her, she tried to catch her friend's eye, her stomach twisting in sudden nausea. "Are you okay? What's going on?"

Had she abandoned Belle too many times, for too long? She'd been gone all night and most of the morning, true, but she'd spent the entire day with Belle beforehand, and she'd thought her friend understood the situation with Lucas. More than understood, *approved*. Of the sex, anyway, if not a potential long-distance relationship.

"I'm fine." Belle flashed her a bright, unconvincing smile, her blond ponytail swinging as she emptied drawers and moved piles of clothing to the nearest suitcase. "And I'm packing, as you can see."

"But…" Tess swallowed. "We don't leave for another week."

Still no eye contact. "I changed my reservations early this morning."

Oh, God. She'd hurt her friend. Distanced herself in favor

of work and Lucas, leaving Belle alone on a vacation they'd planned to spend tog—

Wait.

Belle had been happily spending all that free time with Brian, her designated island fling. What had changed?

"What made you decide—"

Belle shook her head. "I'm not discussing that right now."

Her friend's tone didn't welcome further commentary. But dammit, Tess had to say *something*.

She leaned back against the door. "Our plane tickets are nonrefundable. And we signed up for a sunset cruise tomorrow and a snorkeling expedition on Thursday."

"I have enough savings to cover another ticket and the cost of a few missed activities." Belle waved a hand. "Ask Lucas if he can take time off to go with you. If not, you might be able to cancel the reservations for a refund or go by yourself."

Her lips pressed into a tight, thin line, and she stared down at the suitcase. Then she started packing again. "I'm sorry for flaking out on our plans."

"I don't mind doing things on my own. You know that." Tess still didn't understand, though, and anxiety had kicked her heart into a gallop. "Why didn't you talk to me about this yesterday?"

"I made the decision early this morning." Her friend's strained voice turned wry. "As you know, you were otherwise occupied until just now."

"Did someone—" Fuck, she didn't want to ask, but she had to. She had to. "Did someone touch you? Assault you? Did Brian—"

"*No.*" Belle shook her head vehemently. "God, no. No one laid a hand on me."

"Okay." Her most pressing worry dismissed, Tess could finally take a deep breath again. "You saved for this trip for months, Belle. Are you sure you want to do this?"

Belle closed her eyes and inhaled through her nose, her nostrils flaring with—something. Impatience? Hurt? Anger?

God, Tess was blathering about practical concerns and logistics, when what she really meant was: *I love you. I'm worried about you, and I'm worried about whether I've fucked things up between us.*

Her ex-fiancé was right. She was great at practicalities, terrible at emotions.

"—still pay half of the room costs. It's not your fault I'm checking out early." Belle was responding to Tess's question, her hands trembling as she shoved the last few items into a nearly-full suitcase. "I won't make you pay extra for the rest of your trip."

Belle obviously didn't want to talk about the reasons for her early exit. Still, Tess had to try.

In the past, Belle had always been able to see the unspoken affection behind Tess's pragmatism. But the heart-felt words were important. The question was important. Because, above all, their friendship was important.

"Are you—" Tess moved a step closer. "Are you angry at me?"

At that, Belle finally looked up. "No. No, of course I'm not angry at you. This has nothing to do with you, really."

She sounded tired, her voice dull. She also sounded sincere, but how could Tess know for sure?

"I talked with Lucas last night, and I told him I wanted to spend more time with you." Tess twisted her fingers together. "So if that's why you're leaving—"

"Babe." With a sigh, Belle stopped bending over the suit-case and stood up straight. "I told you, this has nothing to do with you. The only thing I regret about going now is that we won't have another week together. I'll make it up to you soon, though. I promise." She tried to smile. "To be fair, I'll also miss the mojitos. The bartenders here really know how to muddle a damn mint leaf."

Had Brian Whoever hurt Belle, then? Because if he had, Tess was going to track his ass down and shove those gray swim trunks down his throat.

Tess made eye contact with Belle, keeping her voice soft. "Honey, I love you, and I'm concerned about whether you're okay. If you're determined to leave now, I can try to get a ticket on the same flight. We can hang out in Boston for a few days before I have to get back to school."

Leaving Lucas early would gut her, but if Belle needed her near, Tess had to go. No question about it.

"I know you love me, and you know I love you too." Belle's stubborn chin had dropped a fraction, the set of her shoulders softening. She hesitated for a moment before continuing. "I appreciate your concern, babe, and I'm so sorry to cut our time together short. I just need a few days alone to get my head straight."

That was a problem Tess could solve.

"If you want, I can get another room and give you more space." Surely the resort had at least one vacancy. And if it didn't, Lucas might be willing to let her stay with him instead.

Belle shook her head. "I want to go back to Boston, Tess, and I don't have time to argue about this. I need to finish packing, get to the ferry, and catch my flight. Once I'm back at my apartment, I'll call you. In the meantime, have fun with Sparky."

"Belle..." God, she hated to have her friend leave like this, but the ferry's departure time was ticking ever closer. "We'll talk about this tonight? You'll explain more?"

She'd better. If not, Tess would haul her own ass to Boston and drag the story out of her friend by any means necessary.

"Yes, yes. I promise." Belle flapped a hand in the direction of the closet. "Now please let me *pack*, woman."

So Tess did, sitting on the bed and watching as Belle

threw everything into her suitcases and carry-on bag with much less care than usual. Together, they rolled the luggage out into the hallway. Then Belle gave her a quick but tight hug as Tess blinked away tears.

"Love you," Tess whispered again. "Are you sure you don't want me to come with you, at least to the ferry?"

"I'm good." Belle gave her another near-painful squeeze. "Love you too, babe."

Then the door was closing behind Tess's best friend, leaving her alone in the rumpled, half-empty hotel room. Other than the air conditioner's steady roar, there was no sound. Other than the flick of her hair, stray strands sent aloft by the blast of chilled air, there was no movement. Other than her thoughts, there was no company.

Before this trip, she and Belle hadn't seen each other for months. Not since last New Year's Eve, if she remembered correctly. And unless one of them visited the other over the winter holidays this year too, they might have to wait until next summer to meet again.

Still, her ostensible best friend had discarded another week together. Without discussing it beforehand. Without even telling Tess *why*.

Tess had fucked up somehow. If she hadn't, Belle would have explained the situation before leaving, or Tess would have known it already. If she hadn't, Belle would have stayed another week, instead of fleeing the island.

For all of Belle's denials, maybe she'd resented Tess's decision to work over the vacation. Maybe, despite her initial support of a fling with Lucas, she hadn't expected Tess to spend quite so much of her non-planning time with someone else. Maybe she'd been lonely, too lonely to handle staying in the same place any longer.

Or maybe the two of them had been growing apart since the move to Boston, and Tess hadn't noticed. Just as she hadn't noticed when Jeremy stopped loving h—

She swallowed back a raw sound, her cheeks wet and cold.

No. Belle was honest and direct, always. If she said her departure had nothing to do with Tess, she meant it.

Tess had to believe that. She *would* believe that.

With her thumbnail, she traced the stitching on the edge of the duvet. She breathed steadily, again and again, until her chest stopped hitching.

Her best friend had already left. In another week, Lucas would be gone from her daily life too. She'd spend virtually all her days and nights focused on work, without interruption. This year. Next year. Maybe all the years to come.

Somehow, the prospect sounded a lot less appealing than it had only a week ago.

TWENTY-TWO

OVER A LATE DINNER THAT NIGHT, TESS TRIED HER best to stay cheery. She asked Lucas about his day. Laughed at the shenanigans of the kids in his children's lesson. Rolled her eyes at his shameless flirtation and innuendo. Told her own stories about how she'd spent the afternoon.

As he played with her fingers from across the diner booth, she forced a grin. "So then I tried to mount the float *again*, and it flipped over on me *again*, and an elderly woman nearby looked at me with pity and offered to get me water wings."

His head tilted in silent inquiry.

"You know, those inflatable armbands? I thought they were just for toddlers, but evidently not."

He snickered at that.

Ducking her head, she watched the tendons in the back of his hand shift with every stroke of his thumb across her knuckles, every brush of their fingertips.

He lifted her hand, cupping it against the nascent bristles of his cheek and nuzzling into her palm. Then he simply looked at her for a moment.

"You seem tired tonight, älskling," he finally said. "Are you ready to leave?"

She *felt* tired. Tired and old. "Sure."

After giving her hand one last squeeze, he let it go and slid out of the booth. "Let's go to my apartment."

Minutes ago, he'd settled their bill and tucked a generous tip for their server beneath the salt shaker, so there was nothing keeping them in the diner. They walked out together, his arm over her shoulders drawing her close to his side.

The humidity hit her like a sweaty-palmed slap. "Ugh."

"Just think of all the money you're saving on moisturizer." He smiled down at her. "Really, I don't know how anyone can afford *not* to live near Florida."

She wrinkled her nose. "My hotel room is closer than the clubhouse. Let's go there instead."

"Is Belle out with her, uh, friend tonight?"

She swallowed hard. "She left this morning."

His head turned her way. "Left? The room?"

"The island. Her plane should be landing in Boston any time now."

He slowed. "Weren't you two supposed to leave at the same time?"

"Yes." She tugged him back into motion. "That was the plan, but she decided to go home early."

Her voice sounded thin, but he didn't seem to notice.

He bent close and pressed a lingering kiss to her mouth. "I'm glad you didn't leave with her."

Housekeeping had apparently come and gone in her absence, because the duvets on both double beds were invitingly turned down, chocolates wrapped in gold foil resting on the pillows. Two new water bottles, their sides beaded with moisture, had appeared on the nightstands.

Her laugh emerged as a hiccup. "More chocolates and water bottles for me, I suppose."

"That's what you think." After she lowered herself onto her mattress, Lucas grabbed both bottles and handed one to her. "I'm greedy."

223

He opened the other, taking a long drink. Capping it again, he set it on the nightstand, sat down on the bed too, and settled himself against her wooden headboard.

There he remained, arms loose at his sides, eyes on her. In the lamplight, his rumpled hair was edged with gold, the well-honed muscles beneath his thin tee casting shadows across the soft cotton.

That forgiving light erased the damage from years in the sun, and he looked like what he was. An athlete, handsome and vital and...young. So young, when tonight she felt exhausted and dispirited. She might as well have bypassed middle age and hobbled directly into decrepitude. She might as well be four hundred years old.

For a minute, the disorientation of it all stole her words.

Somehow, she'd embarked on an affair with *that* man. Her. Tess Dunn. *Her*. Forty and disheveled and no-nonsense. Practical to a fault. Literally.

Then he held out his arms to her, and she crawled into them without hesitation.

"I'm not usually this tired, not even during my period," she informed his cotton-covered chest, attempting to nestle closer and closer again to his now-familiar scent and his now-familiar warmth. "This is an aberration, brought on by too many orgasms."

His chest vibrated with his amusement. "I can fumble a bit more next time, if you'd like. Pretend I can't find your clitoris. Coming after two or three strokes won't be a problem either, if I set my mind to it."

"Oh, God, not that. I take it back." Spying the gleam of familiar rose-colored fabric on the back of the open bathroom door, she pursed her lips. "Dammit. Belle left her robe. I'll have to mail it to her when I get back."

"Is she all right?" He sounded distracted, probably because he was sliding one hand down her spine, toward her ass. "You seemed surprised that she left early."

Her voice was tight. "She says she's fine."

"So she was just homesick?" His shoulder lifted in a half-shrug. "I guess that happens."

When his mouth lowered to her ear, she moved slightly away. "Not to Belle."

Her tone was sharper than she'd intended, and he was staring at her, brows slightly raised. Dammit. Yet another fuckup in a day full of them.

"At least this means we can spend more time together in the evenings." Letting out a slow breath, he gave her back-side a gentle squeeze. "I know you were worried about abandoning her."

"This isn't something to celebrate, Lucas." Her neck hurt. Tension, probably. "Not even if it means extra time alone together."

"I don't..." His hands lifted from her, and he gave her a little more space. "I guess I don't understand why you're so upset."

He looked genuinely befuddled.

So she explained everything. What she'd said, what Belle had said, how they'd left things, how she still didn't know what exactly had prompted her best friend—her *best friend*—to leave. How her guilt and worry had weighed on her so heavily that afternoon, she'd half-expected to sink directly to the bottom of the ocean each time she fell off her stupid float.

Lucas listened without interrupting until she'd finished. Then he reached for her hand, stopping only a hairsbreadth away. When she bridged the distance and intertwined their fingers, his entire body seemed to relax.

"I'm sorry." His hand tightened on hers. "I suppose I'm so used to my friends coming and going, it didn't even occur to me you'd find it upsetting."

She exhaled slowly. "On the Tour, you mean?"

He nodded. "When you lose, you leave. Even when my

friend Nick and I were in the same tournament, we knew one of us could be gone a day later. Or we might have an entire week together. Two, for the majors. There was no way to predict."

Tess swallowed hard, her eyes prickling. "Until she moved to Boston, I saw Belle every weekday. Without fail. I miss her."

He slid his thumb across the back of her hand. "No wonder you're sad she left early."

"She's my best friend." That, at least, hadn't altered with the move. "The first person I call when I have good news, and the person I cry on when things go bad. I don't even want to imagine what this past decade would have been like without her. I'd have been lost."

His head tilted in curiosity.

"When I broke up with my fiancé, I was, uh…" Her eyes dropped to the veins of his forearms, blue and readily visible. She traced them with a fingertip. "I was in rough shape for a while. I held it together during the school day, but in the evenings…"

Her finger stilled. "After school, I needed company. Distraction. Belle was there every day, supporting me until the worst of the grief was past."

"What exactly happened between you and your ex?" His voice was low. Cautious. "You told me the bare outlines during our second lesson, but I'd like to know more. If you're willing to talk about it."

She hadn't intended to tell him about Jeremy—not tonight, possibly not ever—but maybe it was for the best. Lucas should know before their lives became any more inter-twined how unfit she was to deal with an intimate relation-ship, especially one complicated by distance and age and physical limitations and…so much else.

The words spilled from her, curiously dispassionate. Flat and matter-of-fact.

"He should have broken the engagement instead of cheating on me, obviously." The nearness of Lucas suddenly overwhelmed her. She inched away, letting go of his hand and moving until she sat propped against the headboard too, close but not touching him. "He was right about some things, though. And I should have realized he was dissatisfied earlier. The fact that I didn't…"

She shook her head, carefully not looking at Lucas. All she could see, all she let herself see, were his fists resting on his legs, his tendons and muscles jutting out in sharp relief.

"It was just a symptom of a larger issue." The hem of her shorts frayed under her plucking fingers. "I'm good with practicalities. If you need to call for a plumber or make sure paperwork gets to the right place or pay a bill on time, I'm your woman. When it comes to emotions, though, I'm not especially skilled. At least, not when it really matters."

Lucas cleared his throat in a sort of weird rumble, but he didn't interrupt. When he took another swig of the water, the plastic crackled loudly in his grip.

In a defensive rush, she swung on him. "To be fair, though, I *had* to focus on all those practicalities, because if I didn't do it, he certainly wouldn't. He was always busy researching or writing an article or planning his classes or meeting with grad students or—" Her laugh was sharp and bitter, and it hurt her ears. "Or doing something else with grad students, I suppose."

She'd caught him once. But in retrospect, she knew he hadn't strayed once, or even with one graduate student. So many things suddenly made sense, once fitted into the proper context. The way those young female doctoral candidates couldn't quite meet her eyes at his end-of-semester dinner parties, held at the home she shared with him. The quiet phone conversations he sometimes had in his home office, quickly ended when she appeared in the doorway. The way he always stayed a night or two extra at out-of-town conferences.

All the while, she'd cooked for those parties. Hired the cleaning service that dusted his home office. Made his hotel reservations for those conferences.

"I don't think he ever scheduled a single doctor's appointment. I don't think he ever bought a single pair of his own underwear, not once during the entire time we were together." Her cheeks burned, but not with shame anymore. With sudden rage. "I had a full-time job too, you know. I taught too. I planned classes too, and I didn't have a goddamn TA to do my grading for me. But somehow, the fact that his work was more important than mine became a given, and I don't understand how it happened."

Her fingernails were biting into her palms hard enough to sting. "I don't understand how I became his mother, instead of his fiancée and lover and confidante, but I did. And at least part of that is on me. It has to be."

"Do you feel like my mother?"

Lucas's voice was low. Tight with some emotion she couldn't identify, because of course she couldn't.

She didn't even have to think about her answer. "Absolutely not."

Not just because she wanted his tongue, his fingers, his cock inside her, but because—and the irony would choke her if she wasn't careful—faux-playboy, easy-come-easy-go Lucas seemed to have his shit together in a way her middle-aged fiancé hadn't.

Since their first meeting, Lucas hadn't asked her to do a single thing for him. Not one.

Instead, he'd supplied the food for the picnic, located fluffy booties for her cramping belly, and offered her sweet-tart desserts and chocolates shaped like mountains. He woke up early and arrived to his lessons on time, and he arrived to their dates on time too.

He'd...wooed her. Like an adult, not a boy in a man's body.

His fists on his taut thighs still hadn't unclenched. "Just so you know, I make my own appointments. I buy my own underwear. I pay my own bills. If I make a mess, I clean it up."

She thought she recognized that emotion in his voice now.

"Are you..." God, was she really having to ask this twice in one day? "Are you angry at me?"

"Fuck, no." The words were loud. Immediate. "Shit, Tess, how could you even think that?"

"I told you." The wry smile hurt her cheeks, but she offered it anyway. "I'm not great at emotions sometimes."

Suddenly he was in front of her, straddling her legs. Cupping her face, his thumbs passing in gentle sweeps over her cheeks. Pressing a sweet, light kiss on her trembling lips.

"That's bullshit, älskling," he told her, his tone so tender it took her a few seconds to realize what he'd actually said. "Total fucking bullshit, and you should know better."

When her mouth dropped open, he took advantage.

After a pleasant interlude, he pulled back an inch. "I don't know what happened in your relationship with *Jeremy*"—the word sounded like an epithet—"because I wasn't there. You were." Another sweet, searching kiss. "I can tell you one thing for certain, though: You may be a master of practicalities, but you also have an enormous heart."

"You don't know that." She wanted to believe him. She did. But how could she? "You can't know that, not after a week."

"All right, then. Let me prove it to you." His lips nuzzled against her earlobe. "All your plans for the school. Are they practical? Is that why you're working so hard on them?"

Concentrating on something other than the tease of his breath in her ear was nearly impossible, but she tried.

229

Hungry students. Race-based disciplinary discrimination. Bullying. All the other problems she wanted to address.

Practicality would mean focusing on standardized test scores instead. Would steer her toward saving the school's limited resources, rather than spending more money on the children in their care. Would take her far afield from the initiatives she'd formulated with such enthusiasm, especially given the number of school board members notably unwilling to talk about race and racism.

Belle had already pointed out how much time and effort those initiatives would require. She'd cautioned that Tess might need to scale back her plans to suit a reality in which sleep was still a necessity and not everyone would agree with her priorities.

Tess was committed to them anyway.

So she had to concede the point, if only begrudgingly. "No. They're not especially practical. I figure some of my ideas will meet with significant resistance. Or I'll be told we don't have enough money or people to make them work."

"But something drove you to come up with those plans." He didn't even sound smug, damn him. "If not practicality, then what?"

Swallowing over a dry throat, she told him the truth. "I care about those kids, and I want their lives to be better. I want our school to be better."

Funny. She'd been so caught up in the logistics of everything, she hadn't stopped to consider why she'd chosen to pursue those particular goals. She hadn't allowed herself to acknowledge the raw emotions driving her onward.

Hope. Outrage. Passion.

None of them practical. All of them essential in a good principal.

"You love those kids, Tess. With everything you have." He tucked strands of hair behind her ears and cradled her face in his hands. "And I know you feel like you fucked up with

Belle. But this is what I heard." His eyes on hers were steady. Determined. "You came into the room. You got worried. You asked if she was okay, and she lied. You asked what had happened, and she wouldn't answer. Then you tried to get her to open up by talking about practicalities, because she wasn't ready to discuss how she was feeling or why. And once she'd relaxed a bit, you swung back around to check whether she was angry at you or victimized or hurting in some other way you could fix. She wasn't."

Put so plainly, it didn't sound like such a failure of friendship, such a condemnation of her and her ability to read people and deal with their emotions.

Maybe his reading of the situation was generous, but it wasn't inaccurate.

She took a deep breath, another, for the first time in what felt like hours.

His thumb brushed away a stray, stupid tear. "Tess, maybe she wasn't ready to talk about what happened. That doesn't mean you did anything wrong." He ducked his head close, so close he comprised everything she could see. "Tonight, she said she'd talk to you, and she'll probably tell you everything. But if she doesn't, she may simply need more time."

Tess would hate that. *Hate* it. Lucas was right, though. If Belle needed time to work through whatever she was feeling, she should get it, and Tess needed to prepare herself for that possibility.

"Even if you did screw up with her, it'll be okay. If not now, then eventually." Leaning forward, he nudged her nose with his own, a playful caress. "I mean, look at us. Remember our second lesson?"

Somehow, that memory had already mellowed, had already become more amusing than bitter. "The lesson where we shouted at one another in public and sublimated our unacknowledged sexual tension through harder-than-necessary serves and the ogling thereof?"

231

He grinned. "That's the one."

"Isn't that how all functional adults deal with their issues?"

At her dry response, he huffed out a short laugh. "Let's pretend that's true." He sobered. "My point is, we screwed up. Both of us. We hurt each other, because we're only human."

"Your ego is superhuman. At least when it comes to your penis."

He ignored her snark. "Then we got over it. You and Belle will get over this hiccup too."

She bit her lip. "I hope so."

"I'm sure Belle doesn't expect you to be perfect. I certainly don't. You shouldn't expect it of yourself either." His dimples reappeared. "God knows you shouldn't expect *me* to be perfect, despite my current boyfriend ranking."

She raised a single eyebrow, purely for his entertainment. "Trust me. I don't."

"So try not to worry about your friendship with Belle, okay?" His face compressed into a sudden scowl. "And forget what *Jeremy* told you."

Again, he'd spat out her ex's name, for reasons she couldn't completely parse. Maybe his anger was on her behalf. Maybe it was born from jealousy, or in frustration at how her past complicated their present. Maybe all of the above.

"There's nothing wrong with being a practical person, and there's nothing wrong with how you handle emotions." His statement did not invite argument. "You've already—"

He broke off, and it was her turn to wait. To stroke his bristled cheek and ease him through whatever he needed to say.

"The things I've talked about with you, I don't..." His jaw worked as he found the words. "I don't talk to anyone else like that. It's helped me. More than you know. *You've* helped me."

"If so, I'm glad." Lightly, she kissed the furrows on his forehead.

"Not *if so*, you stubborn woman—"

Then they were mock-wrestling on the bed, his every movement careful of her joints despite his growls and declarations of imminent mayhem. He tickled her until she wheezed with laughter, and then he kissed her, and then they were flinging clothes to the floor, grateful to trade hard words for easy pleasure.

Afterward, she felt better. Lighter and looser, and not just because of the orgasms.

But as they lay clasped together on the rumpled sheets of her hotel bed, she wondered whether he'd defend her quite so vigorously, quite so sincerely, if he knew her better. If he knew her longer. If he knew her in her daily life, rather than on vacation.

Maybe he'd—they'd—want to take whatever lay between them and extend it past the next week. Maybe they wouldn't.

But if he did, if they did—

What then?

What would he think of her then?

TWENTY-THREE

"BELLE WAS FINALLY WILLING TO TALK ABOUT IT this morning." Tess absently gathered a handful of sand and let it sift through her fist in the water, her other hand resting on Lucas's raised knee. "She said I could tell you what happened too, since you weren't likely to spread the story to anyone important. Also, she said you'd be worried because *I* was worried."

True. Undeniably true.

He was impressed, frankly. Despite his limited interactions with her, Belle evidently understood how he felt about Tess better than Tess herself seemed to. He was working on that, of course, but time was slipping away just as fast and just as inevitably as the sand between Tess's fingers.

Four days. In four days, she was taking the ferry to the mainland, and he had no idea when she'd return, if ever.

He wouldn't think about that now, though. Not when she was sitting beside him on their secluded sandbar, no one else in sight, water rushing around her torso and deliciously round arms in gentle surges. The sun was nearing the horizon, and the sky had unfurled banners of pink and gold, bathing her profile in warmth.

"So what's the story, then?" With his forefinger, he traced shapes on her thigh underwater. A heart. A star. A crescent moon. A second heart, one with his invisible initials inside. A sun, its unseen rays as warm as the sweet curve of her cheek. "Why did she leave?"

He turned slightly toward Tess, admiring her one-piece swimsuit for the thousandth time in the past half-hour. The swoop of its neckline dipped low, exposing the deep shadow of her cleavage. The green of the suit, bright as the grass at Wimbledon, flattered her pale skin, turning it creamier than ever. And with the water's eddies, the little skirt on the suit was floating up and away from her thighs.

Since her period had ended—hers were blessedly short, only three days—he'd kissed every soft, dimpled inch of those thighs, then licked his way between them and lingered there as long as she'd let him, first with his tongue and then with his cock. Each time got better and better.

Even when they fucked, they made love. He hoped she understood that as well as he did.

Her spectacular chest rose and fell on a sigh. "Remember how she hooked up with some guy named Brian while she was here?"

Shit. Another dude letting down the home team. "What did he do?"

"They slept together a few times." Her shoulder hitched upward. "Apparently that went fine."

Lucas couldn't help a brief wince.

When she saw it, she laughed weakly. "Yeah, *fine* isn't how I'd want my performance in bed described either. It's the adjective she chose, though. She rated him a seven for technical merit, but only a three for artistry. Apparently, he also tended to skip several required elements."

Required elements? He didn't want to know what those were.

Well, he kind of did, but he wouldn't ask. "She's a fan of old-school figure skating?"

"Newer-school too. If it were up to her, Tessa Virtue and Scott Moir would have nixed all the jumps and just frenched each other during their entire performances." Her eyes grew distant for a moment. "To be fair, that one lift where it looked like he was going down on her? Hot as fuck."

Apparently he'd missed key advances in professional figure skating. "How is that even poss—"

"And I can't count how many times we've watched *The Cutting Edge* together. Almost as many times as she's made me watch that *Gods of the Gates* Aeneas-Lavinia fan supercut on YouTube. I think she considers the guy who plays Aeneas a literal demigod." Her nose wrinkled. "I keep forgetting his name. It's Marcus...something-something."

He snorted. "Very specific."

"Remind me to look it up later." She patted his leg. "Belle would kill me if she knew I'd forgotten again."

Her eyes weren't quite meeting his, and if the sheer force of her grip could turn that fistful of sand into glass, she'd already have cut herself on it.

Enough.

Leaning over, he pressed a kiss to her temple. "Älskling, it's fine if you don't want to tell me what happened with Belle. Really."

"I do." At his skeptical glance, she raised that supercilious brow. "Don't contradict me, Karlsson. It's the truth."

"Then why are you talking about everything *but* that?"

She let out a slow breath and watched him trace a clover right above her knee. "After their last *fine* night together, Brian got a call." Her lips thinned. "From his girlfriend."

Oh, shit. No wonder Belle hadn't wanted to talk about it.

"Tess, I mean it. You don't have to tell—"

"Once Belle understood what was happening, she told him she never wanted to hear from him again." Tess's eyes

236

had narrowed into slits, her rage visible in the stony set of her jaw. "He said girls like her couldn't be picky, and she was lucky he'd been willing to fuck her in the first place."

Girls like her. Lucas could only assume that was a reference to Belle's size.

His chin dropped to his chest, and he stopped drawing on Tess's leg. Instead, he spread his fingers and squeezed gently, a mute acknowledgment of Belle's pain. Tess's too.

"She got dressed, told him to go fuck himself with his Shake Weight, and left." A flicker of a bitter smile tipped her lips. "He's lucky he escaped with his testicles intact. Belle doesn't put up with shit like that anymore."

Even that hint of amusement faded. "She cried so hard, she threw up once she got back to our room." The trident between her brows carved deeper than he'd ever seen it. "So she was hurt, and she was angry, and she wanted a few solitary days to get over what happened. She said she wanted to think about her future too. She moved to Boston for her boyfriend two years ago, but they broke up last month. Now she doesn't know if she wants to stay there."

Tess fell silent.

"That's why she changed her plane reservations," Lucas finally said. "That's why she left."

Tess nodded. "That's why."

With his free hand, he pinched the bridge of his nose. "Shit. Shit, Tess. I'm so sorry that happened to her. What a dick."

"I know. I feel terrible for her." Tess's voice was raw. "I feel lucky, too. No one's ever said anything like that to me. And however our relationship plays out, I know you would never hurt me that way. You're a better man than Brian could ever hope to be, Lucas. Thank you for that."

"No." He turned to her with a jerk, scowling. "Don't do that. Don't thank me for not being an asshole. I don't deserve credit for meeting the lowest possible standards of human decency."

She inhaled sharply. "Okay. I won't."

"Good."

After another moment, she leaned in close and murmured in his ear. "So tell me, then. What *should* I give you credit for?"

Her hand on his knee edged higher, then higher still. Her palm ghosted over his rapidly hardening cock, and he bit off a groan.

"Should I give you credit for how wet I get every time you make that noise?" Her teeth closed on his earlobe with careful pressure, eliciting a helpless shudder. "How you backed me against the wall of your apartment and made me come riding your leg?"

The blood drained from his brain so fast, he had to fight against a full-on swoon. He held his breath as her hand hovered over his eager dick again.

Then she drew back.

"Shit." Her shoulders slumped. "I can't do this here, Lucas. I'm sorry. I thought I could, but it's too exposed. Someone could come along at any second."

He fought the urge to say: *I was about to come along at any second too.*

"That's okay." He could only speak in a pained rasp, but he meant it. "Just…give me a minute."

She scooted away from him, and he turned to stare at her, befuddled by her withdrawal.

"I'm so sorry," she repeated, her face drawn. "I shouldn't have started something I couldn't finish."

The distress in her voice, in her expression, was disproportionate to the situation, and he didn't understand.

"Tess, I don't expect an orgasm every time I get an erection." After taking a deep breath, he managed to wink at her.

"Given how I respond to you, that would mean servicing me hourly. Maybe twice-hourly."

"Mr. Perky." She shook her head, the lines bracketing her mouth fading a bit. "Indefatigable and ever-optimistic."

"I understand why you don't feel comfortable doing anything so...intimate outdoors." Circling his arm around her back, he maneuvered them both until they were pressed hip to hip once again. "Would I have enjoyed a handjob from you here? Of course. Do I want to make love to you on the sand? Obv—"

"Just to be clear," she interrupted. "Even if we owned our own personal island and you could guarantee our absolute privacy, I wouldn't have sex directly on the sand. I'd require a blanket, at the very least. Vaginal microdermabrasion isn't my idea of a good time."

He envisioned that. Cringed. "Understood."

"That said, go on." With a wave of her hand, she urged him to continue. "I'm listening."

Interlacing their fingers, he lifted her knuckles to his lips. "Someday, älskling, I want to see that pale skin in the sun, in the ocean, all of it uncovered and mine to explore. But this isn't the time or place, for reasons you explained very clearly, and I get that. Please don't worry. As long as I have you naked *somewhere*, I'm not disappointed. How could I be?"

She stared at him, hazel eyes distant in thought, for a long moment.

Then she gave a little nod. "I can make sure you're satisfied. At least in that way." It was a vow, firm and determined. "I promise."

He frowned, confused by her vehemence. "Okay?"

She nodded, leaned over, and kissed him on the mouth, hard. Once. Twice.

"Okay," she said.

As usual, Tess waited for Lucas outside the courts, watching from a wooden bench as he finished his last lesson of the day. In theory, he had another one scheduled that evening, but his client wouldn't mind skipping it.

Tess Dunn, Room 1249, much preferred orgasms over advice about her service motion.

No, they didn't bother playing tennis anymore, despite his inflated hourly rate and no-refunds policy. Not with so little time left. Her prepaid lessons had simply become more minutes they could spend together—in his apartment, in a restaurant, in the water—before her looming departure.

They woke in the same bed. They worked identical hours, him on the tennis court, her either on a beach or in bed with her trusty tablet. They took simultaneous breaks for lunch in his apartment. They spent every evening entwined, up until the inevitable moment she shoved him aside to get some non-sweaty sleep.

Three days, he involuntarily thought. *In three days, she gets on that ferry.*

When his clients had returned to the clubhouse, he gathered his gear, hustled to Tess's bench, and bent down to give her a light kiss, cognizant of how drenched his clothing was after another steamy day spent in the summer sun.

"Want to keep me company in the shower before dinner?" He grinned at her. "It may be a clown car, but at least we have enough room to honk each other's red noses."

Her own nose, slightly pink, wrinkled. "Are you referring to my clitoris as a red nose? And saying you'll *honk* it? Because I think my vagina just went completely dry."

"Cut me some slack." Helping her up from the bench, he steered them toward his apartment. "Sexualizing clowns is hard, especially in my non-native language."

"Wait, Lucas." She tugged him to a halt on the sidewalk. "You don't need a shower."

The breeze plastered a strand of her dark hair across her

cheek, and he tucked it gently behind her ear. "Is this about the red nose thing? Because I promise not to honk your clitoris."

"No, it's not about your weird clown shit." She rolled her eyes. "We're going to the beach. You can rinse off in the water, so you don't need a shower." Her head tilted toward the clubhouse. "Just drop off your stuff upstairs. I'll meet you back out here."

Normally, they talked through their options and decided their evening plans together, but if she particularly wanted to visit the beach that night, no problem. Obligingly, he left her by the clubhouse and let himself into his apartment, depositing his gear just inside the door before locking it behind him again and returning to her side.

She took his hand and led him past the family beaches, past the adults-only sandbar they both loved, past the gardens and the rocks and the overlook, to the most distant beach of all.

The nude beach.

At the very end of the sidewalk, a discreetly labeled, sandy path led toward shore. Before the beach and water came into view, though, they had to pass single-file through a narrow gap in a veritable wall of shielding shrubs.

Then the vista appeared before them, all azure waves and palms swaying over the white-gold expanse of shore. The pristine arc of sand was entirely guarded by that wall of shrubbery. And in the early evening, just before sunset, the beach was oddly deserted, empty of everything but a few scattered loungers and a bird or two darting across the sand, hunting diligently for dropped food.

As well as, unexpectedly, a white canvas tent the size of a small room. And a very familiar person in resort uniform standing just outside the tent's entry flap.

Brendan was bent over his phone, texting someone. At their approach, though, he looked up and turned immediately to Tess. "Everything's set up the way you wanted, Ms. Dunn. I double-checked, and there's no one in the vicinity. If you need anything else, let me know."

"Thank you." Tess shook his hand, and Lucas could see the edges of several bills passing from her palm to Brendan's. "You'll put out the sign?"

"What sign?" His brows beetled in feigned confusion. "I wouldn't hang the *Beach Temporarily Closed for Cleanup* sign across the path for no reason, much less block the entrance through the shrubs with a wooden construction barrier. A kid playing a prank must have done that."

With a final salute to Tess and an amiable, congratulatory punch to Lucas's arm, he ambled back toward the sidewalk and out of sight. His jaunty whistling grew more and more distant, until the rush of the breeze on the water drowned it out entirely.

They waited a few more moments, but no voices drifted through the shrubbery. No shrieks of laughter, shouts to friends, or even distant music interrupted the sounds of a beach at sunset.

Tess turned to him. "I remembered Brendan's name from that first lesson, so I tracked him down this morning. I wasn't sure he could arrange things the way I wanted, but he said he could." With her toe, she traced a line in the sand, then erased it with the sole of her foot. "Apparently he was right."

"Tess…" He wanted to tug her close, squeeze her breathless, but he was so damn sweaty, and his woman didn't like mess. "You didn't have to do this."

She ignored that, instead gesturing for him to precede her into the tent. His throat thick, he obeyed.

After depositing her sandals inside the entrance, she surveyed the setup by his side. "It's not fancy. But it's the best I could do, especially on such short notice." Her lips curved into a brief, wry smile. "And on such a limited budget."

How she'd arranged all this so quickly, he had no clue. None.

A wide, two-person wooden lounger had been set up in one corner, its blue cushions covered with a canary-yellow blanket. Within arm's reach, a little plastic table boasted an ice-filled bucket teeming with water bottles and—

How the hell had she located that sparkling pear cider? Sure, he'd mentioned it once or twice in passing as his favorite Swedish beverage, but American grocery stores didn't stock non-alcoholic drinks from Sweden, and neither did the convenience mart in the hotel. He knew that for a fact.

Her tablet rested on the table beside the bucket. Was she planning to work?

She followed his gaze. "It's fully charged, and I down-loaded a couple of tennis matches from earlier today. Your friend Nick was playing, and so was that woman from Sweden. Or if you don't feel like watching tennis, I have a few of Jane Austen's audiobooks on my phone now, so we could listen to them instead."

Foolish woman. As if he wanted to see or hear anything but her tonight.

"I hope you like the food." She nodded toward the insulated bags atop the larger table, just inside the entrance. "I had to microwave everything that was supposed to be hot, since I didn't have access to an oven." Her shoulder lifted in a small, nervous shrug. "But it's all from IKEA, so hopefully it'll remind you of home."

Of course. Of course.

That was where she'd gotten the cider. That was where she'd probably bought—

"There are meatballs, of course. Lingonberry jam. Gravy.

Rosti potato patties. And I got a gooey chocolate cake for dessert."

"Kladdkaka," he said, his voice rusty. "I haven't had that since my last visit home. It's my mom's favorite."

"I packed plates and silverware and napkins. A battery-operated lamp too, so don't worry about eating before dark." She was speaking quickly, her words rushed and higher-pitched than normal. "The food should be fine for a little while longer. I thought you"—she faltered—"uh, *we* might want to get in the water now, while…"

Her throat bobbed as she swallowed hard. "While it's still light outside."

Because he'd said he wanted to see her naked in the sun. In the ocean. Even though she had so many reasons, completely legitimate reasons, to avoid exposing herself that way.

He closed his eyes for a moment. Got hold of himself.

"I didn't expect this from you, älskling." Despite his sweaty clothing, he reached out and folded her into his arms. "I didn't—I *don't*—want you to make yourself uncomfortable for my sake."

"I needed to do something special for you." Her voice was muffled by his shoulder, her hands almost painfully tight on his back. "You don't ask for anything, and you've given me so much—"

He flinched at the bolt of pain. "This is repayment, then? An attempt to balance our accounts before you leave?"

"*No.*" She leaned back to meet his eyes. "This is me, trying to make you as happy as you've made me, because I…" Her jaw worked. "Because I care about you."

His heart unclenched.

Sweet. She was so sweet. *This* was so sweet.

Bending down, he rested his forehead against hers. "Tess, you're enough for me. No grand gestures required."

Her hazel eyes flickered with hurt. "You don't like what I did?"

"Don't like it?" He couldn't help but laugh. "This is amazing. Thoughtful. Humbling. Thank you for all of it." His legs brushed against hers as he edged even closer. "I love it. I love—"

No, he wasn't going to blurt that out on impulse. Before he said it, he needed to examine his own heart and prepare himself for resistance, because he already knew she wouldn't believe him. Wouldn't trust the words, even if she trusted him.

He chose different words, ones she could accept more easily. "I love how much you wanted to make me happy. Even though I don't need meatballs or a tent or you naked in the sun for that. I just need you. Full stop."

Her eyelashes fluttered down, and she bit her lower lip.

"What if I want to be naked in the sun too?" It was a whisper, shyer than any he'd heard from her. "I told you that. Remember?"

He did. The images inspired by that conversation had been looping endlessly in his brain for over a week now.

"But your work..." His thoughts were muddled now. By lust. By hope. "If you regretted this, if you suffered for anything we did together, it would gut me. We can trust Brendan, but there's always a chance someone could ignore the sign and go around the barrier."

She took a deep, shuddering breath. Then she straightened her shoulders, opened her eyes, and met his.

All telltale hints of shyness banished, she cast him a chiding look. "This isn't an impulse or moment of folly, Lucas. I considered the potential problems, and I took steps to control as many variables as I could." Gently, she detached herself from his embrace. "The remaining risk, I'm willing to accept. So I can have what I want. What we both want."

With steady, careful hands, she removed his soaked tee,

his shoes and socks, his loose shorts, his boxer-briefs, until he was bare. Entirely, willingly exposed to her.

Then she reached for the hem of her sundress and tugged it over her head as he gaped at her. She stripped off the swimsuit beneath and tossed both items onto the blanketed lounger.

Chin tipped high, her round body framed by the tent's open flap, she stood there naked.

Espresso hair dancing in the fitful breeze, defiant hazel eyes, lips bitten to lush pinkness, tan nipples crowning pale breasts, a dark brown triangle between ivory thighs. Behind her, the blue, blue ocean rushed to shore, green palm fronds rustled, and the setting sun bathed the sand, her skin, with rosy warmth.

Colors. He didn't remember colors ever being this vivid. So bright they stung his eyes.

She turned on her heel and left the tent. Left shelter in exchange for the open beach, bare feet sinking into the sand. Her dimpled, adorable ass jiggled as she strode toward the water without hesitation, without any attempt to shield herself from his stare or the unforgiving gaze of unseen strangers.

He couldn't move. Couldn't breathe in the presence of such beauty.

She glanced at him over her shoulder, one supercilious eyebrow cocked high. "Coming, Lucas?"

Stripped naked, he followed.

Of course he did.

TWENTY-FOUR

IN THE END, THEY DIDN'T HAVE SEX ON A BLANKET outdoors.

Not so much because Tess was worried about random lookie-loos with cell phones—although she was, if only a little bit, and she'd privately wondered whether she'd be able to relax enough to climax under those circumstances—but because Lucas was worried about her joints.

When she offered, he shook his head. "You need more cushioning and support than that. I won't have you in pain when we leave here."

"You wanted to see me naked in the sun," she protested as he led her out of the ocean and back toward the tent.

"And I have." His grin turned wicked, and his dimples popped. "I saw you naked in the water too."

Oh, she knew where this conversation was going.

A more decorous woman would blush, but she'd left decorum behind about fifteen minutes ago—around the same time Lucas had used the water's buoyancy to hitch her upwards, guiding her until her legs wrapped around his waist and her arms wrapped around his neck. Then he'd taken her mouth in a hard, hot kiss before biting at her neck, palming her ass, and moving her exactly the way he wanted.

In the water, the rock of his hips was so fluid, so easy, as he rubbed his cock precisely where she needed friction. He'd teased her for so long, never quite giving her the speed and firm pressure she needed. Not until she was begging for it, trembling and gasping.

The sun on her face, the lap of water over her flesh, the caressing breeze had all sharpened the sensations. They'd all made the experience glorious and unbearable in equal measures.

In the aftermath of pleasure, her legs were watery and trembling. She was relying on Lucas's arm around her shoulders for support as they walked in the sand.

When they neared the tent's entrance, he ran a possessive hand over her butt. "Best of all, I saw you naked in the sun and water as you came apart, and it was the most gorgeous fucking thing I've ever laid eyes on."

Yup. She'd known he'd end up bragging about her orgasm eventually.

He was so damn smug, radiating intense satisfaction from every pore despite his still-hard dick. She should find that annoying. Would find that annoying, if only her legs weren't still shaking beneath her from the violence of that orgasm.

He'd earned his smugness, and she wouldn't puncture it.

That said, he didn't know what the hell he was talking about. He didn't understand *gorgeous*. He couldn't, unless he located a mirror and saw himself right here, right now.

In the falling light of dusk, he was beautiful enough to break her.

With every step, the thrust of his rampant cock preceded him. The growing shadows only emphasized the bulge of his bicep, the taut swell of his ass, the rhythmic bunch and release of his thigh muscles as they walked.

He slicked his hand down her arm, and the controlled grace in even such a small, meaningless movement literally took her breath away.

He ran a distracted hand through his wet thicket of hair, and it fell into place like magic.

He smiled, and those heavy-lidded olive-green eyes went lambent, his dimples appeared, and she turned liquid enough to pour onto the sand below.

His face was handsome, of course. It was always handsome.

With her, it was also soft.

Muscles alone wouldn't shatter her, but that stubborn, intent, beautiful softness could.

And it did, as he spread her out on that blanket-covered lounger, rolled on one of the condoms she'd packed, knelt between her legs, and made love to her. God help her, *made love*, because there was no way she could call it fucking, and only a fool would term it casual sex. There was nothing casual about it.

He stroked her thighs with his hands and traced her collarbone with his tongue as he moved inside her. He moaned her name. He nuzzled into her shoulder and whispered to her about how much he loved her body, her eyes, the way she held him tight inside and out.

His hands on her breasts were reverent, his eyes on her face gentle. He was attentive to every sign of pleasure and eager to give more. It was all slow and deliberate and tender, the near-violence of their desire secondary to the unspoken emotions between them.

She'd never, ever wept during sex before. But when she came again with a long, low cry, her voice shook from more than just intense pleasure. His face buried in her neck, his gentle fingers still caressing her clit, he came too. His hips jerked, and his groan vibrated against her still-wet skin.

Afterward, eyes dry once more, she produced the bottle of edelweiss-scented oil she'd found at that odd Alpine spa and put the massage lesson she'd taken that morning to good use.

After the group class, she'd asked the instructor about wrists. Specifically, the best ways to relieve pain in that area without causing further damage. Still, before she started, she made Lucas promise to tell her if she was hurting him.

She must not have done too badly, because he didn't say a word. Instead, he simply sat beside her quietly as she rubbed and rotated his wrist and gave him the sort of attention, the sort of care, he needed.

All the while, he looked at her steadily, his face set in solemn lines.

Since it wasn't an expression she'd ever seen directed her way before, she didn't know how to interpret it. So she avoided his eyes and focused on his battered joints and made certain she was giving him absolutely everything she could in this moment.

Because in less than seventy-two hours, once she returned to her daily life, her daily routine, she was pretty sure whatever she had to give him wouldn't be enough. Not for a man who deserved the world. Not for a man who deserved a woman who could *hand* him that world.

The right partner for Lucas would do so without hesitation. Without a job that sometimes took all her available energy.

Without half a lifetime of baggage, of intimate failure, tripping her in the attempt.

She rubbed his wrist and tried to forget the future and made love to him again in the gathering darkness of the tent. And this time, he couldn't see her cry.

At some point in every competitive, high-quality rally, the moment of decision arrived.

If sloppy, unforced errors didn't end the point prematurely, both players generally focused on keeping their shots within the court and biding their time. Waiting for their opponent's shot to fall short. Waiting for that opponent to move out of position. Waiting for a small mistake.

Sometimes, though, a mistake never came. If so, a decision had to be made.

One way or another, the rally would end. The only question was who would force the issue. Who would be the aggressor. Who would take the risk.

Lucas hadn't minded that risk, that responsibility.

In fact, his career had thrived on it.

Sometimes he'd choose a drop shot, one landing as close to the net as possible. If the other player didn't get to the ball in time, the point was over. If the other player *did* get to the ball in time, if he used his new position by the net to angle his next shot far away from Lucas—too far away—the point was still over.

Other times, Lucas would aim down the line and whack a backhand hard enough to shake the fuzz loose from the ball, the shot so fast the man across the net couldn't get a racket on it. If Lucas judged the depth and trajectory of his shot correctly, the point was over, in his favor.

If he didn't, and the ball landed outside the line: Again, the point was still over.

Lucas warmed up on the practice court near the clubhouse, waited for his first client, and thought about Tess, still asleep in his bed after a night when he'd woken her again and again, desperate and hungry and afraid. For the millionth time, he counted the hours until her departure, which—as of that morning—had crept below forty-eight. He considered his future. Hers too.

The inexorable tug in his gut felt familiar. Welcome, in a stomach-churning sort of way.

The moment had arrived.

He was taking the risk.

He was ending this point, one way or another.

TWENTY-FIVE

THAT EVENING, LUCAS WAS...OFF. DISTRACTED. Fidgety in an unfamiliar way.

Maybe he'd simply had a long day, although *all* his days seemed to be long days. Maybe his wrist was sore, although he denied it when Tess asked. Maybe he was tense because this was their next-to-last night together.

Or maybe he'd already decided to let her go and was struggling to tell her. He wouldn't want to hurt her unnecessarily. She knew that for certain, if she knew nothing else.

For once, he didn't cajole her into the shower with him after his lessons ended. Instead, he kissed her on her cheek, pointed out the cupcakes—vanilla bean, with passion fruit buttercream icing—on the counter, and excused himself.

How he'd procured them when he'd either been working or with her all day, she couldn't say, but he definitely had his ways. The cupcakes looked delicious.

Her stomach was churning too much to eat one.

During dinner, they watched his friend's tennis match from the previous day. Lucas kept his hands to himself, his eyes on the TV, and his mouth full of leftover meatballs. By the time they worked together in silence to clear the dishes, she was ready to call it.

He was over this, whatever *this* was. He was over her.

Blinking hard, she took one final sidelong look at him, a lengthy one. Admiring his looks and body, sure, but also his grace. The alert intelligence in his eyes, and the laugh lines at their corners. The scars indicating pain suffered and adversities overcome.

His dimples were nowhere in evidence, but she could pinpoint exactly where they'd appear at some point in the future, for someone who made him grin. Someone who wasn't her.

One more look, as he dried his hands on a dishtowel. Another.

Then she braced herself and got ready to make things easier on both of them. Got ready to go. "Listen, Lucas, I should probably—"

"We need to talk," he said at the same moment, still not meeting her eyes.

So he wasn't going to do this the easy way. The cowardly way. She should have known.

"It's okay." She tried to smile. "I understand. You don't need to say it."

His forehead pinched. "What do you mean, you understand?" He finally looked directly at her, moving a step closer. "What exactly do you think I want to say?"

After a hitching breath, she steadied herself enough to speak. "All night, you've looked really uncomfortable, and I get it. You don't want to hurt me, but it's fine. You haven't made me any promises, and I wouldn't hold you to them if you had."

He braced his fists on his hips, head cocked, the picture of befuddlement. Then his brow cleared, and confusion turned to exasperation. No, more than that. That was anger in the set of his jaw, pain in the way he flinched from her.

Fuck. *Fuck*.

She'd screwed up. Hurt him somehow, when she'd been trying to spare them both pain.

"You think—" He took a visible deep breath. Another. His lips silently moved, and she got the sense he might actually be counting. "Please tell me you didn't just assume I was breaking up with you."

"I…" She stared at the linoleum beneath her feet. "Yeah. I did."

Her cheeks aflame, she wrapped her arms around her middle and waited for the hammer to fall, for his rightful anger to lash at her.

This time, she could actually hear him mumbling to himself. It was almost definitely numbers, but ones she didn't recognize. Swedish numbers.

In her peripheral vision, she could see the moment his shoulders dropped. His chest deflated in a long exhalation. Then his hand appeared in her line of vision, strength compressed into tendon and bone and muscle, capable of incredible tenderness and power both.

She accepted the silent offer. Taking his hand, she let him lead her to the couch.

"Tess…" He settled them next to one another, hip to hip, as always. "I wish you would trust me."

His voice was low. Weary in a way that made her chest ache.

She laid a gentle hand on his arm. "I do. I do trust you."

And she did, more than she'd trusted any man in years and years. She trusted that he cared about her. That he wished her happiness. That he would tell her the truth. That he'd found her sexy and interesting in this brief span of time, here on the island.

She just didn't trust that they had a future off the island.

His lips compressed, but he didn't argue with her, and he didn't shake off her touch. "The reason I've looked so uncomfortable is because I need to talk to you about something."

"All right." She slid her hand down until she was surrounding his with both of hers, a mute apology. But she was a grown woman, and she needed to use her words too. "I'm sorry, Lucas. I just…"

"You just what?" He didn't sound impatient or angry anymore, simply tired.

Her guilt, her anxiety over what he might actually want to say, felt like a literal, physical weight on her aching, slumped shoulders. "I just got worried. I'm leaving so soon, and I don't know what happens then."

At that, he straightened, his thigh suddenly tense and taut beside hers. "Conveniently enough, that's precisely what I want to talk about."

She turned to him, mouth firmly shut this time, and waited to hear what he had to say.

"My contract expires at the end of the year, like I told you. For a long time, I wasn't sure whether I'd renew it or not."

Was he considering another type of work? Coaching? Commentary?

If so, he'd be busier and more distant than ever, but at least he'd be taking advantage of his talents. Stretching himself and discovering what he could do without a racket in his hands.

It would hurt, of course, to have him so far out of her reach. But imagining him buried on this island forever, hiding from his past, hurt much, much more.

He paused. In this light, the circles beneath his eyes were dark as bruises, and no wonder. In lieu of restless sleep, he and Tess had made love throughout most of the previous night. She'd credited that to her own desperation, her own need for him, but maybe she hadn't been the only one worried, the only one unsure of the future.

Another deep breath, and then he continued. "I've

256

decided I won't extend the contract. Over the holidays, I'll visit my family in Sweden for a couple of weeks. Then I'll move to Marysburg."

The words were a punch to her diaphragm, stealing her breath.

She could only gape at him, gasping, unable to parse his intentions or her own emotions.

"I would get my own place at first, but we could eventually move in together." His palm was uncharacteristically damp against her own, his fingers squeezing a bit too tightly. "Either at your house or a new place we bought jointly."

She licked her lips, the buzzing in her ears rendering his voice nearly inaudible.

Then he stopped talking, and all she could hear was static and her heart thudding and thudding again. In panic, in joy, in disbelief, in anger that he was going to make her say it.

He was really, really going to make her be the one to say all of it.

"Tess—" He ducked his head to catch her eye, the movement jerky. "Say something."

Well, he'd asked, and she would.

"You don't have family in Marysburg. You don't have a job in Marysburg." She formed each word carefully, stripping them of emotion. "It's a medium-sized town comprised of a college, a living history museum, high-end outlet stores, and retirees. Maybe people play tennis there, but it's certainly not a hub for the sport."

He immediately countered, "The college has a tennis center, and a Challenger-level tournament is held there every year. When I was recovering from one of my surgeries, I actually played at that tournament."

He'd put that much thought into his decision, at least.

But not enough. Not nearly enough.

"Is the tennis center looking to hire, either now or in the next few months?" Her school-administrator tone had made

257

an appearance, fair but no-nonsense. Inexorable. "I know you have savings from your time as a pro, but would the salary they'd offer be enough for you?"

He leaned back a little, pale beneath his tan.

"I..." His throat bobbed. "I haven't had time to check. But even if they weren't hiring, didn't you tell me I could do anything I wanted? Including non-tennis-related work?"

"Of course you could. You're smart, hardworking, and a great communicator." Her hand was limp in his, shaking, but she maintained steady eye contact. "So if things didn't work out with the tennis center, what other job opportunities would you pursue?"

He waved his free arm, the gesture near-violent. "I'd have between now and December to consider that."

But he knew that was an insufficient answer. They both did.

She hadn't even cut to the frantically beating, pained heart of the matter. But he was forcing her to do it, and she wouldn't shirk the responsibility.

"Lucas, you've known me less than two weeks. For that entire time, I've been on vacation." She pressed her lips together to stop their trembling. "The person I am when I'm working, the life I live during the school year...you won't want that. You won't want me."

When he began to protest, she spoke over him. "I'm not great at nurturing intimate relationships at the best of times. I don't know whether ours can survive long-distance for half a year, and I don't know if it can survive your arrival in a town you chose solely because of me. You'd be friendless and potentially jobless."

His face sagged, and he wasn't looking at her anymore. Instead, he was gazing at the muted television as his friend served into the net, then did it again. Nick had double-faulted. In doing so, he'd lost the game, the set. Lost the match, full stop.

"My friendships don't vanish simply because we don't live in the same place." There was a thread of defiance in Lucas's voice, despite everything. "Look at you and Belle."

"Fair point." She inclined her head. "The rest of mine still stand. I appreciate your offer, more than y-you—"

Her breath hitched, and she had to cut herself off and gather her composure.

"I care about you, Lucas." She strengthened her grip on his hand. Clutched it close for what was probably the last time, because she didn't think they could come back from this conversation. "But what you're proposing isn't practical, and I don't think you really know what you want. Not right now. Not yet. I'm not even certain a casual long-distance relationship makes sense, given the situation."

As she spoke, his head lifted, and he stared at her, brow creased in concentration.

"Practical," he murmured to himself.

Then he gave a little nod, as if in sudden understanding. His mouth remained set and grim. But when his back straightened and he slid his hand from between hers, he no longer seemed lost. No longer seemed damnably *young* and unsettled and rudderless.

"Okay, Tess. Okay." His voice had turned firm again, conviction in every syllable. "I hear what you're saying. I also hear what you're *not* saying."

This conversation was shredding her. Her joints ached as if she had the flu, and her skull was pounding in rhythm with her overworked heart. But he deserved his say, and she couldn't stand to walk away, both literally and figuratively.

"Tell me," she invited.

So he did.

THE STARBURSTS OF LINES AT THE CORNERS OF

Tess's eyes had never been deeper, and she was holding herself like a woman in pain. Stillness punctuated by ginger movements, agony scored between drawn brows and sketched in brackets around her mouth.

Once he'd beaten back his instinctive defensiveness, hurt, and anger, he'd recognized that stance, that expression. After all, he'd seen it in the mirror countless times. He'd seen it from across the net when an opponent was playing through injury.

Lucas couldn't find any indication she'd physically damaged herself between dinner and now, which told him everything. Or if not everything, enough.

Despite the affectless, damnable logic of her words, he saw it now. He saw *her*.

Lucas held up one finger. "You're not saying you don't want me."

She licked her lips, a nervous gesture, and it was all the answer he needed.

A second finger. "You're not saying you don't want a future with me."

Still no argument. No denial. No leavening of the weight slumping her shoulders and dragging her gaze to the floor.

A third finger, and he held his breath for this one. "You're not saying you don't love me."

At that, her eyes flew to his, stricken and damp. But she still said nothing. Not one word. With her silence, the tightness in his chest loosened, if only slightly.

Love couldn't solve everything, but without love, there was nothing to solve.

The fourth and final finger. "And you're not saying you think you'll grow tired of me or consider me a burden during the school year. You're not saying you think you'll stop loving or wanting me if we live in the same place."

Her lips, which she'd bitten raw at some point today, opened. Closed again.

He leaned in close, holding her gaze. Refusing to let her hide. "In theory, then, all your objections, all those practical concerns—and they're valid, don't misunderstand me, and I should have prepared to address them before talking to you tonight—are about me. My needs. My happiness. My future." With a quick glance downward, he confirmed what he'd seen in his peripheral vision. Her fingers, wrung bone-white. Still, he didn't relent. "But I need you to explain something to me, älskling."

She waited wordlessly.

"When exactly did you become responsible for all those things?" He tilted his head in mock inquiry. "At what point did I stop being the expert on my own wants and needs and dreams for the future? That's condescending as hell, Tess, and I expected better from you."

At that, she flinched. "I didn't mean to discount—"

"You told me I wouldn't want the life you lead during the school year, and I wouldn't want you outside of this island." He raised his brows. "As you rightly pointed out, you met me less than two weeks ago. So how can you possibly know that? How can you possibly claim to know better than I do how I'd feel?"

Her mouth worked, her eyes shining with tears, but he made himself finish. Stopped himself from reaching for her and cutting short an argument they needed to have, however painful it was for both of them.

He spoke slowly. Clearly. "Even if I'm wrong and you're right, and I did regret the move, the decision would be mine to make and mine to regret. You're older than me, but you're not my mother, and you're not my assistant principal."

"But it *would* be mine to regret too!" She jumped to her feet, her voice near a shout. "How can you—"

Her rational façade had shattered, and it hurt to watch. Her pain nauseated him, even though he'd deliberately

261

provoked her. Deliberately swung at her protective veneer in hopes of fissuring it and getting at the truth.

Her tears spilled over then, trailing down her blotchy cheeks, and he silently handed her a tissue. "I-if you moved to Marysburg, and we were together for months, and I *lived* with you, and you decided you didn't want me—"

She sobbed, bent over at the waist from the force of her pain, the sound from her throat rough and loud and heartrending.

He wasn't done, but he also couldn't stand to watch from a distance any longer.

In two steps, he was at her side, and within a breath he was cradling her in his arms, letting her hide her face against his chest.

He spoke into her hair. "That brings us to the central issue, I think."

Her shoulders were shaking, and he rubbed her back soothingly.

"Earlier tonight, you said you trusted me. I believe you, Tess. You trust me." He kissed the crown of her head, resting his cheek there. "I don't think you trust yourself."

Her arms were wound so tightly around his waist, he could barely breathe. Or maybe that was his own emotion, his own grief and anxiety.

"All that pragmatism, älskling. All that rational doubt, covering all that fear." She made a wounded sound, thin and shaken, and his own sight blurred. "You're enough for me, Tess. You're worth a risk. But I can't convince you of that if you won't let me."

His t-shirt was wet over his chest now, as if his heart were bleeding.

"Shhhh." He stroked her hair, resting a supportive hand on her neck as she slowly calmed. "I'm done now. I'm done. Deep breaths. In through the nose, out through the mouth."

The exercise, one he'd practiced using biofeedback and deployed during fraught matches, helped both of them.

Eventually, she spoke against his chest, her voice small and choked. "That'd be easier if I could actually breathe through my nose."

Leaning to his side, he snagged another tissue and handed it to her. The loud honking sound that followed made him smile, if only for a moment.

"Did you want to say anything?" he asked. "Or are you done too?"

More honking. A long pause. "I'm done. For now."

"We both need some time to think." He pressed his lips to her temple. "Is that fair to say?"

When she raised her head from his chest, her eyes were bloodshot and swollen, her nostrils damp. But her nod was firm.

He wished the next bit weren't necessary. "So let's give ourselves a night apart and meet again tomorrow."

Her eyes grew wet again, and he knew why. They had so few hours left, too few to spend them on anything unnecessary.

But this *was* necessary, and they both understood as much.

"Okay." She was hoarse but calm again. "We'll talk tomorrow night?"

Her last night on the island. Maybe their last night together.

Minutes ago, she'd said even a casual long-distance relationship might not make sense, which terrified the fuck out of him.

"Yes. Definitely." This wasn't goodbye, he reminded himself. Not even close, if he had anything to say about it. "I'll text you tomorrow about when and where."

With her first step backward, he forced himself to let her go. To trust her, trust them, and have faith she wouldn't hide herself away until her departure. Or, worse, follow her friend's example and flee immediately.

She gathered her belongings awkwardly and tried to smile as she offered him one last hug, fierce but brief. Then she left without another word, the door clicking quietly shut behind her.

He looked up at the blank white ceiling, blinking hard.

Foolishly, he'd forgotten one key detail. While his willingness to end a point, to be aggressive and take a risk on the court, had earned him a major, it had also cost him countless other matches, ones he should have won.

Commentators had bemoaned his joints of glass, of course, but they'd also repeatedly pointed to one other flaw in his game, one more area for growth: rally tolerance. The willingness to wait until the *right* moment to strike, not just the moment his patience ran out. The ability to stay collected, keep working a point, and put himself in the best possible position for victory *before* he hit that drop shot or sent a scorching backhand down the line.

It would come with more experience, they'd said. With time.

But he'd run out of time. Just as he was running out of time now.

He had work to do before he saw Tess again, and that was fine by him.

Those commentators might have lamented his fragile joints and his lackluster rally tolerance, but they'd never criticized his capacity for hard work or his will to battle.

He still had both.

Tess had helped him see that. Helped him see *himself* again.

No, he wasn't letting her go. Not without the fight of his life.

TWENTY-SIX

For a while, Tess simply sat and stared into darkness, hugging a pillow to her chest.

The hotel room's armchair looked more comfortable than it was. The seat hardly gave an inch beneath her, and the fabric was stiff. Good for durability, no doubt, but not comfort.

Right now, she needed comfort. God, did she need it.

One way or another, she was leaving this island, leaving Lucas, in a day and a half, which was distressing enough on its own. Even worse: When she considered the future beyond that, she drew a complete, terrifying blank. At least when it came to her relationship with him.

After his jaw-dropping offer, after their subsequent argument, she had no idea what to think anymore, no idea what to believe. About him, herself, or what they both wanted and needed. What they both feared.

Or maybe that was wrong, because she did know two things: He wanted her in his life, and he hadn't feared a future with her in it. Not the way she feared a future with him.

Then again, he'd never had a long-term romantic relationship. He wasn't dragging his intimate history behind him like a set of chains, ghosts rattling unseen in the darkness.

Usually, when those ghosts clanked and moaned, she ignored them. Pretended not to hear them until they disappeared, and she could claim they didn't exist at all, or if they did, they didn't matter, didn't affect her in any meaningful way, certainly didn't circumscribe how she lived and loved.

Lucas had forced her to acknowledge them tonight.

Maybe it was time to look those wraiths in the eye, so she could understand why they'd arrived and what they demanded from her. She'd learned to live with them, even while denying their presence, but maybe—

Maybe it was time for an exorcism.

Her laptop booted up quickly, and the e-mails were easy enough to find. After she'd discovered Jeremy with that poor grad student, he'd written her message after message. Hourly at first, then daily. Then once a week, before he'd finally had to acknowledge she wasn't going to respond. She wasn't coming back.

She could have changed her settings to make those messages bounce. She could have switched her personal e-mail address to something he didn't know. At the very least, she could have left those letters unread. But even if she'd never, ever given him the satisfaction of a reply, she'd had to know.

Why, after so many years?

Why, after she'd offered him everything she had?

Why, when she'd loved him?

Why, when he'd said he loved her?

Even years later, the worst messages—the ones written after his pleading turned to rage—remained pristine in her memory, each word crystalline, their edges razor-sharp.

No man wants to fuck his mother, Tess, come on.

You're so good at arranging things, but people don't want to be arranged.

If you'd paid more attention to my feelings, and less to your schedule, I wouldn't have—

Some people aren't made for love or marriage. I suppose you can't help being that way.

At least she was warm. You won't even return an e-mail after ten years together, you cold bitch.

Some of the most cutting passages stung less now. After encountering Lucas, she no longer doubted her desirability to the right man. And she didn't know about marriage, but love had come to her easily enough. So easily it frightened her.

The rest of Jeremy's bile…well.

Somewhere along the way, she'd internalized it as fact. As objective truths offered by a man who no longer needed to spare her feelings.

But Lucas had dismissed Jeremy's accusations without even knowing their source. Not just tonight, but repeatedly. He'd staunchly defended her ability to read and respond to emotions. He'd said her pragmatism stemmed from love—or fear. Either way, he'd insisted, there was more to her than the perfect administrator, the practical helpmate.

She supposed she could see for herself.

For the first time since that shattering afternoon in a shared bedroom, she read the e-mails from before that day. Messages she and Jeremy had written to one another as they'd dated, moved in together, gotten engaged, and lived as a committed couple. After a minute of thought, she accessed the old texts too.

What she read didn't exonerate her. Not really.

It also didn't convict her.

A man in his thirties—then his forties—shouldn't have begged her to buy socks or schedule haircuts for him. He shouldn't have committed her to cooking for his students without asking first. He shouldn't have gotten angry when she needed to stay late at work and couldn't immediately proofread his article for him.

But if he insisted on doing those things, he then should have understood that she was fucking *tired*. Too tired for frequent sex or even flirtation. He should have understood that she was treading water as fast as she could, showing her love as best she could, in the only way that still felt possible for her.

Then, if all else failed, he should have either suggested couples counseling or broken their engagement before he fucked someone else in their bed.

So, yes, at some point, she really had started addressing her fiancé with the exasperated, exhausted fondness of a mother, rather than a lover. She'd focused on the minutiae of their life together, rather than the greater picture of how their interests, their hopes and passions, had diverged. She'd stopped responding enthusiastically to sexual overtures and innuendo, ignoring them whenever possible and tolerating them when necessary.

But she'd only become his makeshift mother because he'd behaved like a child.

And before all that—before they'd moved in together, before the laundry and the toothpaste purchases and the doctor's appointments, back when he'd been her lover instead of her charge—she'd asked him about his dreams. Taunted him with glimpses of the lingerie she planned to wear that night. Commiserated when none of his students finished the assigned reading, and the tenure committee was demanding yet more documentation, and his journal article didn't generate the acclaim he'd hoped.

She'd told him she believed in him, and more than that, would love him no matter what.

You are so good to me, he'd written. *When I'm with you, I feel like I can do anything, Tess. Like we can do anything as long as we're together. Thank you for loving me.*

All the accusations, all the petty quarrels of their life together, no longer made her cry.

His message of love did.

Once—so long ago—she'd loved him and he'd loved her. Once, they'd made sense as a couple. Then they hadn't.

Neither of them had acknowledged that central, heart-breaking truth. Instead of dealing with her emotions in a better way, she'd buried herself in work and practicalities. Instead of dealing with his emotions in a better way, he'd cheated on her. And instead of dealing with *that* in a better way, he'd blamed her for everything. Made her responsible for their breakup in the same way he'd made her responsible for so much else in their relationship. Told a story of their time together that contained just enough truth to be credible to both of them.

Just enough truth that she'd believed all of it. Every word.

In doing so, he'd relieved his own guilt and shame.

In doing so, he'd conjured ghosts and set them at her heels.

But the evidence didn't lie. She wasn't faultless, but she wasn't a cold, practical automaton incapable of love either. She wasn't inherently, irreparably flawed and doomed to alienate any man who dared love her.

With a swipe of her forefinger, she dismissed the texts on her cell phone. One tap later, her contacts list appeared. Another tap, and she was calling her best friend.

"Hey, babe." Belle's voice was normal again, thank goodness. Breezy and confident, instead of shaken. "What's up? Shouldn't you be boning Sparky right about now?"

Fuck, she wanted to talk to Belle about Lucas. But before she could contemplate her future, she needed to reconcile her past.

"I want to ask you something. I've asked you before, but I need to know you're being completely honest with me. No feelings spared." Tess switched on the bedside light, suddenly impatient with the darkness. "Promise me."

"Uh…okay," Belle said, sounding befuddled. "Yeah, I promise. What do you want to know?"

Before Tess could falter, she rushed into speech. "All those things Jeremy said about me, about how I wasn't good with feelings, and I was more practical than loving, and I acted like everyone's mother, are you sure that stuff wasn't true?"

There was a long pause, and she cringed.

Dammit, she shouldn't have asked again. And if she was going to ask, she shouldn't have demanded total honesty, because Belle would give it to her.

"Well…" Another pause. "Sometimes you do get kind of maternal and managerial, but only in the most loving of ways. And if I tell you to knock it off, you do. Immediately. The other stuff is complete fucking bullshit, though, as I've told you before. You should know better."

Lucas and Belle were nearly echoing one another. It was uncanny, really.

Tess exhaled. "Thank you. I—"

"Which of my friends held me every time I cried about my brother and didn't let go of my hand during the entire memorial service?"

It was less a question than an outraged demand for justice, so full of love and loyalty and remembered grief that Tess wanted to cry. Again.

"Me, although any friend—"

But Belle wasn't nearly done. "Which of my friends helped me apartment-hunt in Boston? Which of my friends cheered me up every time I got depressed by my job search there? Which of my friends immediately offered to cut short her hot affair with a twenty-something athlete so she could keep me company as I pouted about some random asshole fuckboy?"

"You weren't pouting. You were h—"

Still not done. "I've told you again and again. *Jeremy Boller*—"

Belle spat out the name like a mouthful of poison, and she sounded so much like Lucas in that moment—again!—that Tess suddenly wanted to laugh *and* cry.

"—is a gaslighting, cheating, man-child *asshole* who didn't deserve a single one of the tears you shed over him, and the fact you even have to *ask* me whether he was right about you *again* makes me want to track him down and staple his *nuts* to his stupid *chin*, assuming I could even find it under that horrible *muskrat* he had growing on his fucking *face*."

There was no holding back the laughter, not after that.

Belle's indignant screech echoed over the phone. "Don't *laugh*. That motherfucker's going to be wearing his testicles as goddamn *earrings* when I'm done with him."

When Belle got overwrought, she started swearing and emphasizing words. Lots of them. It was one of Tess's favorite things about her best friend, truth be told.

"I love you," Tess said.

There was a distinct *harrumph* before Belle responded, sounding grumpy as fuck. "I love you too. I suppose you're going to tell me I have to leave his balls intact."

"You've already heard my lecture about assault charges and jail time, so I won't repeat myself." She couldn't help another snicker. "A muskrat?"

"That was one scraggly-ass beard, babe. You could do better." Belle's voice brightened. "Come to think of it, you *did* do better. How's it going with Sparky?"

Tess told her. And by the time they ended the call, the ghosts of her failed engagement had stopped clanking. At least for now, and maybe forever.

Right. That was done.

Now she knew what to do. Now she knew what to believe.

Her most important romantic relationship to this point had cracked under the stress of daily life together, true. But she knew how to give love, and how to receive it. She knew how to be there for those she cared about—her friends, her students, her coworkers, and all the other people in her life. She might be overly practical and managerial on occasion, but she knew how to apologize when she fucked up, and she knew she definitely *would* fuck up on occasion.

Lucas would too. Because they were human, both of them, as he'd said.

Because of Jeremy, she knew not to let those fuckups snowball into something too big to recover from. So maybe those ghosts had served a purpose, after all.

Above all else: She knew she loved Lucas, even after a startlingly short amount of time together. He deserved that love more than any other man she'd ever met. If he still wanted her, if he still wanted to take a chance on her, on them, that was his choice, and she'd take that chance along with him.

If.

That was the word haunting her now. Her new ghost, come to call with a decided *clank*.

If.

TWENTY-SEVEN

For the first time since Lucas's arrival on the island, he called in sick to work. He was suffering from terrible stomach cramps, either from food poisoning or too much time in the heat.

Either way, he definitely couldn't give lessons that day, and not the next morning either. Not until Tess had boarded her departure ferry for the mainland, anyway.

The lie caught in his throat and itched beneath his skin, as did the thought of disappointed, inconvenienced clients. But a man had to have priorities, and a certain intransigent, terrified principal-to-be was his.

He'd fucked up last night. No question about it.

Their evening on the nude beach, she'd essentially explained everything he needed to know about how she approached risk, and he hadn't listened. Not well enough.

This isn't an impulse or moment of folly, she'd told him. *I considered the potential problems, and I took steps to control as many variables as I could.*

After that—and only after that—she'd allowed herself to have what she wanted. What they both wanted.

Then, literally the next day, he'd approached her with a

273

high-stakes gamble and given her absolutely no reason to believe he'd thought it through sufficiently. He hadn't considered potential difficulties and concerns and counterarguments she might offer. He hadn't theorized how best to address her worries.

In short, he hadn't eliminated as much risk as he could. For her. For them.

No wonder she'd considered his decision to move a fleeting impulse. Pure, stupid folly. Yes, she'd responded from fear. But he hadn't given her any reason not to be afraid, had he?

Tonight, he had one more shot at convincing her. Today, he'd prepare.

He'd already compiled his list of topics to research, people to contact, and tasks to complete. By the time he saw her that evening, he'd have his shit together and his arguments in place. He'd have positioned himself for a winning shot as best he could.

Rally tolerance. He was learning. Better late than never.

AROUND LUNCHTIME, HE TEXTED HER TO MEET HIM at the clubhouse at seven.

In the end, the timing was tight, but he marked the last item off his list ten minutes before she was due to arrive. And after a quick shower, one last review of his plans, and a near-panicked jog down the stairs and through the clubhouse, there she was, standing outside the door and looking precisely as tense as he felt.

When he unlocked the door to her, though, she immediately stepped into his arms, which lowered his heartrate all the way from *barely survivable* to *rabbit-like*.

He held her and kissed her cheek.

"Hey, älskling," he said into the fine, soft hair at her temple.

Her response was just as quiet. Just as tentative. "Hi, Lucas."

After claiming her hand in his, he led them both upstairs to his apartment. Neither of them said a word along the way. He waved her to his couch and offered her a drink, which she refused with a shake of her head.

She perched on the edge of the couch cushion, tired hazel eyes pleading as she looked up at him, hands twisting between her knees, and he didn't want to wait any longer. Neither of them could withstand much more tension without breaking.

So he remained standing and took his shot. Again.

This time, prepared.

"Last night, I—" she began, and he didn't let her finish.

"May I speak first?" Interrupting her was rude, but he didn't want her to condemn them both to loneliness before he'd had the chance to change her mind. "Please?"

Her entire body stiff, she nodded. "Of course."

He couldn't tell whether she was braced for pain or poised for flight. Either way, her posture made his arms ache to hold her again.

"Today, I contacted the players' association with a proposal. We haven't worked out all the details, obviously, but I suggested a new partnership between the association and disadvantaged American schools. One created and coordinated by me."

Her mouth had dropped open in shock, and he took a certain amount of pride in that. "It would involve players who live or train in the U.S. adopting certain schools and periodically visiting to give talks and mentor students. Interested kids in need would receive free tennis lessons and be given access to training facilities and necessary equipment. Funds would also be used to eliminate school lunch debts for everyone, not just students interested in tennis, because as you've told me, hungry kids can't perform at their best. On court or off."

He reached for the laptop on his coffee table and turned the screen to face her.

"Here's the written proposal I sent them. It's brief, but it's a start." A tap of the touchpad, and he flipped to another page of typed notes. "The money aspect might entail my having to set up a foundation and do some fundraising, but that's workable. I've already contacted my lawyer and an accountant to look into everything I'd need to do."

Her eyes were wide, stricken with so many emotions he couldn't identify them all. But he definitely saw love there. Admiration. Maybe best of all: pride.

In him. He was making her proud. He was making himself proud again, at last.

"That's…" Her twisting hands stilled. "That's incredible."

"Even if the association rejects the proposal, I'll still adopt a school myself." Another tap. The appropriate home page appeared, its banner image dominated by a three-cornered black hat. "*Your* school, Tess. Marysburg High School, home of the Fighting Tricornes. Which is a pitiful mascot, to be honest, but I suppose you can't help that."

"Lucas, I…" She shook her head, shock still parting her lush lips.

When she trailed off, he took advantage of her silence and continued. "I'm excited by the proposal, and I can't wait to make it reality. So thank you for helping me stretch myself. Thank you for believing I had more to offer the world than just my skill with a racket."

"Don't thank *me*." This time, her voice was steady. Resolute. "You're the one who envisioned all this. I had nothing to do with it."

His tone matched hers. "But without you, without what you've told me about your school and your students, the proposal never would have occurred to me. Without seeing you brainstorm and work out the logistics for your own ideas, I would have struggled more to put the proposal together. Without your love and encouragement, I wouldn't have had the confidence to make all the phone calls and write all the letters and explain why I'm the right person to coordinate this kind of partnership."

At the word *love*, she collapsed back into the couch, as if in need of its support.

"I understand the importance of your work, to you and your community. I see myself fitting into your life, your school, in various ways, including this one." Sitting beside her, he pressed his hip to hers, allowing the contact to anchor him. "I clarified a few other things today too."

She blinked at him. "Holy crackers."

"Turns out, I actually know the coordinator of Marysburg University's indoor tennis complex. It's Sasha Kasterov, who played on the ATP Tour with me a few years back. Not a big name, but a good guy." He took her hand in his, unable to tell whose was trembling more. "He doesn't have a job opening right now, but he thinks he might in the spring. If he can get more sponsors and funding for the tournament, he'd like to hire someone to coordinate the event while he deals with the daily functioning of the facilities."

"You would be amazing at that." Her smile was shaky but genuine. "Then again, you'd be amazing at anything you chose to do, Lucas. You have to know that."

Fuck. If she kept being so sweet, he wouldn't be able to finish this without either kissing her or crying.

Squeezing her hand steadied him. "I volunteered to help him plan and promote the event this fall, so I can get a better sense of what the job would entail. But I think I would enjoy it, and I think it would suit my strengths. The ones you forced me to enumerate in detail, because you're relentless and loving and fierce." Unable to resist, he pressed a quick kiss to her soft lips. "In the meantime, he said he could hook me up with people who might want coaching from a former top-five player."

"You'd have work in Marysburg," she said slowly.

He inclined his head. "I'd have work in Marysburg. I could line up clients ahead of time, before the end of my contract here." Ducking down, he made direct eye contact, because this was important. "Let me be clear, though. Whatever you decide tonight or next week or next month, I'm leaving this island at the end of the year. When that happens, I'd like to move to where you are. If you object, I won't. But I'll still leave here, even if you don't want a life together. I'll still adopt a school, even if it's not yours. I'll still find work I love in a community where I can set down roots, even if it's not Marysburg."

Her hands weren't trembling anymore, or cold. When she intertwined his fingers with hers, their warmth felt like a benediction.

Maybe this time, he'd aimed true.

Maybe this time, he was winning more than a point.

"All this"—he pointed to the laptop screen—"is about you. I won't deny that. But it's also about me and the kind of future I want. I'm not simply drifting passively in your wake, Tess. I want to be your partner. In every sense of the word."

He leaned forward. Another two taps on the touchpad, and the e-mail he'd written the resort's recreation supervisor appeared on screen. "No matter what, I'm taking several weeks off this fall. If necessary, I could spend that time looking for work and housing outside Marysburg, but I'd rather spend it with you instead." When her forehead creased anew, and her lips parted, he held up a staying hand. "I know you can't take that amount of vacation during the school year, and I don't want you to. My goal is for us to experience a few weeks of your normal schedule together."

This time, she didn't even try to interrupt. Instead, she

appeared to be waiting patiently until he was done, her eyes wet, her lush mouth tipped at the corners with the beginnings of a smile.

"Consider it a test run. I can stay at a hotel, or I can stay with you. Either way, I'll volunteer with Sasha, nail down plans with the players' association, and look at rental housing while you're at work. Maybe I'll even schedule a few lessons with potential clients. The evenings and weekends, we can spend together, and if you need to work at home or decide to have dinner with your friends instead of me some nights, so be it. I want a real taste of what our life together would be like."

One by one, he was anticipating her objections and fears. Controlling as many of the variables as possible, so she could take a risk and give them what they both wanted.

"The visit might be disastrous." He smiled at her. "But I doubt it. Either way, we'll know more than we do now."

Lifting their joined hands, he pressed them over his heart.

It wasn't really his, though. Not anymore. Not for almost two weeks now.

"One more thing." Softly, he rubbed the tip of his nose against hers. "I love you. You can tell me it's too fast, too much, but that won't change anything. It's a fact. A scientific truth. The sun rises in the east and sets in the west, the tides come and go, we'll eventually grow old and die, and Lucas Karlsson loves Tess Dunn."

Her cheeks were damp now, her voice thick. "I think we need to work on your grasp of scientific theory."

"I want to be at your side for all of it. Every sunset, every low tide, every day of your life, as long as I'm alive and breathing on this earth." His own voice was a pleading croak now, equally choked, and he didn't care. "Give me a chance to prove it to you, älskling. Please."

When she drew back from him and stood, his muffled

sound of grief should have humiliated him, but he was too bereft for pride. Too bereft to keep speaking, keep arguing.

Instead, numb with misery, he simply watched her reach for her purse.

He'd missed his shot. Lost the point, the game, the set, the match.

He'd lost everything.

Rather than taking her purse and leaving, though, she unzipped it and dug inside.

"I'll forward the e-mail confirmations to you later, but I printed these at the resort business center this morning. I wanted some sort of concrete physical documentation to show you. Feel free to call me old. I can take it." She handed him a folded sheaf of papers, and he fumbled to hold them. Struggled to read them through wet eyes. "I need to be at school as much as possible this year, but I can take several long weekends if I prepare far enough ahead of time."

When he simply stared at her, too overwhelmed to piece together what she was saying, what she'd handed him, she stroked his cheek. "The plane tickets are nonrefundable. I'm coming to see you at least three times this fall, whether you want me or not."

"I do." It was barely a sound, and as much as he could articulate. "You know I do."

Another stroke of his cheek, tender and warm. "I know."

After more digging in her purse, she produced something small. Removing the papers from his grasp, she laid them on the coffee table and deposited a key in his palm.

When he closed his fist over that silver key, the movement sudden and fierce, she bit her lip. "I'm not ready to say you can move in. But I went to a hardware store on the mainland today and made you an extra key for my house, because you're welcome there, and I want you with me, and I want us to figure out how a daily life together could work. Because I love you."

He bowed his head and fought for control.

"This isn't practical, you know." Her palms cupping his face tipped it upward, until she could meet his blurry gaze. "Not something a reasonable forty-year-old woman would do."

He nuzzled into her hands. Rested there, content. "But?"

"I trust you." Her lips courted his, clinging for a sweet moment. "I trust myself."

"We can make this work," he said against her mouth. "We *will* make this work."

It was a declaration. A vow made with the force of everything he held dear, everything he'd dreamed, everything he was.

"I agree." She smiled at him, her hazel eyes bright and warm and more beautiful than he could express in any language. "Let's prove it."

EPILOGUE

LUCAS'S SHOT WHIZZED OVER THE NET TO TESS'S side of the court, but getting to it would require running. An intense burst of speed, culminating in a dive for the ball and a frantic swing of her racket.

Nope.

Instead, she leaned on that racket and watched the ball pass by, then turned back to Lucas. "Nice shot."

"I didn't mean to hit it that hard. Sorry." In the partial darkness of the late-evening tennis court, the gleam of his grin shone from the shadows. "I got distracted and forgot what I was doing for a moment."

The sight of her in a sports bra tended to have that effect on him. At least she hadn't whacked him in the nose with a ball yet, although the night was still young. Unlike her.

As of tomorrow, she was forty-two. Back to fourteen years older than her boyfriend, instead of thirteen. She was also back to the gorgeous island where they'd first met.

A fair tradeoff, in her view.

She shook her head. "You know I'm always going to suck at tennis, right?"

"I know." He strolled toward her. Bending over to rest both elbows on the net, he regarded her with amusement. "You know I don't give a shit, right?"

"I know," she said.

Jesus, she was sweaty enough to singlehandedly keep any local desalinization plants in business. How had she forgotten the muggy heat of the island, even after such a long absence? Far enough away from the breezy shores, every breath felt like gargling soup. Given the occasional insect, chunky soup at that.

She directed a longing glance in the direction of the beach. "How badly do you want to keep doing this?"

He raised his brows. "It was your idea to play tennis the night we arrived, älskling. I wanted to watch you try on all your swimsuits so I could determine which one was most likely to fall off in the water. Then convince you to wear that suit exclusively. Then remove it with my teeth."

Dammit, she wanted that too. She really did.

Stay focused, Dunn. You have plans to execute.

"I thought it might be nice to return to the scene of the crime." She walked closer to the net and pressed a quick kiss to his mouth. "So to speak."

"You did draw blood here, if I remember correctly." He kissed her back, then wiggled the bridge of his nose, as if checking for damage. "But if you want to go where we first met, we have to head to the ocean. Although you're basically underwater as it is, what with all that sweat glistening over your—"

She gave him a gentle whack on the shoulder with her racket. "Skank."

He spread his hands, the picture of outraged innocence. "I was talking about your water bottle. It's sweating. Covered with condensation. Sexy, sexy condensation."

His eyes were definitely not on her water bottle.

"Want to go to the beach?" For her purposes, the more private the location, the better. "How about that little sandbar on the adults-only end of the island? I know we didn't actually meet there, but it's so peaceful."

They could both use a little peace. More than a little, to be honest.

Her work life hadn't slowed over the last two years, and neither had Lucas's. On a daily basis, he was running his foundation and coordinating the partnership between underprivileged schools and the players' association—all on top of his part-time duties at the tennis center. Since a chance meeting at the Challenger-level tournament earlier that year, he'd also started consulting regularly with Lilly Tulu, who was recovering from yet another surgery and willing to travel to Marysburg for his guidance.

Despite all that, he still had energy to burn at night. So much energy.

God bless Mr. Perky.

Tess's own daily schedule was equally packed. Although she'd managed to delegate some of her administrative duties at school, weekdays still teemed with meetings and paperwork. As of that spring, she had regular physical therapy appointments for her knee too. The time those appointments took still rankled her, but even she had to admit it: They helped. A lot.

To his credit, Lucas hadn't pushed her, and he didn't say *I told you so*. Instead, he helped her with the exercises, accompanied her to the doctor when he could, and incessantly discussed which new sexual positions a healthier knee would make possible. Which was the best possible motivation for continuing her appointments, something he definitely understood.

For a European playboy bro, he was awfully clever. Which was one of many reasons they'd moved in together just over a year ago.

Two weeks later, she'd earned her new title at work.

Cressida had delayed her retirement as long as possible. But last August, Tess had officially become principal of Marysburg High.

Her dream. For a long time, her only one.

Not anymore.

"The sandbar it is." Lucas took her racket and tucked it under his arm. "Why don't I return everything to the clubhouse while you rest for a minute?"

Lifting her damp hand, he flattened her palm against his cheek and nuzzled his bristles against her tender skin until she shivered at the prickle.

"Am I going to need the rest?" she asked, her voice husky.

His teeth sank into that soft swell of flesh just below her thumb. Not enough to break the skin. Just enough to excite her.

At her gasp, he smiled slowly. "Yes."

"Why are you bringing your tote bag?" Lucas removed it from her shoulder and swung it over his as they walked to the beach. "I've got the towels, I put the room key in my swim trunks, and you don't need sunscreen at night."

She didn't break stride. "I wanted to bring something... special. You'll see."

"Ah. I *do* see." He sped up, just a little. "Naughty, naughty, Principal Dunn."

She wasn't even nervous. Why wasn't she nervous?

Within minutes, they'd arrived at their destination. The adults-only tip of the island, where the shush of the waves mingled with the flutter of a breeze through palm fronds.

In this spot, it was almost completely dark. Private.

Perfect.

Only feet away, the water lapped at the shore. And just

beyond the point where that water seemed too deep, past the few fraught feet where she'd struggle to keep her head above surface, the sandbar waited for them.

This time, she knew Lucas would ease her through the frightening moments when her toes no longer touched bottom. He'd support her so she didn't need to worry. Hold her hand as she forged ahead.

Inevitably, the sand would rise again to meet her. Then they'd sit hip to hip, swaying in the gentle, unceasing advance and retreat of the ocean. They'd let the silky sand dissolve through their fingers and swirl their hands through the warm, buoyant water.

They'd be. Just be. Together.

Paradise. But no more so than the house they now shared, their daily lives full of meetings and frustrations and laughter and the look on Lucas's face each and every time she came home.

Lit from within. Incandescent with love.

So no, she wasn't nervous. She was as buoyant as that swirling water.

She couldn't wait for the sandbar. She couldn't wait another moment.

When she fell to one knee in the damp sand, Lucas swore and dropped everything. "Tess, are you okay? Did you twist your knee? Because I can call for—"

He was crouching down, his hands grasping her shoulders, his brow creased with worry as he frantically scanned her for injuries.

Yup. He'd completely missed the point of all this.

The rings helped, once she fished their velvet boxes from the depths of the tote bag.

Men didn't usually receive engagement rings, but she didn't want a long engagement anyway. Not this time. She figured he could use the band as his wedding ring too. And she absolutely loved the design she'd picked for both of them. No diamonds anywhere to be found. Just wide circles inscribed with the date they'd met.

The day her dreams had multiplied and started coming true.

"I love you, Lucas Stig Karlsson. As long as I live, I'll want you by my side. As long as I live, I'll stay by yours." She smiled into his astonished face. "Will you marry me?"

Silence. He didn't say a word.

Nothing.

Nada.

Okay, now she was getting a *teensy* bit nervous.

"Tess..." He stared down at the platinum bands cradled in her palm, and then—to her shock—started laughing. "Älskling, I have two rings in my suitcase back in our room. Along with tickets for Vegas, in case you wanted to cut our trip here short and get married right away. That would be my preference, incidentally."

Oh, thank God. "Mine too. The black oblong boxes have rings in them?"

He nodded.

She grinned at him. "I thought those were sex toys."

"I know you did." He winked at her. "The sex toys are in a different bag."

Then he was on his knees too, her hands in his, the rings she'd chosen pressed between their palms. "Tessa Bethany Dunn, I love you. I'll always love you, and I'd be proud as hell to call myself your husband. Will you marry me?"

Her kiss, her smile through her tears, served as her answer.

———

MUCH LATER, WHEN THEY WERE BOTH WEARING

their rings and skirting the border of public indecency charges, she pulled slightly away from him, panting.

"Lucas…" When the breeze ruffled his hair, she smoothed it with unsteady fingers. "We should go back to our room. In about half an hour, servers are going to start bringing every single item from The Sands's dinner menu to our room."

A smile spread slowly across his face, and his dimples popped. "You're giving yourself what you want."

"All of it. Practical or not." Her breath caught as he squeezed her ass, the gesture possessive and approving. "It seemed like a fitting start to our engagement."

"Definitely," he said, nipping at the sensitive spot just below her ear. "And it would definitely be fitting if I did *this* too."

"Maybe illegal," she managed to say as his hands roamed freely, "but very fitting."

After another breathless interlude, he gave her one last kiss, reluctantly disentangled himself from her arms, and got to his feet with a groan. "We need to go. Shame on you for distracting me, Principal Dunn."

She shook her head at him. "You're incorrigible."

"You're welcome." His rumbling voice was smug. So very smug.

If she didn't love him so much, she'd probably find that annoying, rather than sexy.

Alas.

"Lucas…" Even though she could do it on her own, she still held out her hand to him. "Will you help me up?"

His eyes went soft. Taking her hand, he eased her to her feet.

"Always, Tess." He stood by her, hip to hip. Her friend, her lover, her fiercest ally. Her heart, strong and true. "Always."

THANK YOU FOR READING *40-Love*. ♥ IF YOU'D LIKE to stay in touch and hear about future new releases, please visit me at oliviadade.com and/or sign up for the Hussy Herald at https://go.oliviadade.com/Newsletter.

PREVIEW OF SWEETEST IN
THE GALE

ONE

THE FIRST TIME GRIFF TRULY NOTICED CANDY Albright, she was yelling about Frankenstein.

Well, maybe not yelling, per se. More issuing various pronouncements about Mary Shelley's magnum opus at such a volume that witnesses at that faculty meeting would never, ever again confuse the story's eponymous scientist with his vengeful, humanoid creation.

Over the course of five very loud, very entertaining minutes, she announced the various actions she'd taken to clarify the matter to the student body. Including—but by no means limited to—a planned puppet show. A goddamn *puppet show*, the apogee of her Frankenstein Is *Not* the Monster Initiative.

She was vibrating with passion, unabashedly herself, more alive than he'd felt in—

Well, that didn't matter.

What did matter: It was the first time since his move to Marysburg that he'd smiled.

In various start-of-the-school-year English department meetings, he'd only vaguely registered her presence and her name. Which was both a mystery and a travesty, given the way she seemed to gather all the light in the room, only to expel it in a sort of didactic supernova.

Overlooking Candy was a mistake he didn't intend to repeat.

For the rest of the school year, then, he made a point of observing her. Listening to her too, which wasn't difficult, given her admirable lung capacity.

She never disappointed. She always snapped his attention into sharp focus.

Stalwart. Stubborn. Shrewish, some might say, but they'd be wrong.

Since that first Marysburg High School faculty meeting, almost a year ago, the sight of her marching down the hall, all martial intensity and unshakeable confidence, had heartened him, even on his worst days. She cared about so much. Students and colleagues and stories and language. She was a constant reminder that determination and belief still existed in his world.

Which was why, when he saw her shuffle into the faculty lounge the following August, he immediately straightened in alarm.

"Good morning," Candy said, the words barely audible.

She'd spoken into Griff's right ear, but that wasn't the issue. His colleague's voice, so gloriously booming and decisive, normally made her angle of approach irrelevant.

Not today. She'd murmured the standard greeting, rather than making it seem like an order—you *will* have a good morning, *or else*—and she did so without her usual direct eye contact. Instead, she'd kept her head down, her gaze on the memos she'd just removed from her staff mailbox, still facing that honeycombed wall of wooden slots.

It didn't sound like a good morning. It didn't look like one either.

Nevertheless, he echoed her words, studying his colleague as discreetly as possible as she flipped through her mail.

With her shoulders slumped, her head bowed, and her hair shorn, the pale nape of her neck seemed...vulnerable. Not a word he'd have ever imagined using to describe her. Even more alarmingly, her usual schoolmarm cosplay, as he liked to think of it, had vanished.

Instead, she was wearing stretchy black pants, an over-sized, faded tee, and sneakers. Which made total sense for a returning teacher prepared to set up her classroom for the upcoming school year. He'd donned worn jeans and his own faded t-shirt for this day's efforts, which would likely involve moving chairs, desks, and books between and within classrooms.

But Candy Albright didn't let good sense get in the way of her convictions, and at some point she'd evidently become convinced she should clothe her solid frame in a blouse, cardigan, pearls, and a long skirt each and every day she appeared at work. That she should pull her ashy brown hair back into a bun with the assistance of a wide headband, her eyebrow-length fringe of bangs brushed to the side. That she should secure her horn-rimmed glasses with a chain around her neck, even though she always, always had them perched on the bridge of her aquiline nose.

Rain, shine, school day, teacher work day, faculty retreat... it didn't matter. She altered not, as Shakespeare might have said.

Before this moment, then, he'd literally never seen her with her hair down. But sometime during the summer, she'd cut it too short for a bun. Instead, it framed her round face in smooth, jaw-length arcs. With her chin down, that swoop of hair swung forward, obscuring her expression from his sight.

The barrier bothered him more than it should.

It wasn't his business. He shouldn't inquire. The two of them were—and would remain—friendly colleagues, rather than friends. For so many reasons, his instincts had consistently guided him away from bridging that gap.

Still, he cleared his throat. Opened his mouth.

But before he said anything, she offered him a curt nod and trudged out the door of the faculty lounge. Belatedly recovering his own good sense, he waited sufficient time to ensure she'd reached her classroom before following her path to his.

Her room might adjoin his, and he might watch her from afar, but that was as much intimacy as he could handle.

Alas, I have grieved so I am hard to love.

Not that love had anything to do with it. Not at all.

THEY BOTH WORKED THE ENTIRE DAY AT THE school, sometimes encountering one another in the English department office or the copy room or—once again—in the faculty lounge, where he reheated the turkey sausage chili he'd made over the weekend while she retrieved a Diet Coke from the old, rattling refrigerator.

At each encounter, she greeted him with another dip of her chin and nothing more.

No talk of new department initiatives. No blustering insistence that he get more sleep, because she'd spotted the bags under his eyes. No demands that he tell her if he needed help moving or organizing anything.

She responded to his own offer of help with a mumbled assurance that she was fine, thank you anyway. He had to lip-read during that particular exchange, she was so muted.

He didn't want to worry. He wouldn't.

Most of their time, they spent inside their classrooms. And even through a wall, the screech of moving furniture told him what she was doing. Setting up her classroom, angling her desks and chairs just so. Exactly what he was doing.

Later in the afternoon, though, those bursts of sound

ceased. Like him, maybe she was fastening laminated posters to the wall or covering her bulletin board. Labeling folders and reviewing opening-day lesson plans.

At some point, as the sun sank toward the horizon outside his classroom windows, he took a break. Leaned his desk chair back. Snacked on a handful of pretzels.

Thought, unwillingly, about Candy. Again.

After their encounters today, he'd found himself loath to turn on music as he worked. He'd kept close to the wall adjoining their two rooms, his own newly-assigned classroom silent. Just in case.

He'd seen that particular greyness before. In the mirror, three years ago.

He reached for his reusable water bottle, which was sitting at the edge of his battered, paper-covered desk, and tipped it back. Swallowed hard.

If she needed him—

Rather, if she needed *anyone*, he wanted to hear. Especially since no other teacher had started their classroom setup quite so early, and the school echoed with emptiness after the administrators and maintenance staff went home for the evening.

Because of the encompassing silence that night, he heard the short, shocked cry, the crash, the thud. The awful moment of silence, followed by something that might have been a whimper.

He didn't have time to contemplate the matter further, because he was already racing out his door and wrenching hers open—why was it closed, when she never closed her door except when teaching?—and scanning her classroom for signs of trouble.

They weren't hard to locate or interpret. A chair rested on its side before her half-finished bulletin board, and Candy lay crumpled on the floor near its metal legs, eyes clenched shut.

She'd stood on the chair. Overbalanced. Fallen on the unforgiving tile.

Half a dozen strides, and he was there.

"Candy?" When he knelt beside her, that same tile bit into his aging knees. "Talk to me."

To his relief, her answer came immediately, its irony sharp enough to relieve his worst concerns about a concussion. "Certainly, Mr. Conover. Name your subject."

Normally, she called him Griff. Caught in such a helpless, vulnerable position, however, little wonder she'd grasped for the dignity and distance of his surname.

No blood. No unnatural angles in her limbs. Thank the heavens.

That said, some serious injuries weren't obvious to the untrained, naked eye. "Tell me where you're hurting."

She let out a single, heartrendingly raw sob, then pressed her wide mouth into a tight line and breathed hard through her nose. "I'm p-perfectly well, thank you."

If he hadn't been so worried, he would have yielded to the familiar, charming mulishness of her declaration. Given the circumstances, though, he couldn't let the clear falsehood stand.

"That seems more aspirational than truthful, I'm afraid." His hands hovered over her, his eagerness to help her from the hard floor at war with his common sense. He could cause further damage by lifting her head into his lap, and he knew it, but leaving her like this—if only for a moment longer—galled him. "Can you move?"

"Of course I can move." She sniffed, her pretense of unconcern only somewhat undercut by her trembling chin. "I'm a bit bruised, that's all."

Her legs shifted first, straightening in a seemingly easy motion. Then she raised her head. Rotated it cautiously but without signs of distress. Wiggled her torso.

"If your back and neck feel okay, do you want to try

sitting up?" He offered his hands, ignoring how they trembled fully as much as that stubborn chin. Jesus, she'd scared the hell out of him. "Here. Let me help."

She mustered a small smile. "Although I appreciate your offer of assistance, I'm more than capable of—*fuck!*"

With a gasping cry, her attempt to lever herself up ceased, and she curled in on herself once more, cradling her left arm against her body, panting through obvious pain.

He'd never heard her use an obscenity before. If only these sorts of situations prompted them, he hoped he never would again.

"Okay. Okay." Frantic, he peered out through the doorway, hoping to see their security guard, but he wasn't sure Carlotta even worked so late during the summer. "I'll call an ambulance. Or drive you to the emergency room."

"*No.*" It was an instant refusal. Firm and loud and definite.

He ignored it. Why weren't his keys in his jeans pocket? If he'd deposited them on top of his desk, he'd have to leave her long enough to get them. Shit.

"I'm going to my classroom for my keys, but I'll be right —" Already on his feet, he gaped down at her. "What the hell are you doing?"

Somehow, while he'd been patting his pockets, she'd raised herself to a sitting position using her right arm, her left still pressed against her chest. "Getting up, clearly."

She was trying to maneuver herself to her knees, her face deathly pale where it wasn't blotched with livid pink. Once more, he found himself reaching for her but unable to touch. This time, because she hadn't given him permission.

"Candy..." He met her red-rimmed gaze. Held it. "Please don't hurt yourself trying to do it alone. I can help. I *want* to help."

Her eyes turned glassy once more, and his gut churned at the sight.

Then she blinked hard, lifted a hand, and accepted his. "Okay. On the count of three. One...two...three."

Together, they got her kneeling. Her palm was damp against his, her grip firm, the skin-to-skin contact electric in a way he didn't have the time or inclination to parse.

He put her good arm around his shoulders. In halting movements, she rose to her feet with his assistance, still breathing hard through the pain.

For a few seconds, she remained huddled against him, allowing him to support some of her weight. He bore it gladly.

"Thank you," she eventually said.

The words were unadorned but decisive. Loud enough to hear easily.

He looked down at the graying crown of her head, wondering when that booming voice had become such a comfort to him. "You're welcome. Let's get you to the hospital."

She moved away from him then, her chin turning pugnacious in an entirely familiar way, and he braced himself for a fight.

After glancing down at her left arm, though, still bent protectively close to her chest, she sighed. "Your keys are in your classroom, you said?"

He let out a slow breath, almost giddy in his relief. "Yes."

"I'll gather everything I need and meet you in the hall." Her throat worked. "Thank you again. I don't—"

She cut herself off. Gazed up at him, brow creased in seeming confusion.

"Thank you," she repeated.

He forced himself to turn away from her.

"No problem," he said over his shoulder as he headed for the door.

Only he wasn't sure that was entirely true. Not for either of them.

"IF YOU DRIVE ME BACK TO THE SCHOOL, I CAN make it home just fine." Perched on the hospital bed, Candy pointed meaningfully at her left arm. "See? My arm might be broken, but the splint will keep everything stable until the swelling goes down and I can get a cast. And I didn't take anything but Tylenol, so my head is perfectly clear."

The doctor had wanted to write a prescription for stronger painkillers, but she'd refused with so much loud adamance, the man had taken an actual step backward, his white coat flapping.

A bit of missing context, Griff presumed. "Yes, but it's still going to be awkward. I'm happy to help you get settled, if you want."

"Thank you, but you've done enough," she said, looking down that straight nose at him.

The pronouncement did not invite argument, so he didn't offer one. Not about that, anyway.

He shoved his hair out of his eyes, recalling the doctor's instructions. Following his instincts. "Fine. But you'll need to elevate your arm above your heart whenever you can."

"Yes." Her gaze narrowed dangerously. "I also heard what the doctor said. There's nothing amiss with my hearing."

Well, that made one of them.

He deliberately ignored her growing ire. "You can put some ice in a towel or plastic bag to help with the swelling, but only over the splint. Fifteen to twenty minutes every few hours."

"I understand that." Each syllable sounded like ground glass. "I do not require you to reiterate all my instructions."

Apparently, his instincts when it came to Candy were surprisingly sound. As she grew more and more irritated, that awful grayness receded. Her cheeks turned rosy, her brown eyes sharp. Her shoulders squared, and her voice got louder.

Broken arm or no broken arm, she looked more herself right now than she had since June.

He wanted that confident, truculent Candy back. For her. For himself.

So he continued talking, injecting a bit of extra pompousness into his tone. "You should wiggle your fingers as much as possible."

"You—" Her brows snapped together, and she flung her uninjured arm in the air. "Are you aware that I was *in the room* while Dr. Marconi told me what I should and shouldn't do? Did you somehow *overlook* my *very presence?*"

Honestly, this was the most fun he'd had all day. "I thought I saw you, but I wasn't entirely certain. It's harder to recognize you without that whole bouffant thing"—he swirled his hand over the top of his head—"you used to have going on up here."

Her mouth dropped open in outrage. "A tiny bit of volume does not equal a *bouffant*. I'm not a refugee from the mid-1960s, Mr. Conover!"

"More late eighteenth-century France, then?" He sat back in his chair, crossing one ankle over his knee. "You *are* fond of proclamations. Very Marie Antoinette of you."

She sputtered, her nostrils flaring.

He smiled at her in a particularly obnoxious way. "Anyway, I won't go inside, but I'll follow you home, just in case. And I'll wait in your driveway until I see the lights come on."

"*Fine.*" It was more a growl than an actual word. "As long as you stop talking, right this second, you can follow me home."

That seemed like a fair tradeoff to him.

Besides, Shakespeare had the right of it. *Nothing can seem foul to those that win.*

So he obediently kept his mouth shut while she received

her discharge papers and swiped her credit card for her emergency room copay. Still silent, he drove her to the school parking lot, and then followed her small SUV across town.

It was after midnight, and she was returning to a dark, empty house. Just as he would, as soon as he ensured she was safely home.

After she let herself into the front door and flicked on the interior and porch lights, she lingered in the doorway. After a moment, she raised her good arm in something that wasn't quite a wave. More a gesture of acknowledgment.

Within that halo of golden light, he could read her lips. *Thank you, Griff.*

Then the door closed, and he drove home. Showered. Got in bed. Blinked at the ceiling as his brain inevitably returned to its favorite preoccupation.

Candy Albright. Again. Still.

She fascinated him for so many reasons.

Twenty-plus years of teaching, full to bursting with students and colleagues and discussions about poetry and plays and novels, had in turn taught him well. He'd learned at least one thing for certain.

Not everyone could decipher subtext.

Not even if they noticed its presence, which many people —too enmeshed in their own thoughts, their own concerns— did not. Not even when it was pointed out to them by, say, a longtime teacher who wanted his ninth graders to pass their end-of-year English proficiency test, and also wanted them to take pleasure in the way simple words could contain multitudes. Universes secreted away, but open to explorers with sufficient curiosity and persistence.

Even those who *could* decipher subtext didn't always wish to perform the labor. He hadn't required a teaching degree for that revelation. A decade of joyous, sometimes-contentious married life had clarified the matter sufficiently.

Yes, subtext was difficult. Fraught. No question about it.

Still. Since that first faculty meeting, he'd been amazed. Nay, stupefied.

People seemed to think Candy Albright was as straightforward and direct as her pronouncements, as if she possessed no subtext at all. No river running swift and hidden beneath the craggy, immovable, desert-dry boulders of her words.

Worse: No one, as far as he could tell, seemed to wonder about context either, or consider the simplest and most obvious question. The question he trained his ninth graders to ask over the course of a school year together.

Those times when he couldn't successfully occupy himself with other matters—times like these—he did wonder. He did consider. He asked himself *why*.

Why her students claimed to fear her, yet seemed entirely certain she would spend hours after the last bell working with them on their college application essays. Which she did. He'd seen her night after night, bent over a desk, red pen in hand, attention sharp as the tacks studding her bulletin board on the students and papers before her.

Why, when she worried and grew exasperated, she borrowed the words of mobsters instead of poets and threatened—unconvincingly—to put hits on those causing her distress. She, an English teacher of considerable repute, who guided her seniors inexorably through poetry and prose and the vagaries of the AP English Literature and Composition exam.

Why a woman, so often humorless as a dirge, had a laugh as loud and honking and unabashed as hers. A cascade of sound, its joyful draw undeniable. Though he had done his best to deny it anyway.

Why a woman so brash and unafraid and amusingly *certain*—a tidal wave in human form, a *force*—had arrived weeks early to set up her classroom, face grey and wan. Hair shorn, also greyer than the previous year. So quiet. Too quiet. Even before her injury.

Why, in short, Candy Albright was Candy Albright. The cocksure Candy Albright of last year, and the bafflingly diffident Candy Albright of today.

He shouldn't wonder, of course. It didn't speak well of him that he did. Or rather, *how* he did, with fascination and anxiety and something like urgency.

He wondered anyway.

Finally, once the bedside clock ticked past two in the morning, he punched his pillow, turned on his side, and forced his eyes shut.

This preoccupation—this foolish, damnable fascination with Candy—was a mere academic exercise, the allure of a puzzle yet to be solved. At most, the automatic, perfunctory concern of a coworker. Nothing more than that.

Please God, nothing more than that.

SWEETEST IN THE GALE: A MARYSBURG STORY COLLECTION WILL be available soon! For more news and release-day alerts, sign up for my newsletter, the Hussy Herald, at https://go.oliviadade.com/Newsletter.

ALSO BY OLIVIA DADE

ABOUT OLIVIA

Olivia Dade grew up an undeniable nerd, prone to ignoring the world around her as she read any book she could find. Her favorites, though, were always, always romances. As an adult, she earned an M.A. in American history and worked in a variety of jobs that required the donning of actual pants: Colonial Williamsburg interpreter, high school teacher, academic tutor, and (of course) librarian. Now, however, she has finally achieved her lifelong goal of wearing pajamas all day as a hermit-like writer and enthusiastic hag. She currently lives outside Stockholm with her patient Swedish husband, their whip-smart daughter, and the family's ever-burgeoning collection of books.

If you want to find me online, here's where to go!
Website: https://oliviadade.com
Twitter: https://twitter.com/OliviaWrites
Newsletter: https://go.oliviadade.com/Newsletter

ACKNOWLEDGMENTS

This novel went through more iterations—more *vastly different* iterations—than any book I've ever written. Accordingly, I have many, many people to thank. MANY.

Some of my trusted friends read the story when it was a 40K novella, rather than a full-length novel. Mica Kennedy, Karen Booth, Ruby Lang, and Kate Clayborn: Your time and insight and feedback meant the world to me and improved this story immeasurably. Thank you so much!

Next, two wonderful friends bravely read this book when it was (briefly) an 80K deep-dive into angst. Therese Beharrie and Ainslie Paton, I am so grateful and so very sorry.

Finally, two intrepid, loyal souls read both the initial novella *and* this third, final, less-angsty version of *40-Love*. Emma Barry and Erin, you deserve medals of some sort. Thank you for helping me polish the remaining rough edges of the story and reassuring me I'd finally gotten it right.

I also owe a big thank-you to Sarah Younger, who championed *40-Love* from the beginning and coaxed me to make it longer and more Swedish. :-)

Sionna Fox is so patient with me and generous with her time and skills. Leni Kauffman—the artist who created my glorious cover—has earned my endless admiration. Thank you, both of you.

Finally, I edited this book amidst a pandemic, with my family close by at all times. Which was...uh, challenging?...at times. But they tried their best to give me the time and space I needed to work, because they take me and my writing seriously. I love my husband and daughter for that, just as I love them for countless other reasons. Thank you, now and always.

CPSIA information can be obtained
at www.ICGtesting.com
Printed in the USA
BVHW031032300520
580606BV00001B/247

9 781945 836145